THE DEVIL'S PENNY

Bernard Carlton

authorHOUSE®

AuthorHouse™
1663 Liberty Drive
Bloomington, IN 47403
www.authorhouse.com
Phone: 1-800-839-8640

Published by AuthorHouse   02/21/2012

ISBN: 978-1-4678-8346-7 (sc)
ISBN: 978-1-4678-8347-4 (e)

Contents

Chapter 1   An Unwelcome Encounter 1

Chapter 2   The Manifestation of the Penny 8

Chapter 3   Another Mouth to Feed 42

Chapter 4   The evil becomes manifest 54

Chapter 5   Love Found 82

Chapter 6   The Penny Takes Hold 113

Chapter 7   Retribution 137

Chapter 8   The Front 152

Chapter 9   The Foxhole 173

Chapter 10 The Return Home 193

Chapter 11 The War Goes On 222

Chapter 12 Arrival at the Squadron 244

Chapter 13 A Strange Episode 264

Chapter 14 New Horizons 280

Chapter 15 Going Home 312

CHAPTER I

An Unwelcome Encounter

THE GUNFIRE STARTED AT 4.30am sharp. Twenty two artillery batteries opened up simultaneously along the Verdun section of the front, Generals wanted lost territory back!

A solitary bugle somewhere in the camp shrilled an alert, bleating out its piercing dissonance over and over, calling soldiers to their action stations. The bugle call was the equivalent of a spoken order and was expected to be obeyed as such.

Motorised supply columns were already busy loading from the massive stacks of shells stretching hundreds of feet in length standing 20 feet high and twice as wide that formed the main ammunition dump. The bombardment had gained momentum such that artillery batteries were firing uninterrupted streams of explosives towards their unseen foe; supply columns had no time to lose.

Engineers had fashioned a railhead to bring in supplies, a spur from the French main railway system that brought in munitions to replace the ordnance disgorged by the batteries in endless torrents. When a 'push' of such enormity as this was under way, two or even three mainline trains a day would move in and out of the rail head depositing tens of thousands of tons of arms. The track had been thrown over roughly levelled ground in pre-fabricated lengths to be bolted together to take the railway closer to the guns when territory was gained only to be torn up and transported back again as it was lost.

The counter assault now under way came hard on the heels of German gains and was unpalatable to both sides having been launched so soon after an encounter that had claimed many lives.

'Here we go again!' is an expression of weary acquiescence uttered by foot soldiers regardless of nationality when in receipt of orders to engage in battle by command of superior authority. It was quoted now as preparations for close order engagement took form. Foot soldiers would be first into engagement after 'softening up' bombardments from the artillery. Formed up in battle readiness they crouched in multiple rows stretching the full length of the forward trenches. The smell of fear was palpable and ever present. Small arms ammunition in support of this chaotic, senseless confrontation-to-be, had been handed to each man as they shuffled without enthusiasm into their positions. Small but lethal pellets of death that each man hoped they would make the enemy swallow whilst trusting that they themselves would not receive one!

They were to face a strong, remorseless enemy and each man knew it, they were also aware that the foe was made up of Mother's sons, sweethearts, suitors, husbands brothers, cousins and among themselves, friends—just like themselves.

Trepidation leeched through lines of anxious minds as they thought of the moments to come; when the whistles shrilled they would scale the ladders to the parapets and march blindly forward in rigid order into the onslaught of flying metal that was at this very instant being loaded into the opposing machine guns. Without choice or hope or opportunity of dissent they must go forward to meet their fate or be disgraced and shot dead by their own Officers!

Charles and Tommy were glad they were not foot soldiers, they were at readiness in the first aid orderly's dug-out carved into the rear face of a forward trench. They wouldn't go 'over the top' until the second wave had departed, only then could they be sure that there was work for them. (or so the field medical orderly's manual instructed).

As he waited for the action he knew was imminent, Charles' attention was drawn to a coin concealed within his clothing, he could feel it burning into his flesh, it was becoming a furnace, he knew there was nothing he could do to calm it and wished he could be free of this evil thing that had come to him. A thing that he was powerless to be rid of, a thing that dominated him and wanted nothing but to take the souls of human kind. A thing that would stop at nothing to get them.

He took the trinket from his pocket and bound it tightly in his blood stained handkerchief—perhaps Lucifer would settle for that, but no, it burned stronger for the contact with what had once been life giving essence of a loving mortal.

Charles became aware of a feeling in the pit of his stomach that something was about to change, something *extraordinary* was about to take place, something *far* more sinister than the battle about to unfold. The penny didn't feel as it normally did, it was if it had gained new power that had elevated it beyond influence. Could it be that the talisman considered there was nothing further it could gain from its present courier and was seeking a new one? He thrust the foreboding to the back of his mind and snapped back to the moment; whistles were shrilling their signal for another wave to advance.

"Come on Tommy!" he yelled and threw himself at the ladder dragging the awkward rolled stretcher with him and towing a bewildered young lad at the other end. They ran headlong forward through the thud of bullets, Charles could hear a faint call for help barely audible above the din; around the men earth was being thrown up by mortar fire, debris stinging their faces as they pressed through the treacherous strafing. Tumbling breathless into the hollow of a depression carved by a spent shell they encountered a young soldier who was, in battlefield terms, not so much badly injured as badly frightened. He'd suffered a bullet wound that had taken away some of his teeth and parts of the soft flesh of his lower left cheek. The peculiar feeling of air passing through the wound as he gasped in panic had led the boy to believe that there was nothing left of his jaw!

Charles did what he could to ease the boy's panic and gave him a small shot of morphine to calm him down and ease the pain as he cleaned and dressed the wound. The man would certainly live but if he survived the war he would never again sweeten young ladies with what had once been handsome Adonis features.

The Germans had countered the challenge in a trice and in rebuttal were heavily shelling the Allied lines. Third and fourth waves of wretched men were ordered from the trenches into the jaws of iniquity in the hope of gaining a clod or two of useless earth before they in turn, succumbed to the misery of injury or were called to make the ultimate sacrifice for the greater glory of King and Country. Charles and Tommy laboured with selfless energy treating injured and wounded men, transporting them to the safety of their own lines where they could be attended by surgeons with more elevated skills. The fallen would remain where they fell for there were living to tend!

The two men worked without either orders or direction traversing the course of 'no man's land' countless times to where help was needed. It was inevitable that sooner or later they would find themselves pinned down. They had been forced to take refuge in a makeshift hollow beneath murderous mortar and machine gun fire.

Both men were exhausted from the relentless physical effort and mental stress of dodging bullets and conveying the wounded. Their stomachs told them they should eat but there had been no time to stop for such luxury and in any case the field rations they had been issued with they had opted to leave in the trench in favour of replacing the space and weight by carrying more dressings and medical supplies.

More pressing than the need of food though was their desperate need of drinking water. The canteens of water they carried had been given to the afflicted for comfort and reassurance and had long since been empty.

Earth flew over the depression in torrents as bullet after bullet picked away at the ridge that had been thrown up around the hole by the shell that had made it.

"I could murder a bloody drink!" cursed Charles.

"I'll get you one." blurted Tommy and before Charles had chance to grab him he was over the top and gone.

Charles was stunned that his remark had brought forth such an unintended effect. He felt utterly dejected and desperately miserable about what had transpired for although he had known this youth just a bit more than a day, he had come to respect him as a brother and would not at any price have let him face death for nothing more than a little personal comfort!

He felt as if he had been skulking in this stinking pit for days yet realisation dawned on him that the hour could be little past mid-morning. Laying on his back he gazed skyward in sullen silence at thick billowing smoke thrown up from the engagement above driving across the opening. If it could have been seen without the frenzy of battle then the day would have been pleasant enough with little wind and benign, balmy sunshine occasionally smiling from silver-edged clouds in a backdrop of powder blue.

Charles lay there unsure of what he should do, feelings of guilt pervaded his uneasy mind as he thought of what might have befallen his comrade. The penny was tearing into him, blazing in its concealment conveying that it was expecting something greater than the evil toll thus far. He felt deserted, his confidence at a low, had the unusual gift of courage his ownership of the penny had bestowed upon him now been withdrawn?

What happened next was extraordinary to say the least for over the rim of the foxhole came rolling a very unexpected character.

A very unexpected character indeed!

Of all the people on the battlefield that Charles might have expected to see it turned out to be the one individual he would never have thought of—Major Thomas Grace-Williams in person!

Even before Charles could speak the major had drawn his pistol and was levelling it at him. The smirk on the Major's face told Charles that this was not the act of an Officer on the battlefield making ready to further the honour of his regiment.

"I always knew my chance would come Jenkins". He hissed from clenched teeth, "Out of the cover of battle there was no chance for me to settle my score with you so I've watched and waited for this opportunity for some while. Fate at last provided opportunity—your life is now mine to take and there's no one to bear witness—I mean to make the most of it!"

The Major's eyes narrowed to hate filled slits, mouth twisted in a wicked snarl.

"On your knees Jenkins and beg for your life!"

A calmness stole over Charles as he faced the stark reality of this act he knew to be revenge for the beating he had dispensed to the Major all that time ago when the war was being talked about but not thought to be likely. He smiled from the irony of it all and said nothing. Better to die a man than grovel before an individual who thought nothing of dishonouring himself and the service that had placed its trust in him as a leader. Charles wondered how on earth he had come to this, he resigned himself to his situation and in deference to what he knew must be, his mind slipped back to a happier time.

CHAPTER 2
The Manifestation of the Penny

T HE NOISE IN THE smoke filled stamping room was ear shattering as the heavy steam presses crashed and thudded their way through the daily task of minting the Empire's coinage. Charles had come to the stamping room at the age of 13 and was now a trusted hand working a press turning coin blanks into currency.

There was, as far as could be determined, no particular differences about the Winter's morning of the last day of January 1912. It had begun with a biting sharp frost. Charles had walked the six and a half miles from his home to the mint not heeding the cold, just grateful it was dry. It was persistent drizzle he most hated, it seemed to penetrate the coarse weave of his clothing to reach his bones. Working in damp clothing made the day extra long and miserable for there was no heat save that of the steam press and his body that could dry him out. The walk, even at his brisk pace, had taken a fraction more than an hour to accomplish and passed in silence save for the morning chorus of the awakening bird population. Taking position at his press at seven o'clock sharp he set about producing bright new pennies for King George the Fifth, his realms and dominions.

Collection and accounting of new coins was a matter of exceptional importance and was treated with extreme regard to put it in conservative terms. That a single coin could escape the tight control of its hawk-like supervisors was unthinkable yet just such an event transpired on that fateful January morning, the result of which would have far-reaching consequences. It happened just a few moments after Charles had set his press to work. Without any change of sound or tempo a single new penny popped from the press-head, missed the collecting tray and landed moist with coolant at his feet. He glanced at the coin in amazement, attention captivated by the wisps of silver vapour that rose in lazy curls from this bright and gleaming new coin. He had the strangest intuition that it was somehow intended for him though he knew he would never be able to explain this sensation—not even to himself. Charles was more than aware that if he claimed this errant coin and was caught with it in his possession the repercussions would be severe. Yet in the sure knowledge of this and the frightening possibility of transportation to the colonies, temptation got the better of him. He darted a quick glance about him to make sure he wasn't being observed and without disrupting the tempo of production, stooped and lifted the coin with the deft sleight-of- hand of an accomplished magician. In a sweeping movement he thrust the coin into the single pocket of his thick serge trousers. Charles was unaware that, through this single act, he had entered into a contract and would live to rue the day the coin had come to him but for now he felt elated and somehow invincible. The penny reposed in concealment awaiting its moment, for this was no ordinary coin, it was an ill-begotten trinket that was destined to become the instrument of countless chilling occurrences and the perpetrator of many evil misfortunes. It would come to be known as a harbinger of death, a poisoned chalice, the tender of the devil himself, the ***devil's*** penny!

Hour upon hour he toiled at the press, stamping out coin after coin in monotonous repetition for there was but one break at mid day for rest and relief. As the day lengthened, his young and demanding stomach, began sending pressing messages that it was time to eat again; time to go home!

From beyond the stamping room walls the steam siren wailed heralding the end of the working day. Charles, relieved that another boring day was over, released the steam control and watched as the large cylindrical piston retracted to its resting position before beginning the task of cleaning. The machine would be inspected by the shop supervisor and would need to be spotless before he would be free to vacate it!

At the sound of the second siren, workers collected the few belongings they were permitted to carry and formed themselves into columns that led to narrow, single file exit gates placed side by side and to the officials that stood sentinel on them. It was the practise of these supervisors to select at random a number of individuals that they would subject to a thorough body-search with the express intent of deterring theft. Not so much of coins for that was impossible, but more to prevent the petty theft of easily concealed materials.

As Charles neared the gate through which his line would pass, individuals before him were being singled out for search with meticulous attention. His heart plummeted to his boots as he recalled to mind the penny still concealed in his pocket, he knew beyond doubt what would happen to him if it was discovered. The shock of the recollection compelled him to stop in his tracks to the extreme irritation of the man behind who responded by giving Charles an almighty shove sending him staggering into the men in front of him. Turning away from the growls of protest, Charles glared over his shoulder at his assailant and was about to protest until prudence intervened. The man was a veritable giant and from the hardened sinew that packed his bulging shirt it was clear that he would have floored Charles.

"Stupid Sod!" scathed the giant waving Charles forward, "Get a blinkin move on—we wanna get 'ome tonight!"

Charles resumed his place in sullen resignation closing the gap that he'd caused. He was inwardly seething but level headed enough to know that it was far more sensible to swallow pride and accept this unpalatable state of affairs than to invite trouble.

The distraction had relieved the immediate consternation Charles had felt on remembering the penny he'd stolen but the relief was short lived. The coin now pressed warm into his thigh, it seemed to be determined to make him aware of its presence.

Apprehension returned to hang over him like a dark cloud. Drawing nearer to the inspection area he began to shake, feelings of nausea swept through him sending shivers through his body even though he was hot and clammy. The distance between him and the supervisor diminished inch by inch. His head was pounding and felt as though it was being pierced by razor sharp spikes making the veins at the side of his head pulse and stand out like grotesque earthworms. With each shuffled step he took, the fear in him mounted.

Dark blue stubble had formed on his chin as the day had drawn on, it now stood out in stark contrast to the ashen colour of his fear ridden face. Charles' eyes bulged in their deep-set sockets and were welded to the face of the check-out supervisor, it was obvious to *anyone* looking at Charles that something was very much troubling him. To the sharp, unyielding eyes of the well trained supervisor he was an obvious target.

His expression revealed the secret!

"You!"

The supervisor pointed at Charles, fixing him with steel-hard eyes. Eyes that were blacker than the darkest winter's night. Eyes that burned deep with such piercing ferocity that they conveyed a permanent expression of displeasure befitting his position and adding to the air of intimidation he deliberately conveyed to those beneath him.

"Come on lad, look sharp now!" he barked.

Charles had stopped again, legs rooting him to the spot, all the while the coin pressed hot into his flesh. The devil's tender was taking *joy* from the quandary. Breath now came to him in short staccato gasps as he fought to get air into his lungs and push back the panic that was making his face distort as if in the throws of a seizure. The room took on a drunken rotation, sound around him faded, legs buckled like rubber yet he strove with all his might to regain balance and fight off the attack. Searing pain tore at his chest and the last thing he was aware of before succumbing to oblivion was sending a half-filled jug of water crashing to the floor as his arms thrashed in search of support.

"All-right, stand back, ***stand back!***" the supervisor shouted at the small band of workers that were gathering around Charles,

"***Stand back*** and give the man some air."

"That chap looked proper ill a few minutes ago!" volunteered one of the onlookers.

"Yeah that's right guv." chipped in another, "He went as white as a sheet and near passed-out a good five minutes ago. This bloke here,"—he motioned with his thumb in the direction of the giant, "gave him a wicked shove 'e did . . . . Ill 'e is I reckon!"

The supervisor stepped back to better distance himself from whatever ailment might be confronting him and nodded in a dismissive manner. He hadn't time for all this nonsense, there was still a lot of workers to check through the gate and the delay was making them restless.

Driven by irritation rather than compassion, he summoned an assistant to take two cleared men and carry Charles to the infirmary for attention. He would call on him and check his person as soon as the line was clear. Although not aware of this turn of events or his good fortune, Charles had been manoeuvred through the search area with the stolen trinket undetected in his keeping! He was similarly unaware that the sinister force that had been at work in instigating this outcome, wielded power beyond human comprehension and had drawn him deeper into the macabre contract!

The balloon-bosomed infirmary matron took Charles under her ample wing and thrust a bottle of mind-blasting smelling salts under his nose. The shock of the powerful odour jerking his head as if it had been struck by a club. Charles came instantly to a state of confused consciousness. As his strength returned and his mind began to clear he drew himself up in the wheel back infirmary chair and brushed away the assistance his companions had been affording.

Satisfied that her patient was no longer in need of support, the Matron thanked the men and ushered them out of the infirmary to rejoin the stream of departing workers then returned with a cup of tea for the lucid but still groggy Charles.

He took the cup of hot sweet tea from the Matron's out-stretched hand and cupping it with his fingers, sipped in silence. The Matron scrutinised his every move intently as she searched for signs of whatever had caused the boy to pass out. She pressed Charles with endless questions about his habits and general health and was quite enjoying the diversion. The commotion had been a welcome opportunity for the well intentioned benefactress to exercise her skills. It afforded purpose both to her employment and to the facility she maintained.

Discovering nothing of obvious detriment to his health she took the almost empty cup from him and set about taking his pulse and examining his eyes, cupping his chin in her hand and swivelling his head from side to side to better scrutinize their movement. Again finding nothing, she shook her head in perplexity and concluded her investigation by taking his pulse a second time.

Pledging solemn assurance to the Matron that he would go straight home, take a hot bath and go directly to bed, Charles was released through the infirmary 'staff only' side-door into the thrashing wind and sweet cool of the evening outside, but sweetest of all to *freedom!*

Setting out from the large iron gates of the mint a little shaken, he forced himself into a brisk walk and as each pace put distance between him and that treacherous incident, his spirits lifted. The tension created by the affair diminished with every step he took; feelings of dread and horror were replaced by feelings of euphoric well-being, feelings almost akin to those of invincibility he had experienced on receiving the penny. In time to come he would come to understand why these unfamiliar events were taking place and the price he would be bound to pay for his freedom.

The fragrance of the fresh evening air was sweet on his nostrils and heavy with the scent of damp grass over which floated weak odours of wood smoke. He thought himself lucky to be foot-loose in this beautiful un-cluttered countryside and even the freezing drizzle that was now falling failed to stifle his gratitude for the retention of this freedom.

An accumulation of water droplets that had gathered in the canopy overhead released themselves to cascade over him lending stinging cold refreshment to his weary body and stirring new vigour in his blood. Smiling, he turned up the large collar of his coarse serge over-coat. Drawing the coat more tightly about him he pressed resolutely on, head bowed to shield against the shrill wind. His mind shut out his surroundings as he marched thinking deeply about the events of that day.

"What in the world could I have been thinking of?" He mumbled.

Over and over he repeated the question as he recalled with dismay the act of theft that had brought the coin to him. His light weather tanned complexion gave way to livid crimson as he remembered passing out, *fainting,* before the very eyes of his brawny workmates. It was this perhaps that disturbed him the greatest, he knew he would find it difficult to keep his head up and retain his pride when next he encountered them. He strode on converting the energy of embarrassment into a vigorous pace in the hope of distraction. At least it helped him on his way.

Almost without being aware of the distance he'd covered, Charles arrived at the cottage. The creak of the wicket gate swinging under the pressure of his hand brought his mind back from its meanderings. Looking up in astonishment he took in his absent minded arrival and became aware that he was out of breath; pausing for a moment he took time to recover.

Raising his head he stared at the single oil-lamp relaying its welcome from the window overlooking the path that led to the cottage door. Charles watched the lamp cast out shafts of warm, comforting light that danced and flickered mellow beams reflected through moisture swept in waves upon the wind.

In the room beyond the lamp as dominant as life itself was his Mother, scurrying this way and that as she went about her ritual of fetching and carrying so that all would be ready for the men-folk returning from work.

A half-smile crept across Charles' sallow countenance softening his furrowed brow as he surveyed the comings and goings of this implacable, bustling matron lady of their simple homestead.

In sheer defiance of the penetrating wet of the inhospitable weather Charles remained in his position of obscurity, his heart gladdened by the scene unfolding before him. He could not have known that the coin would see to it that he would look back on this scene in years to come with a longing that would bring him close to utter despair.

He snapped from the daydream as the comprehension of what might have been lost that day came back to him;

he shuddered as he sensed the fingers of more than one kind of coldness creeping through his saturated clothing! Charles stirred himself and made his way to the door, eyes misted by moisture that was not rain. He was home!

The old wrought iron latch clacked as he raised it with his right hand; pushing the door before him he stepped into the tiny flag-floored living room. The breeze that followed him caused the edge of the room to chill in spite of the radiating warmth of the open range coal fire. The large black-leaded range with iron ovens at each side sandwiching the fire was exuding not only reviving energy but was conveying to Charles the odour of coal and wood-smoke suffused with the enticing smell of the evening meal bubbling away in the pots and pans! It was a greeting that is peculiar to many old stone cottages but the hallmark of this one.

The large cast iron kettle with its huge twine-wrapped handle, steamed in readiness for the scalding cup of tea that would help Charles put the cold behind him. Peeling away his saturated garments, he hung them on the wooden pegs driven into the cottage wall beside the doorway where they would dry in readiness for the day to follow. He tugged the heavy hob-nailed working boots from his weary feet and placed them to one side at the outer edge of the hearth away from the direct heat of the fire so that the thick leather wouldn't harden from the heat. There were calluses enough on his feet to give testament to the lessons he had learned through childhood of drying footwear too fast!

Slipping on an old well-worn hand knitted cardigan, he reached up to the soot stained wooden mantle shelf that crowned the fireplace and took down his pipe, only then did he speak!

"Evenin' Mother!"

"Charles." she nodded, acknowledging the greeting in an almost flat, dispassionate way

"Weather's bin a bit like it—I had a notion of buying a boat to come home in!" He joked.

His mother responded with a hollow laugh and continued with her activities without looking up. Though in her late thirties, his mother had a young and melodious way with her laugh that was both endearing and appealing. In normal circumstances her neat frame responded in synchrony with her laugh, but as their eyes met Charles could see that mirth was not reflected in either her face or her actions as he felt it should have been.

She averted her eyes and continued the fetching of plates and paraphernalia to the table slanting her head at an angle to better disengage her eyes from those of her son as he sought to scrutinise her movements. Charles was aware that something was not in its proper place but was unable to identify where the anomaly lay. He could also sense that his Mother was trying to avoid eye contact.

"Something wrong Mother?" he enquired, "You're not your usual self I fancy!"

She stopped with her back to him and placed her hands before her on the white scrubbed wooden table, fingers outstretched in spider-like form; she stared at them unmoving and with supreme effort tried to collect herself and gather whatever strength she could to resist the temptation to clear her conscience of a burden that had now become unbearable.

"Mother? ventured Charles again, his voice rising in consternation as the single word tailed off.

Without a sound her shoulders began to rise and fall and as her proud head sank onto her chest her will gave way; she succumbed with reluctance to the tears that had been waiting for the opportunity to spill since she had become aware that she was with child but without husband!

In that moment she cursed her husband for having died so young in that worthless stone quarry and wished they had remained in the beautiful Welsh valley in which they had both been born and raised. Unable to continue working coal because of injury, her husband had been dismissed and forced to find employment wherever he could and thus they had left the valley they had loved and moved to a dwelling closer to the quarry.

She cursed herself in utter despair for the loneliness of being without a partner and the circumstances that had led her to a momentary lapse in a life-time of irreproachable restraint and for the unwanted fruit of the unfortunate encounter.

As the clear silver moisture of her tears fell one by one upon the table, Charles sped to his Mother's side and placed an arm about her shoulders. In a voice that was heavy with suppressed emotion he ventured,

"Whatever it is that's troubling you Mother, we'll face it together, you me and Tom. We're family and we'll stick together!"

He paused in the hope of response but receiving none added,

"Won't you tell me what it is?"

She inclined her head toward him and through tear stained eyes examined the face of this still very young man. Care-lines already furrowed his brow and he was ageing more swiftly than was fair for such a young heart. She wondered how on earth she was to tell him.

God knows it had been difficult enough feeding and clothing Charles and his brother Tom, younger by two years, with only Charles' wage coming in! True it was supplemented by the few coppers given to Tom in return for the employment he had been newly given at the farm. Pay in the first year was never much, it was more a token than anything since employers believed that they were doing a measurable favour in engaging those starting out, thus affording them status and providing the first step towards manhood and eventual independence.

She brooded on how hard it was to keep bread on the table for the three of them, the thought of yet another mouth to feed and another body to clothe and keep was abhorrent in every sense!

"I wish Father was here my Son,—that's all," she lied, not wanting to burden the lad with such devastating news at so early a stage whilst there might yet be a chance that the situation could right itself. She had thought of somehow ending the pregnancy but her moral senses were outraged even by the thought of such an action.

She determined that she would bite her lip and wait for a more favourable time and more suitable circumstances to share her secret. Faithful to her indomitable nature she brushed away her tears and with them her misery and resumed her interrupted table preparations.

Charles was man enough to recognise that there was something more than the loss of his Father at the back of this, his searching eyes remained locked upon his mother seeking some sign, some notion of what best to do.

He knew that to press his mother in the hope of winning her secret would only result in an obstinate and immovable silence, he accepted that he would have to play the waiting game. Transferring his eyes to the fire for a second, he half-turned in his Mother's direction and with composure and wisdom beyond his years announced with genuine feeling.

"When you're ready mother, I shall be waiting, and here is where I'll always be when you have a need of me!"

He looked across at her as she moved towards the table with the last of the utensils and added as an after thought,

"I'm sure you'll tell me when you have a mind to!"

"Be off with you lad and call your brother," she retorted gesturing toward the rough—hewn stairs with her thumb.

"Whatever next!" she added in feigned indignation and clicked her tongue in reproach. She conveyed an image of stern self assurance to her boys but beneath that sharp, collected and confident exterior lay unimaginable doubt and uncertainty.

The three of them sat in silence as they ate the simple beef and suet stew, grateful for its satisfying taste and wholesome nourishment. Charles helped himself to a second serving, polishing it off in fewer seconds than it took to refill the plate and mopping up the juices with a door-step slice of coarse brown bread baked by his Mother in the side oven of the range.

The two lads cleared the table and whilst Charles emptied the hearth of ashes, Tom fetched cut wood and placed it beside the fire in readiness for the day to follow.

The chores done, the oil-lamp was reduced to the dimmest glow to conserve precious fuel and the tiny room drew silent as it slipped into the hands of the fire-devils emerging from the range to dance and flicker their merry jigs upon walls and ceiling. Charles relaxed almost to a doze as he puffed at his re-kindled pipe, half-closed eyes reflecting the orange glow from the hearth. Deep inside them at that moment there could be seen a measure of pure, undiluted contentment.

He thrust a languid hand into his trouser pocket and there it was!

His blood ran cold as he recognised the familiar feel of the penny. The events at work earlier that day pressed back into sharp focus propelling him from the chair as if scalded, heart pounding in his breast like he had been about to be strangled.

Charles took out the coin and was astonished to find how warm it still felt. He decided it was nothing but body heat and reached above the mantle to deposit the coin in a scraped-out mortar joint until such time as he could think of what best to do with it. One thing was certain, he couldn't take it back to the mint with him and risk the inevitable accusation of theft!

He yawned and stretched himself and early though it was, tapped out his pipe in the ash pan. Bidding a sleepy good night to his kin he made for the stairway.

Gripping the thick rope that ran up one side of the stairwell to steady himself, he clumped up to the three rooms that formed the upper story. Drawing aside the heavy jute curtain that draped the entrance to his room he undressed as fast as he could in a bid to retain as much body heat as possible. The day had taken the best from him as he flopped into the freezing bed.

He awoke bright and early as was his custom but even then was a good half-hour behind his Mother who was already busy in the gloom below. Pouring ice cold water from the earthenware jug on the dresser, he filled the wash-bowl and sluiced his upper body with energy and purpose bringing a rosy glow to his healthy young cheeks. Charles completed the ablution with vigorous towelling to get blood coursing through his sleep dulled muscles.

Throwing on his clothes he clattered down the open wooden stairway to the hearth to absorb the remaining warmth from the embers of the almost spent fire.

"As soon as you please Charles!" called his mother, from the adjoining room. He knew at once that she was waiting for him to re-kindle the fire that served not only as heating for the whole cottage, but also as the sole source of heat for cooking. Charles threw himself into the task making good use of the now dry wood placed by his brother the night before. He threw on a paraffin block raking it into the base of the logs where it sprang to life raising the room from oppressive gloom to animated life. Squatting on hands and knees he blew into the fire and within a few minutes had a magnificent blaze going to greet his kin and bring a little cheer to the new day.

The fire-devils that had been biding their time in slumber, now awoke and refreshed their frenetic grip upon the shadows speaking with vigour the crack and spit that is the language of their own!

Taking up the large fire blacked kettle that hung in the ingle-nook hearth, Charles made for the door which he unlatched, opened and stepped through in a single movement kicking it shut with his heel. As he did so, a mixture of bitter cold air and sleet pressed through the opening as if to challenge the right of the fire to its domain. The chill of the swirling eddies came as a shock forcing him to throw his free arm across his face in an act of defence. He wished at once that he had put on an over garment of some kind. He pressed in haste through the freezing weather to the well-head cloaked in the blackness of early morning. Dawn would wait a while longer before the fingers of its first light would come creeping over the horizon!

Icicles hung like duelling swords from the gabled cover that served to house and protect the windlass and rope that suspended the heavy wooden dipping bucket. As Charles turned the heavy iron handle, its clanking broke away some of the overhanging icicles creating a musical ping almost as if they were glad to be liberated from the entrapment of an unwanted resting place. Above the whistle of the biting wind he could hear faint splashes as the falling shards hit the water below; the sound was soon lost to Charles however, his attention diverted to the numbness of his fingers and the violent shivering that was making his teeth chatter.

He hoisted the bucket as fast as he could in an attempt to work up body heat and with stiffened fingers decanted the water clumsily into the kettle losing almost a half of it as he did so. Driven by cold and a sense of extreme necessity, he scurried for the house with what he had!

Bursting through the door he thrust out the heel of his heavy working boot and kicked it shut with a loud thud as he made directly for the life-reviving warmth of the blazing fire. He dumped the freezing kettle on the hot range evoking a loud hiss from the contact and stood before the fire rubbing his hands together to restore feeling.

Charles basked a moment or two in the sheer pleasure of the heat before tossing on a few more logs. Although they were not needed, the action imparted to him a sense of satisfaction, almost of achievement!

With feeling returning to his fingers, he lifted the half-filled kettle and hoisted it onto the hinged iron cradle built into the hearth and swung it over the fifteen inch high flames that were now licking from the fire. The smell of burning wood pervaded every corner of the house; through it, moments later, came the odour of pan cooked bacon and fried doorsteps of bread as Charles busied himself with the making of the first meal of the day!

Just once a week, on Sunday, each member of the family would experience the luxury of a single fried egg to complement the everyday breakfast of bacon and fried bread. The remaining eggs from the few hens they were fortunate to own, were used for baking bread and the occasional cake.

Charles looked after the fire as was expected of the eldest male of the family but, since he was at the fire anyway, he had elected to tend the breakfast pan to give his Mother a short break from the endless duties of cooking and household chores. It was a task he accepted without fuss even though he sometimes felt a little foolish at doing what was generally accepted to be the work of the lady of the house.

He reached up and carved a generous slice from the cloth-covered, salted and smoked sow belly hanging beside the hearth and popped it into the pan. The boiling fat protested and spat as if in objection to this addition but Charles ignored its dissent humming an unmusical melody as he continued with his task. Mixed smoke and frying odours curled high into the house stealing through every room and acting like cheese in a mouse-trap to stir his Brother and bring him clumping down the stairs with an empty belly and a strong sense of expectation!

Like all young men, he was always hungry and there was nothing like a good night's sleep to work up a young man's appetite!

As he approached within an arm's length of Charles, Tom's stomach let out an almighty and unmistakable rumble telegraphing his gastronomic condition and his need of early sustenance. Charles turned and was about to voice his disapproval but held back as he was greeted with a cheery grin that threatened to split his Brother's countenance in two!

"Crikey!" exclaimed Tom, "I could eat a ruddy horse!"

He craned his neck and looked around Charles' shoulder at the pan,

"Got any done yet?"

"Wait your turn Tom," chided Charles, "Mother hasn't eaten yet and she's been up a full hour!"

"Sorry." mumbled Tom. He pulled his thick leather belt in a notch and settled himself at the side of the hearth where he could receive the benefit of the warmth from the fire and at the same time keep his eye on the pan. His tummy rumbled again!

Charles paused for a moment, half-turned toward his brother and fixing him with a steady gaze asked,

"You had a wash yet?"

"Sod off!" came the truculent reply.

Charles was taken aback but was quick to regain the initiative.

"No wash—no breakfast mate! An' I'm pretty sure *I* can make room for another helping."

"There isn't any water left in the jug—you used it all *mate*!" retorted Tom. He was beginning to irritate Charles for it seemed that Tom was not only finding his feet now that he was a working man, he was also finding his tongue but employing it in a most annoying manner.

Charles spun on his heel and raising the cooking fork to within an inch of Tom's face blasted out:

"Take the pail and *fetch* water, and while you're there, you have a bloody *wash*!"

Tom flinched at the sight of the fork, eyes widening with dread; he was in no doubt that he was about to be impaled upon it. He made to take a step back but as he did so, the wood pile he had formed the night before caught his ankle, propelling him into the wooden hearth chair with a thump. His long un-combed hair fell forward covering his entire face giving him the appearance of something resembling a cross between a mop leaning against a sack of potatoes and a shaggy sheep-dog.

Charles burst into laughter as Tom let forth an un-modulated shriek of anguish that brought his mother hurrying from the kitchen curious to know the reason for this uncharacteristic early morning commotion!

"What are you two up to? you're making enough noise to wake the dead, if you haven't enough to do that you have time to play games then I'll soon find something for you!" She scolded.

She eyed them both with disdain and fixing her steely gaze on Tom she waved a finger at him and barked impatiently, "Tom get up and get proper dressed this minute and when you've done,—fetch water and wood!"

She scurried away in the direction of the kitchen muttering under her breath, "The devil finds work for idle hands alright!"

Even as she made the remark she recalled her own plight and the work the devil had found for her. A cold chill gripped her and her head began to swim. Reeling, she thrust out a hand to the doorway and grasped the frame to steady herself. Beads of clammy perspiration stood out on her forehead and her complexion became deathly pale transforming her face into a ghastly white mask.

Easing her grip on the doorframe, she slid the hand above her shoulder and leaned forward clutching the pit of her stomach with the other; she felt wretched and strength had all but drained from her. Charles could see that something was wrong, he lifted the heavy pan from the fire and placed it to the side of the range and in a few brisk strides he was at his mother's side. Without a word he placed an arm about her and turned her toward him, taking her hand from the doorway he placed it on his shoulder. He drew her trembling body to him and eased her head to rest on his other shoulder. There they remained, motionless save for the stifled sobs his mother was trying to hold back so tightly that their energy drifted to the silent heaving of her shoulders.

Charles gripped her with a firmness that drained the blood from his knuckles, tears welled in his eyes, gathered and ran from his face to mingle in his mother's soft hair.

It was in this moment that Tom returned. He halted at the door uncertain of what had taken place in his absence, he was certain that something terrible must have happened or his mother wouldn't be hanging on to Charlie this way. He looked on in silence as he eased the door shut and gingerly replaced the latch not wanting to make a sound or even breathe out loud for fear of making the situation worse. He listened tight lipped for some whisper, some inkling of what this state of affairs might mean but Charles had his back to him and his mother's face was obscured, buried in Charles' shoulder.

Through the gloom he could see little of what was transpiring so, driven by curiosity he edged closer, ears pricked for the slightest sound.

Collecting her strength, she eased Charles from her taking care not to hurt his feelings, with a fleeting glance at him she departed to her kitchen, her haven. This was her sanctum sanctorum, the place where she dreamed her dreams and to where she would come when she felt need of solitude.

As her glance had swept over him, Charles caught the glint of moisture imparting polish to his mother's clear eyes. He could also see a sadness approaching despondency in them and cursed himself for the inadequacies of his youth and his lack of knowledge of the ways of women.

"Charlie?" Whispered Tom.

Charles stood rock-still, staring in wistful silence at the kitchen doorway, an unbecoming frown creased his young countenance. A frown that was slicing his skin into deep furrows, worry-lines that would soon make themselves a permanent feature. His mind had turned inward and had become so engaged in anxiety over what had just passed that he was both blind and deaf to all around him.

"Charlie!" snapped Tom, digging Charles in the kidneys with the crook of his elbow,

"What's going on?"

Charles turned and regarded his brother with hostility, he fixed him with a cold, un-blinking stare but offered not a word.

The eyes of the two men locked for a moment, Charles raised a finger and was about to deliver a strong remonstration to his Brother when he noticed the look of uncertainty, of worry and fear in Tom's eyes. He yielded at once transforming his irritation at his Brother's ignorance into feelings of understanding and compassion. He stretched out his hand in a gesture of consolation and placed it on Tom's shoulder.

"It's alright Tom," he said softly, "Mother's a bit under the weather and I fancy she may have some sort of bad news to be giving us shortly."

He turned his head in the direction of the kitchen doorway to re-affirm that his mother was not listening; detecting no sign of movement he continued, "I don't mind telling you that I'm a bit worried about leaving her alone today but there's nothing to be done for it!"

"I could ask the boss to let me go after the milking Charlie, I could make up the time on Sunday an' I know he'd be happy about that!"

Tom lowered his eyes to his feet and shuffled with embarrassment as he went on,

"If that would be any help that is?

"You're a good 'un Tom,—truly mate, I think that'd be just grand and I know it'd be a great comfort to mother."

"That's done then," said Tom with an air of finality.

"You alright mother?" Charles called in the direction of the kitchen.

"Of course I am," returned the curt reply, "Land sakes lad you take too much on yourself . . . . I never felt better," she lied again. "Hadn't you both best be off to work,—have you seen the time?"

The lads glanced first at each other then at the old wooden clock, even without seeing the time they knew they were late.

"Heck!" they cried in unison and dashed for the door grabbing their caps and coats as they went!

Charles was sensitive to the lateness of the hour as he marched, simply by the feel of things around him, given his present financial circumstances it would be a long time before he would be able to own a time-piece. For the present, his body aligned time with nature and measured its passing by natural events that are ever present and plentiful as long as you know where to look for them!

He fortified his brisk pace with powerful long-legged strides to make up for the time lost at the cottage and was soon perspiring so freely that, despite the fine clinging sleet, he was forced to unbutton his coat to let his body ventilate.

The birds were singing their morning tribute to the opening day in a diversity of song that would in normal circumstance be a joy to Charles but the lateness of the hour had robbed him of this pleasure and drove him to lengthen his pace. His breath was now coming in short, strenuous gasps parching his throat from the strain.

Thus he arrived at the mint and presented himself to the booking-in clerk to sign the attendance register just two minutes before the closing deadline.

The clerk eyed him with unconcealed scorn, his piercing eyes stabbing barbarous glances over his pince-nez spectacles in silent challenge to the right of this young person to employ sheer effrontery in presenting himself to a superior in such a depleted condition *moments* before the serious business of His Majesty's mint was to commence! Charles signed, darted a wan smile in his direction and was gone.

The long, shrill blast from the siren heralded the beginning of the working day. One by one engines clattered to life developing energy to drive the myriad of overhead shafts and pulley wheels that powered the conglomeration of machinery. Ascending commotion accompanied the hiss of escaping steam from warming die presses. The rattle and clack of overhead leather belts grew louder as shafts and wheels gained momentum. The expanding din, now interspersed by dull, hesitant thuds, intensified in volume as each operator worked his press up to speed until the familiar crash and clank convoluted to become a cacophony of un-harmonious rhythm bleating out the notes of a discordant symphony.

Blue smoke gathered and began its curling journey to the fanlights above whilst minds drifted in search of pleasing distractions as each operator became submerged beneath the burden of endless repetition!

Thus the days passed, one after another except for Sunday, the day of rest and religious celebration upon which best boots were cleaned, fresh clothing donned and neckties worn as families attended their chosen place of worship.

Ministers would climb pulpits with great deliberation from where they would survey the sinners below in attitudes of lofty contempt, roaring forth in animated disdain sermons of intended redemption. It struck fear into the hearts of the most hardened of men and reduced all to a state of intrinsic obedience and piety. On this day, at the conclusion of religious celebrations, old friends were re-met and new friendships kindled. Young men would stand around in small groups making sheep's eyes at the young fillies chaperoned by their kin in the hope of being introduced to a future partner. Gossip as well as news would be exchanged. Nothing could escape the ritual and no stone would be left un-turned in the search for controversial topics, good news was accepted with equanimity whilst bad news was welcomed with eager relish and with special particular if it concerned the demise of some unfortunate soul! Small wonder then that no-one courted mischance!

The oil lamp in the cottage window was all but snuffed as Charles arrived home. The occurrence set his mind racing with anxiety, it was out of character for his Mother and unusual in the extreme. He had been aware of subtle changes in her manner since the evening that he had arrived home with the penny. Although some weeks had passed since then, she had still not confided the reason for her evasive behaviour. Charles could see for himself how uneasy and irritable she was becoming, she was not her usual self at all! For all that, he was unable to bring himself to broach the subject of her discomfort; he had said he wouldn't press her, he had said that he would wait until she was ready and therefore wait he must. His word was his bond and bond was honour and he would never break it whatever the cost to him!

He swung the gate shut behind him and strode to the door; even as he raised the latch he sensed rather than felt that something of sinister consequence was about to unfold!

Stepping into the gloom of the near dark room, Charles was staggered to find that the usual cheery fire was but a few embers of spent timber smouldering in the hearth. A sense of dread rose deep in his breast as his eyes adjusted to the gloom in the space before him. The cold and damp of late February had driven the heat out of the room and replaced it with a chill that penetrated the very bones of the body yet there was his mother, sat at the almost spent range staring at the pots and pans that should have been boiling and bubbling above the iron fire-grate. She was clad in a thin cotton dress with a light shawl of wool over her shoulders, her face bore an expression of tormented despair that twisted her features into a hideous mask of grey wrinkles. Her eyes were unseeing, expressionless and un-blinking, clouded by an opaque film imparting to her countenance the appearance of the living dead.

Charles was dumbfounded, rooted to the spot. His legs felt as if they were made of lead and his hand had locked upon the door latch.

"Mother?" he called but there was no response.

"*Mother*?" he called again, seeking the reaction he so desperately wanted to see. His faltering voice was heavy with consternation and fear. It was the same sort of paralysing fear that had gripped him so rigidly on the day he had received the penny. Now that consuming fear was preventing him from moving further into the room, it was a fear of the worst possible kind!

Obsession flooded over him in a powerful wave shaking him free of the dread and propelling him to his mother's side.

"NO!" he bellowed, the word bursting from his dry lips,

"NO!" he cried again shaking his mother's shoulders,

"NO, NO, *NO*!" he repeated time and time again shaking her lifeless body but there was no response, no movement, no feeling. He flung off his over-coat and under-jacket and wrapped them tightly about his mother brushing away the tears that were coursing down his cheeks with the back of his hand. He forced from his mind the coldness in the room that was needling at his body.

He thrust three paraffin blocks into the embers of the fading fire and dropped to his knees, blowing with all his might he could feel pin-pricks starting at the back of his eyes. With a dull 'pouf' the fire sprang to life energised by the volatile blocks onto which he threw tinder-dry kindling and split logs, almost at once warmth began to penetrate the room and drive back the numbing cold and all consuming gloom. Charles turned once more to his mother, she was exactly as she had been when he had first found her, there was no movement, no sign of life. Fearing the worst, he strode to the door he had left open and shut it smartly; fetching blankets, he added them to the coats that hung on his mother's body.

He took her hands in his and rubbed them with a fierceness that surprised him, next her fore-arms then her feet, then in turn moving from one to the other in a ceaseless sweep driven by desperation. The heat of the fire on his back was truly welcome but he shuffled to one side to enable it to work the better on his mother, drawing her chair closer he swivelled it around to afford her the best exposure to its reviving radiance.

The tiniest of sighs broke from her blue lips and sent Charles' spirits soaring. He rubbed the harder for the encouragement, overpowering relief mingled with feelings of elation and light-headedness. Above the crackling of the growing fire Charles became conscious of high-pitched chuckling resembling that of a deranged fool and was stunned beyond belief to discover that the sounds were coming from his own throat!

With imperceptible slowness the film that had stolen over his Mother's eyes began to recede, her features regained colour casting out the hideous death-mask appearance. The pallor of her drained features began to brighten as life returned to her face. Charles fell to his knees and embraced his Mother, hugging her tight to him.

The kettle hissed a scornful warning as it boiled over into the powerful heat of the fire sending clouds of dense, moist vapour into the room. Relinquishing his embrace, Charles reached out and swung the iron cradle suspending the kettle away from the fire; he set about putting the boiling water to good use by making a pot of tea. It was an uncalculated action, automatic almost in its performance yet in its sheer simplicity it was a unique act of celebration, a traditional gesture of refreshment, of family welcome, of home coming!

As strength returned to her, Charles' Mother cast off the drapes about her shoulders and rose without hurry to her feet. She reached with feeble fingers for a heavy shawl that she had left draped over the back of the fireside chair. It was warm from the blaze of the stifling fire. She placed it about her shoulders not so much for warmth but more for the comfort and ease of mind it brought her. The coats were a warm and thoughtful necessity she knew but were impregnated with a mixture of the stale odour of male perspiration and mould, as were most garments worn by humble working men. In that moment she felt no wish to be reminded of men.

She returned to her seat at the fire, drawing her chair a distance from it to prevent the wool of her shawl being curled by the heat. Charles positioned himself to one side of the hearth and watched, not a word passed between them. Darting a fleeting glance at him her heart softened, the tenderness of his years showed clearly in his face, his eye-brows had drawn together and his features had become ashen with anxiety and uncertainty. Her Son's soft brown eyes were unblinking as he followed his mother's every move. She glanced again at him and felt pity that she had not done more to smarten his dishevelled and untidy clothing. A tiny smile stole across her thin lips as she noticed for the first time, how baggy and poor fitting they were.

"You're a good lad Tom!" she whispered.

"It's Charles mother!" Chided Charles in playful correction.

She looked up at his face, half-lit from the light of the fire and managed a weak chuckle,

"Heaven forbid!" she mused,

"As if I don't know me own son, what in the world am I coming to?"

An awkward silence stole between them and as it gathered pace it became difficult for either of them to find words to sever it.

Charles' mind raced as he searched his head for something to offer, something that would help her feel more at ease, *anything!* He was still struggling with this when his mother made an announcement that hit him with the force of a heavy hammer. Her words slammed into his brain with an effect that astounded him, shaking him to the very core and sending his mind reeling in shock.

The words came in a whisper but with a heavy burden of finality, they came like the cutting edge of a mighty cleaver.

"I'm going to have a baby Charles!"

He was thunderstruck from the weight of her declaration and just stared, mouth wide in astonishment. She raised her eyes and engaged his in unfettered resignation. Experience of life would lend her the confidence to hold her head up in defiance of a situation she knew would be incalculably difficult to endure and from which deep disgrace and isolation must befall the family. She knew also that, in his lack of understanding of the ways of life, the true import of such an unfortunate incident would be almost impossible for Charles to comprehend.

Their eyes remained locked for what seemed like minutes; strength determination and obstinacy in hers, astonished incredulity and doubt in his. It was a while before Charles gathered composure enough to enquire in a faltering voice,

Wh . . . How?" He stammered pleadingly, his voice betraying the confusion that had robbed him of the power of coherent thought at the time he was most in need of it. Words would just not come no matter how hard he searched!

For some weeks past, she had been dreading the moment she would have to tell her sons of her situation and it was dread of this and the shame she knew it must bring that had led to her mental break-down. Now that her secret was out she felt strength rising within that had been lacking for some time, an inner calmness and confidence that somehow things would work out! She embraced the feeling with gratitude for she knew now that if she led the way, the shame and ill-feeling that this unplanned event would bring to the household might be borne without lasting bitterness or resentment among the family.

In the months to come the strength of her sons would be her only sustaining support and would give her the courage and fortitude she would need to weather the snipes and wicked innuendoes of those that had once been pleased to number themselves among her trusted 'friends'. Thus it was imperative above all, that she held tightly to her the loyalty, trust, and love of her two young lads.

Charles searched his mother's eyes for several long minutes before regaining composure, finding no solutions in them remarked plainly,

"I knew there was something terrible wrong mother, I knew it all along! It's been a while since father died an' I s'pose it's been hard for you what with me and Tom to raise!—I don't know how it came about and I don't want to know unless you have a mind to tell me, but is there any chance that whoever it is will do the decent thing and wed you"

"No my son", she replied.

"He's wed already—that is he is *now*, at the time this happened he made a promise to me though heaven knows why I should have been foolish enough to believe him! I've known him since we were children and I've always known him for no-good!"

"Tell me who he is and I'll break his bloody neck!" vowed Charles, furious that his mother should have been tricked, used and discarded in so abominable a manner. He hadn't given a thought for the far-reaching effect that the event would have; hadn't visualised the scorn and derision that would haunt every move he made, every step he and his family would take!

"That won't help Charles, what's done is done and nothing can change that, we must be good and ready for what is to come and be thankful for whatever friends are left to us—," her voice trailed off reluctant to continue, she shifted her harsh gaze to her feet. She alone understood the hardships that were to come. A sudden shiver took her as a mental picture of what the future might hold passed in fleeting anguish through her mind. She drew her shawl tighter about her in an act of self-protection and began rocking her chair. She had withdrawn into herself shutting the door on reality and the present and without uttering a word had made it plain that further conversation would be pointless.

Charles moved a few steps closer to her and resting his hand on her shoulder gave it a gentle squeeze. She reached up with her hand and placed it on his, her fingers beating out a silent tattoo upon it as she moved deeper into herself and her innermost thoughts.

When Tom was given the news, he took it with indifference and apart from asking what was to be done, dismissed the whole thing as trivial! It seemed that the two years between him and his brother might just as well have been twenty—such is the sweet unawareness, the ignorance of youth!

Months wore on and the child within grew stronger with each passing day conveying to all but the blind, the news of its coming! Friends began to drift away one by one, not wishing to be seen associating with a family into which would be born a child with no declared nor discernible father. Such things were not done for not only was it considered to be immoral but was regarded as an act of despicable sin, the perpetrator to be shunned and scorned. The child would surely be no good! Decent society would offer no tolerance or understanding. The mother, the child and the family would be afforded no help, no relief, they were not to be spoken with and propriety would demand that upstanding folk should cross the street rather than risk an encounter with them.

Needless to say they would no longer be welcome at church nor tolerated at Chapel for the nature of the sin was of sufficient infamy that redemption or understanding must be out of the question, wasted indeed! There was always the workhouse for such miscreants. An establishment most suitable for such people whose worthless lives would in any case be short because of their irredeemable nature! Seen through the eyes of their peers and superiors, transportation to the colonies would be a more suitable and befitting solution to their situation since it would rid society of wasters and at the same time provide much needed labour at places where demand was always at a premium due to the unfortunate and most inconvenient mortality rate!

As the months wore on, fewer and fewer folk would have anything to do with the family and although Tom was maintained in employment at the farm he was no longer gifted the vegetables that he used to take home for the family. Had it not been that his employer was as much in need of Tom as Tom was in need of employment, it was certain that he would have been dismissed.

The loaves of coarse bread that Tom used to obtain from the son of the hamlet baker in exchange for some of the excess vegetables he was given were now also denied him as he found door after door closed to his company! These things were of little importance to him and were as nothing in comparison with the finger-pointing and name calling that followed on his heels as he passed daily to and from the farm!

Thus the family diet gradually reduced to whatever could be cultivated within the confines of their own small patch of land for none it seemed would now afford them compassion or assistance of any nature. The procurement of flour and salt for the bread they must now bake themselves had passed into the hands of Charles who was still able to buy from a tiny store run by a Mrs Freeborn at the village beyond the mint. It was fortunate indeed that gossip had not yet travelled that far!

CHAPTER 3

Another Mouth to Feed

C HARLES CRADLED THE BABY in his arms afraid to hold her too firmly lest he should hurt her, but wanting to hug her to him from sheer joy! She was the most beautiful creature he had ever seen and he felt a strong and exhilarating bond with her at once. Feelings stirred in his heart that he had never experienced before. He was certain beyond all shadow of doubt that his purpose in life was to protect her, to see that she grew up safe and happy, untroubled by the vagaries of their meagre existence!

The moment of her birth had been something of a miracle in itself; the preparations for the confinement had been concluded weeks before and Charles had been well briefed by his Mother regarding what was to happen.

To say that he was ready would be sanguine indeed for the lad was terrified about the part he was expected to play and more than a little concerned about what would happen should the child arrive when he was away at work. With Tom at the farm and Charles at the mint, his Mother would have no-one to help her or see her through. No friends now remained that could be called on to take care of her so everything would rest on him and his Mother's strength. Thoughts of death in childbirth visited him almost every night as he lay in his bed listening with dread for the first sound of the new arrival. How would he know? What would he do? Would he be capable enough to do the right thing if his Mother lost consciousness? Doubts were now so much a part of his life that he hadn't noticed that winter had given way to spring and spring to summer and that he was now approaching nineteen years old!

As doubts multiplied, concentration at work had become more and more difficult for Charles so that his production quota had fallen below the expectations of the mint. It came as no surprise to him to be summoned to the supervisors office and informed that he was no longer required. Charles pleaded for the opportunity to work out the rest of the day; the family would need the money to clothe and feed the newborn in the days to come, but it was to no avail. He was escorted to the gate and given a shove to help him on his way.

Charles had been well enough paid considering his age and for all its boredom, had tolerated his employment in order to ensure that his family could enjoy a tolerble existence. What were they to do now? He dreaded the thought of having to burden his Mother with this new blow that would add to the misery that was already building up for the family. He made his way home without enthusiasm. His mood brightened as his mind recalled the few salted hams they still had left in the pantry and the winter vegetables in the garden. He would make the family a decent meal from them so that at least they would eat well for a day or two whist he sought new pastures!

It was a strange occurrence indeed for Charles to be arriving home at noon but here he was with but a few hundred yards to go. He had passed the entire journey in deep contemplation of the predicament that had befallen him and somehow despondency had receded and given way to optimism. He consoled himself by asserting that he would put things right, he would see that everything would turn out for the best whatever life had yet to throw at them!

An unusual scene confronted Charles as he approached the cottage gate; tethered outside was something he had never seen there before.

'That's odd' he murmured, addressing himself, 'a pony and trap'?

Passing through the cottage door he heard it for the very first time—the unmistakeable sound of a baby's cry! There were voices upstairs and none of them were Tom's *or* his Mother's.

Without shedding his boots he took the wooden stairs three at a time wondering what to make of this unfamiliar situation when he was drawn up in his tracks by a woman he had never set eyes on before. She barred the way to his Mother's bedroom with her well proportioned frame, a single finger pressed tight against her pursed lips.

"SHhhhh!" she warned, "Your Mother needs rest and time to see to your little Sister".

Charles' mouth hung open, there were a million questions racing through his mind but all he could stammer was,

"Who in God's kingdom are *you* Missus?"

The woman chuckled rippling the fat around her midriff and replied with good humour,

"I am Doctor Moody's Wife my lad. Doctor Moody and I have been aware for some time of your Mother's condition and have been passing by each day during the Doctor's house calls. It was fortunate indeed that such a call brought us to your door at the very moment that your Sister began to arrive, so it is that we were at hand to see to everything for her."

Charles could no longer suppress the anxiety that had been lingering in his heart since learning that a child was to come, nor the dread he had harboured knowing that he alone might have to deliver the infant. An enormous wave of relief washed over him, if only he had known that the Doctor and his Wife had been taking an interest in his Mother. It was as if a dark and heavy veil had been lifted from the skies to reveal the sunshine of a glorious day!

"I-I-I," he stammered, unable to draw upon the words he so desperately needed to thank these caring and wonderful folk who had put aside the edicts of Society and religious hierarchy to help a being less fortunate than themselves.

Gathering his wits Charles ventured,

"I don't know how we can ever repay you M'am," He shook his head in regret, "I have just my lost my job and the only real income this family has; we are penniless!"

The finger again made its way to the pursed lips and with a smile Mrs Moody whispered,

"We all have our difficulties in life my lad and I'm sure that when the time comes you will repay us many times over, all it needs is opportunity and God's blessing!"

"May I see my Mother?"

"Not for a while yet, when the Doctor is finished I will wash her and change her into clean clothing then, after the baby is fed, I will take you up to see her but remember, she will need lots of rest!"

"In that case I'll go and get on with making food but please see that Mother knows I'm here and thinking of her—and my Sister!" he added in sweet afterthought.

He made his way to the kitchen and set about peeling potatoes, cutting them into small segments to make them easier for his Mother to digest. Once they were in the pot with water he set off to the garden to pull turnips and carrots, he would make stew his Mother would be glad to eat! Life seemed sweeter somehow.

Charles swung the cradle suspending the large pot over the fire and threw on more wood. There was enough shop bread for this meal as long as they used it sparingly but from now on they would have to bake what they needed themselves. Charles must ask his Mother how to bake for whilst he was at the mint there had never been time enough for him to learn. He stared into the fire his mind for the time being contented with the state of affairs. Relieved of the worry of what to do in child birth, he drifted into a grateful half-sleep.

The scalding hiss of pots boiling over accompanied the distant wail of a hungry newborn wrenching him from slumber and a world of pleasant meanderings to the reality of the vows he had made and the duties he had newly undertaken which honour and self-respect would demand he fulfil!

He swung the pot away from the blaze to allow it to cool and added the ham he had prepared in the kitchen, the result was beginning to give out the odour of a sound meal! Charles added a pint of good home brewed ale he was fond of making (and indeed drinking!) and a little stock left over from a Duck he had been lucky enough to find shot by the gentry but for some reason had not been picked up.

It seemed that a month of afternoons had passed before Doctor and Mrs Moody came down the stairs, Charles glanced up from his pot tending and rose to his feet as the Doctor approached.

"How is she Doctor?" he asked.

"Mother and child are both well and healthy my son, but see that your Mother stays in bed for the next few days until she has recovered enough strength to cope; strong though she is, she has endured a great deal of pain and extreme discomfort, will you do that for me"?

Doctor Moody smiled and with a gesture towards the upstairs added,

"You may go and see your new Sister now but don't stay too long"!

Charles made to move then checked himself. He thrust out a hand and took the Doctor's in his shaking it vigorously,

"I can't thank you both enough, you have been so wonderful and generous. I hope the folk around will realize what good Samaritans you both are"!

"Tush my lad, only doing what God intended"! returned the Doctor, "I'll call again the day after tomorrow but if you should need me for any reason, send your Brother and I will come at once"!

The Doctor turned to leave, hesitated, then turned to face Charles again and remarked,

"Mrs Moody tells me you have been released from the mint and it occurs to me that, since I am no longer a young man, you might like to take up employment with me. I am in need of someone to drive my trap and tend to my pony that I might be relieved of the burden of bridling, hitching and stable cleaning. I am afraid that the wage will be only 10/5d per week and is probably much less than you deserve but it is all we can manage at this time. Will this be of any help to you my Son"?

"Help Sir, *help?*, it would be downright marvellous and would make all the difference in the world to us"! Charles exclaimed,

"Only thing is I never learned how to drive a pony and trap"!

"Nothing to it"! winked the Doctor, "I will teach you all you need to know and perhaps a few doctoring tricks as well such as first aid so that you can be of constructive help to me should an emergency arise." The Doctor thought for a second then suggested, "Perhaps if your Mother is well enough you would be kind enough to start on Monday?"

"I will be at your house at seven o'clock sharp Sir and will be proud to stay until you have no further need of me"!

"Very good my boy, I will look forward to it"! concluded the Doctor as he followed his Wife through the open door into the fresh summer air of the July early evening

As the door clacked shut, Charles sped up the stairs to his Mother's room. Pausing at the curtained door he listened to be sure not to disturb her if she was busy with the baby, there was nothing but silence.

He rapped gingerly on the door frame taking care not to disturb the heavy door curtain and waited. There was no acknowledgement. The silence was disturbing, he was growing both concerned and confused by the lack of response. If his Mother was not well enough to respond he should go in, if on the other hand she was resting, the last thing he wanted was to wake her. He turned to leave but impulse and caution made him draw the curtain just a tiny bit and peek in. It was the first time he had ever seen the face of a newborn child. She was fast asleep and snuggling tight to the body of his dozing Mother.

She was bright pink and wrinkly and was the tiniest living creature Charles had ever seen.

Her eyes were screwed tight shut as if the light hurt though there was not much of it! Her mouth was tiny and formed like a perfect rose bud about to open, she was sucking her lower lip with funny little smacking noises. She held one tiny arm above her head waving it occasionally as if in greeting; her fingers, oh! her fingers, so small and beautifully formed, opening and closing as if asking for something or perhaps calling him.

Charles was captivated, this was **his** sister, his very **own!**

Hiiisssssss! The stew attempted to extinguish the fire.

Charles let the curtain fall back into place and made his way downstairs with the subtlety of a galloping rhinoceros,

"Crikey"! he blurted, "I haven't taken off me boots yet"!

He swung the pot further from the heat, the stew bubbling like a living thing, had taken on the appearance and the aroma of a fine meal.

'By the time Mother wakes, Tom will be home and the food will be ready for us all' he muttered to himself. 'Time I got myself a pint'!

He made his way into his Mother's kitchen and drew a quaff of fine ale from the wooden flagon that his Father had made when teaching Charles the rudiments of beer making. He held the rough cast glass tumbler up to the light of the tiny kitchen window, his chest swelled with pride as he examined the crystal clear liquid given added polish by the remains of the evening sun. God was in his heaven and all the world at peace.

He carried the beer through to the warmth of the range and reached for his pipe before sitting down in the fireside chair, for once he felt really good about things. He had lost his job, found another at very little loss, and gained a sister all in the same day, but best of all, his Mother had received the gift of compassion and support when she most needed it by folk Charles had judged as uncaring!

He was on his second glass and almost aglow when Tom arrived.

Bursting breathless through the door Tom began to bleat.

"Oh Charlie"! he began, "That farmer *knows* I 'ave to be 'ome early to tend to Mum, but he keeps finding stuff for me to do and won't let me go even though I work extra on Sundays for nothin"! "What are *you* doin' home so early"?

"Don't fret Tom, Mothers had the baby, it's a little girl and she's lovely"!

Tom stood there dumbstruck, mouth wide open. Finally and with effort he collected himself enough to ask,

"Kin I go an' see 'em"?

"Not for a while" replied Charles, "They're both sound asleep and the Doctor says we must leave 'em be"!

"Has she got a name yet"?

"Course she has, its MOTHER you daft bugger"!

"Not *Mother*, the *baby*"! Tom retorted.

"Till Mother wakes up I don't know any more than you old Son, we'll just have to wait and see"! Charles winked and that seemed to satisfy the needs of the situation.

"What's that lovely smell"? enquired Tom, his nostrils flaring to better catch the aroma of the simmering stew.

"Supper lad, but not 'till Mum wakes up—She's in more need of it than us"!

"Sod!" cursed Tom pulling in his belt as if to say 'If I don't get fed soon I'll perish'!

Charles smiled and returned to his pipe, raising his pint he mused upon how unpredictable and fickle life could be. Without knowing it he had come of age as a man, not by years but by actions and had established his position as head of the family.

Both men sat before the range exchanging the occasional word here and there whiling away time until finally Charles could restrain impatience no longer.

"I think I'll pop up and see if Mother is awake"! he announced with an abruptness that startled his Brother.

Tom shot a glance at him, grateful that this turn of events might lead to his getting something to eat, his belt would pull in no further. Charles rose from the chair, tapped out his pipe which he placed on the rack that his Father had made for his own pipes and turned to make his way upstairs. As he did so there came the shriek of a hungry infant—loud enough to blast the crows from their nests and the rabbits from their underground bastions.

"Charles"! came the almost inaudible cry, "*Charles*"!

Again Charles took the stairs in groups of three and in a trice was at the bedroom door.

"I'm here Mother"! he exclaimed, "I'll *always* be here"!

"Come in my Son", she called over the baby's wail.

He strode quiet as he could to his Mother's side and took her hand in his.

"I've made stew for you as soon as you're ready to eat Mother".

She looked at him and squeezed his hand with affection.

"I've fed your sister and I feel so hungry myself I could eat a donkey my Son. Your stew will be perfect, couldn't have wished for anything better but I feel too weak to come down, may I have it here"?

"Just give me a couple of jiffy's Mother"! he exclaimed and turned to leave. The baby had stopped wailing now and was sleeping once again. He paused to take another look at her and could feel joy rising to fill every corner of his heart.

It was some time before Charles had finished running back and forth between his Mother's room and the range downstairs; his Mother was indeed as hungry as she had said and ate several bowls of the stew with great relish and praised her Son for the fine job he had done. She washed the repast down with two earthenware mugs of strong hot tea following which she brushed her hair before asking to see her other Son.

Tom greeted his Mother with a powerful hug and the effort of it drew an audible rumble from deep within his empty belly.

"Haven't you eaten yet"? Charles demanded crisply.

"No Charlie, I've been waitin' fer *you*"! quipped Tom, peeved that he should be challenged in such a manner when all he was doing what his Brother had asked!

Charles sensed that he was being unfair and retracted his comment.

"Sorry sunshine", he declared, "Didn't mean to upset you, why don't you get yourself downstairs, there's plenty left in the pot and for all the time you've waited you deserve it"!

Tom winked at his Mother, looked with indifference at the infant and without a further word made his way down the rough wooden stairway.

"I don't think he knows what to make of it all Mother", mused Charles staring after his Brother. His voice was subdued almost as if he was talking to himself but his Mother had caught the intonation.

"It'll take time for him to work things out Charles. This is all so new to him and 'though he's close to manhood he has a little more growing to do; in more ways than one"! she gave her Son a wistful look not really expecting a reply for there was not much to be said!

The room fell silent as Charles fought for something eloquent to say in response, something to reaffirm his own newly acquired adulthood and his Mother's acceptance of it but as if often the case in such circumstances, nothing would come.

"I think I'll rest for a while now Charles, it'll not be long before the baby is awake again and I must take my opportunity whenever I find it. I'll call for you when I need you again"!

Charles nodded and turned the solitary paraffin lamp as low as he could without it making smoke. He had wanted to ask his Mother how to make bread but had thought the better of it—she was tired enough and needed rest not questions. He would work it out for himself.

As he descended the stairs he received a sharp reminder from his own belly and was suddenly aware that he was famished. Passing into the living room he made for the pot but Tom had indeed helped himself for there was barely enough stew left to feed a grown man and all but a small slice of the heavy bread remained.

Charles felt his heckles rising but there was far too much on his mind to waste energy complaining, he was grateful for what there was and surprised at how well his culinary effort had turned out!

CHAPTER 4

The evil becomes manifest

C HARLES WAS REALLY TAKEN with his new occupation; driving a pony and trap was fulfilling indeed and he was overjoyed at being outdoors in the fresh, clean air instead of having to breath the constant smoke and dust of his former place of employment.

It transpired that the arrangement between the Doctor and himself was to be more akin to friendship than to an employer/servant relationship. The Doctor had been as good as his word and whenever time could be found he gave Charles detailed tutoring in the construction and oddities of the human frame and how ailments, diseases and accidents should be dealt with. In return, Charles made a first class student absorbing the information with careful attention and putting it into practise wherever an opportunity presented itself. Charles was so appreciative of all that the Doctor was doing for him that he had taken to working long into the evening delivering medications to patients and carrying out dressing changes and the like. Hitherto, the Doctor himself would have to have seen to these irksome everyday tasks which, in his advancing years, were becoming more tiring and demanding of his time.

The relationship between the two men had developed in such accord that Charles had become completely entrusted with his duties without there being any need for supervision from his employer. They were well found these two and well pleased with each other!

Fate is a fickle mistress however and what has all the outward appearance of bliss and contentment can sometimes turn out be nothing more than a cloak masking misfortune and horror for the new skills and abilities that Charles was enjoying were not *naturally* found!

It had been a long and difficult struggle convincing the chapel minister that an illegitimate child is better baptised and accepted into the family of God than shunned to follow a path empty of enlightenment and thus placed in the path of evil. On each occasion that Charles had visited the chapel to plead consideration for his innocent Sister, the minister had chosen to preach sermons about the sins of the flesh rather than make any commitment regarding the child. Faced with Charles' unrelenting persistence however, the Minister at last gave way and a date was arranged for a mid-week baptism that was to be strictly family and the announcement of which was not to be conveyed to anyone!

In hindsight, the minister felt all but mortified that he had agreed to permit the baptism and was filled with anxiety about what his deacons and chapel elders would do if they found out that he was administering God's blessing to a child not born in wedlock.

Charles' Mother was thrilled with the news and spent weeks in the making of a beautiful Christening gown for the child and in preparing the family's best clothing for the special day. Although there were to be no guests with whom to share this significant event, she cleaned the cottage from top to bottom and prepared a splendid feast for the family to share in celebration of the baptism. When the day arrived, the Minister appeared somewhat less than enthusiastic about his duty and conducted the baptism with an attitude that suggested he had a bad smell under his nose and shards of glass in his shoes! After pronouncing, "I name this child Sophie Rosanne," he set about winding up the ceremony with all haste; his face radiated an expression of relief that was plain for all to see!

It was of no importance to the family, the deed was done, honour and propriety were satisfied and they could hold their heads up once more safe in the knowledge that the little girl could never be placed in unhallowed ground!

It was customary for the eldest male of the family to provide a memento of such an occasion to the newly christened child but, opportunity and prospect being limited for Charles, he decided to give his Sister the only possession he owned that he thought was worthy. Watched by his Mother, he retrieved the coin he had secreted above the mantle shelf all those months ago and announced to the family that this was to be his gift. The coin was as bright and shiny as the day it had popped from the press and had reposed unhandled in its place of seclusion, yet as Charles retrieved the coin it felt strange—felt warm to his touch!

Charles handed the coin to his Mother and as he did so his spirits fell. He had an immediate and overpowering feeling that he had done something inherently wrong, that he had *injured* somebody!

"My how . . . . how *warm* this is Charles!" his Mother remarked. She turned the coin over repeatedly,

"How on earth have you managed to keep it so polished?"

"It came direct from the press Mother, it hasn't been passed from hand to hand yet nor felt the tarnish of perspiration!"

"It's a lovely gift my Son and I'm sure Rosanne will treasure it as she grows older for it bears the year of her birth! I'll place it beneath her mattress to bring her good luck. She's sleeping soundly now so I'll pop it up when I retire!"

She placed the coin on the table as Charles set about opening the elderberry wine that he had made specially for the occasion and the three tucked into the splendid and very welcome feast that lay upon the living room table. They exchanged animated, jovial conversation, enjoying each others company into the small hours of the morning unencumbered by the isolation that they would fall back to in the weeks to follow.

As eyes began to droop from the unaccustomed lateness of the hour and the effects of the potent home brewed wine, the three decided that it was time to make for bed and thus the day's festivity drew to a close. Passing the table, Charles noticed that the coin had been overlooked by his Mother and still lay there, he picked it up with the intention of handing it to her at the top of the stairs but for some reason, perhaps due to wine and tiredness, he put it in his waistcoat pocket instead.

As the days had worn on, Charles had developed little by little into a very competent medical attendant indeed. To admit to his contemporaries that he was a nurse would have been unthinkable in those times for no male person outside of the military could *ever* have considered such an occupation without becoming the butt of derision. Nursing was thought to be best confined to the female population because of their natural aptitude and abundant compassion brought about by generations of child bearing and tending physical misfortune! This was something of a strange state of affairs when viewed in the light of society's prerequisite that only *men* should be Doctors of medicine, but thus things were. The day to day conduct of life and its professions had been clearly delineated by the peers and superiors of society who were nothing if not intransigent and would have no truck with departures from the accepted norms!

Charles was about to set off on his walk home after cleaning and stabling the pony when he heard the distant siren.

He'd heard it many times before as it called off the old shift and signalled the start of the new at the Colliery just a few miles to the south west but this time it was very different. The usual short blasts were long and prodigious, almost continuous as they telegraphed an obvious warning that something dreadful had transpired. He returned to the stable and set about re-harnessing the pony which was, to say little of it, most reluctant to oblige, darting its head from one side to the other in an effort to avoid the bridle. Though Charles knew nothing of collieries, a vocation he had avoided because of his predisposition to shy away from confined spaces, he guessed that some form of accident had taken place and that the Doctor was sure to be needed.

He could hear the Doctor's telephone ringing in the distance and knew that time would be of the very essence if there were injured men to take care of.

He led the pony, still resisting in its trap, from the stable just as the Doctor appeared with his leather bag quite out of breath,

"Well done Charles—I see you have anticipated what has happened. It seems there are several injured men for us to tend."

He paused as he placed his bag on the floor of the trap in front of the passenger's seat. Turning to Charles, a look of consternation clouding his countenance, he remarked,

"There is likely to be blood and missing limbs Charles, you have never experienced that—will you cope?"

"I will do my best Sir!" exclaimed Charles with a feeling of extreme unease. He had witnessed accidents at the mint where careless men had lost fingers in the unforgiving steam presses as they slammed down on the anvil block and had been present when one had lost his life after a steam pipe had fractured scalding him such that his skin was falling from his face in delicate lace like gossamers. He had helped this man, still conscious and walking in severe shock, to the infirmary where he collapsed and passed away before Charles' very eyes. The shock of this had been indescribable and was so deep it had distressed Charles beyond imagination yet somehow he had held on to himself and had mercifully transcended the incident though he had never been able to tell anyone about the horror he had felt.

The memory of that ineffaceable incident came flooding back to him in this moment; he felt mortified by the thought of what the scene at the colliery might do to him! Pulling himself together he climbed into the trap and turned his mind to the pony that was still trying to remind Charles that its day was done and wanted nothing more than to munch hay and dream equine dreams in its cosy stable!

Charles would have none of it and with a double slap of the reins on the pony's back they set of at a brisk trot. Darkness was casting its long shadowy veils upon the countryside and it would soon be time to light the marker lamps on the trap, with any luck they would arrive at the colliery before that would be needed.

The siren wailed again, this time nearer and much louder, the situation must be worse than Charles had thought—help must be needed badly, he stirred the pony into a steady canter.

The siren would fetch all off-duty colliers and infirmary staff back to the pit head to help with whatever rescue attempts were being planned, even off-duty engine men and pump hands would turn up to lend whatever assistance they could. Colliery accidents were usually catastrophic events and mostly took place deep beneath the earth where explosive gas and flood waters were ever present; such was the case now.

The mining community were a proud, self-reliant group who tended to keep themselves to themselves and rarely passed the time of day with folk from outside. They lived together in houses provided by the colliery owners in close proximity to the pits they served and all the skills needed to run those pits, from shaft sinkers to bricklayers, were drawn from that community. They were honourable chapel going folk who looked after each other to the point where no Policeman had ever been needed to adjudicate or dispense justice within their community. Their code of honour was at the very heart of who they were.

The front doors of the terraced houses that lined the hill leading down to the Colliery were all wide open spilling mediocre light from their oil lamps into the street and illuminating the womenfolk standing outside, arms akimbo, watching the men as they scurried downhill. They looked at each other with worn faces and tired eyes, many of them had husbands and young sons underground and they knew, and felt, well enough the horror of loss of kin!

The scene at the pithead was chaotic, smoke was rising from the main shaft which meant that a fire was still raging between the pit bottom and the many galleries and tunnels below. It also meant that this shaft could not be used to evacuate men for the fear of lowering the rescuers into the fire.

The colliery manager, a well qualified mining engineer, was busy on the telephone trying to raise the manager of an adjoining colliery in the next valley. The collieries had not long been linked underground in the working of a rich seam being chased from either end by both entities and this proved fortunate indeed for it offered an alternative rescue route for those trapped beneath the surface.

Injured men lay around the pithead on dirty bedding fashioned from rough sackcloth and straw, some were unmoving and some were very clearly in pain judging by the cries of anguish that escaped when trying to move them or make them comfortable.

The Doctor climbed from the trap as Charles secured the pony and stuffed the brake shoes beneath the wheels.

The manager replaced the ear piece on its candlestick and grasped the Doctor by the hand.

"Thank God you've arrived Doctor Moody, the infirmary staff are all here somewhere but they cannot cope with many of the more serious injuries, you are sorely needed here!"

"Where might I find your principal medical officer?" enquired the Doctor.

"The PMO is in the lamp room, a part of which has been cleared to fashion a makeshift hospital. There are a number of amputations needed that he is attending to. I suggest you join him there!"

Very well!" replied the Doctor, "Come Charles."

They made their way through the pithead yard under the powerful illumination of acetylene flood lamps set up to aid the rescuers. The scene about them was horrifying; medical helpers were attending to the lesser injured brought out of the shaft before the fire had escalated. Some had seriously lacerated skin whilst others had suffered compound fractured limbs through crushing.

"I'll go to the colliery medical officer Charles and find out what it is he would have us do, in the meantime take my bag and see what you can do for some of these poor fellows, you know what to find in it!"

"Of course Sir," said Charles and made his way toward a solitary nurse who was quite clearly in need of physical help.

He looked down at the man's badly mangled leg, the nurse was pressing her blood covered fingers into a severed artery trying to stem the pumping blood.

"Thank God you're here at last Doctor!" she exclaimed with relief,

"I can't take the pressure off this vein long enough to apply a tourniquet, can you help me?"

Charles had not heard her greeting, his mind was racing as he fought back the memory of the death at the mint and tried to remember the drill that the Doctor had drummed into him when dealing with such cases.

"Doctor?"

The nurse appealed again bringing Charles out of his debilitating dark thoughts and dragging him into the present.

He took a leather lace from the mans boot and bound it securely above the injury making it tight by using a pencil to form a windlass, he then set about cutting away the man's shredded clothing so that the wound could be cleaned effectively.

"Wash your hands" he instructed the nurse, "and fetch some clean dressings and surgical spirit. This man seems to have lost a lot of blood and we don't have too much time!"

The nurse scurried off without a word in the direction of the infirmary. Charles removed the bottle of surgical spirit from the Doctor's bag and began cleaning away the congealed blood and coal dust from the wound. What he saw as the muck came away caused him to break into cold perspiration; shattered bone was protruding through the skin and was shredded into disjointed splinters, how on earth could he *possibly* deal with this? How could he be *expected* to deal with this?

He wished the Doctor would return and relieve him of this agonising and unwelcome task that he was neither trained nor prepared for! But the Doctor didn't come, instead the nurse reappeared carrying the items he had called for. She opened her mouth to speak but was prevented from doing so by Charles.

"We need Doctor Moody or your Doctor right away!" he barked.

"This man is losing his fight for life and I'm pretty sure this leg will have to come off!"

"But they're *both* up to their necks in the hospital sir, there are a lot more casualties in there and more are expected from the emergency pithead any minute!" the nurse retorted. "Whatever needs to be done will need to be done by *us*—there's no time to wait for anyone else!"

Charles was stunned, he had been totally unprepared for this but could see that she was right, he was no more qualified than she was but something *had* to be done and done *NOW*!

"Without a further word, he took the scalpel from the Doctor's bag and cut away the man's trousers just below the crotch.

"Clean the area around the whole of the upper fracture," Charles gestured to the nurse indicating a wide band just above the knee, "And douse it liberally with this," he continued, waving the scalpel toward the surgical spirit.

He turned and grabbed the shoulder of, a passing collier and demanded.

"I have to remove this person's leg, can you get hot pitch for me?"

"There's always some fer caulkin' in the battery room, 'ow much do you want Guv?"

"Just get me half a bucketful but keep it as near boiling as you can, it mustn't be cold when you get it here, but be *double* quick for the love of God!" instructed Charles as the man departed.

"I'm going to give you the chloroform bottle and pad lass," continued Charles," Can you manage that for me?"

"I've never done that myself before Doctor, what if I get it wrong?"

The nurse was apprehensive about taking on this task knowing that too little chloroform could result in the patient being woken by pain but too much could cause him to suffocate and die!

"Don't worry yourself nurse, there are too many things that could go wrong to count but if we don't act now the man will die *anyway!*"

The nurse applied herself to the task as best she could as Charles prepared the few tools that the bag afforded. Skin clamps, bone saw, scalpel. He released the tourniquet for a few seconds to prevent the onset of mortification but not so long as to lose too much of the man's precious blood.

Charles and the nurse piled extra covers on their patient, both aware that they would have to take special precautions if they were to prevent the possibility of him contracting hypothermia during the operation that was about to be performed. He had become so engrossed in the action to hand that he hadn't noticed how profusely he was perspiring.

"Got yer pitch Gov. but you'll 'ave to 'urry 'cos it'll get cold quick out 'ere!"

The collier had returned, it was now or never!

How the two of them got through the next ten minutes will always remain a mystery to Charles. They somehow had coped with something that a qualified Doctor untrained in surgery would have shied away from but they *had* done it and the patient's breathing appeared to be rhythmic and his pulse steady and strong!

At that moment Doctor Moody reappeared and having inspected what the two had just done congratulated them both on their fine workmanship and the quality of the surgery they had performed.

"It wasn't so much me sir as the good Doctor here," the nurse informed Doctor Moody. Charles heard what she had said for the first time and looked at her in astonishment, he noticed also how young and pretty she was. He was about to correct her when Doctor Moody intervened.

"Charles," he ventured, "The main shaft fire has been extinguished and a rescue crew are going underground to see if there is anyone else to bring up.

They are in need of a medical man but neither I nor the colliery medical officer can be spared and in any case, I am a little to old to be crawling on all fours, can I count on you?"

"I'll go with him"! interjected the nurse looking at Charles with new found respect and admiration.

"No my lass," the Doctor was adamant, "Underground is no place for a girl and I fancy you will be very much needed here until the injured have all been attended to!"

"He's right", affirmed Charles as the Doctor added.

"There are yet more injured to be treated in the lamp room and in any case you would not have the physical strength to be of much help, stay here nurse and work your magic!"

The girl blushed and averted her eyes from the two men as she nodded her reluctant acquiescence. It seemed Charles had acquired a disciple.

Charles finished cleaning the implements he had used with a strip of clean linen dipped in surgical spirit, the only autoclave that could sterilize them properly was in constant use in the makeshift hospital and there was no time to divert to alternatives.

"Heaven knows what'll happen if I need them again," he muttered to himself, "They could be contaminated in all manner of germs and viruses!'

Collecting the bag he walked alone to the pit head frame where the team to go underground had already assembled. The men there eyed him with scepticism and a little suspicion, he was obviously very young. They shrugged off his appearance and accepted him reassured that he must be old enough or he wouldn't be a Doctor.

"Bin underground before?" enquired the team leader, a wizened man in his late thirties with leathery features and huge knarled hands calloused from years of coal shovelling.

"No!" returned Charles, "But I'm strong and willing to do whatever must be done—never too late to learn!"

The man chuckled, the lad clearly had spirit if nothing else to recommend him!

"In to the cage lads", ordered the leader and one by one the men filed into the single decked narrow cage taking with them timber for shoring, shovels and picks, lamps, blankets, fresh drinking water, splints, first aid gear and a myriad of various bits and pieces to aid in the rescue attempt. The long narrow cage, slung between four guide wires, was suspended by a single wire rope that passed from the steam driven winding drum in the engine house, up and over the pit head winding wheel before turning vertically down to suspend the cage. The system had been installed in 1896 and was for those times, the very latest innovation in winding technology.

As one cage descended from the top, so the other ascended from the bottom of the shaft in counterbalance. The system relied upon a single wire wound around a huge horizontal windlass drum to connect both cages. As one wire paid out from the top of the drum, the other was gathered in at the bottom and vice versa. Recalling this to mind, the Manager suddenly called to the rescue team,

"**Stop!**—Out you come lads!"

The rescuers looked from one to the other but none had any idea of what this delay was in aid of. They knew well enough not argue with an order from the manager however and cleared the cage in haste.

The Manager picked up the pit head telephone and gave orders to the engineman in control of the winding to swap the positions of the cages.

The banksman in charge at the pit head knew exactly why this was being done and called loudly,

"WINDING—Stand clear of the pit!"

With a soft 'Choof, choof choof' the snorting, hissing steam engine turned the giant winding drum sending the cage on its 800 yard journey into the depths of the earth raising a thunderous rattle in the shaft as it did so. In a few moments the cage that had been at the bottom slowly appeared amongst the paraphernalia of objects that formed the upper end of its journey. It was hot and smoking but at least it was intact. The manager had ordered this action because he was afraid that the suspending wire to the lower cage might well have been weakened or even burned through and separated by the fire and if this *was* the case then the rescuers could themselves have been propelled in free-fall to their own deaths as the loaded cage fell out of control from the loss of counterbalance!

The waiting men looked at each other again and this time grinned—glory be the grace of God and the persistence of wise men!

Doused with copious drafts of water from the fire hose, the cage was quickly cooled, inspected and given the all clear, the team embarked once more. The pithead banksman signalled by bell to the engineman that there were 'men winding' and closed the outer safety gate. The cage rose a few inches in slow motion so that the banksman could retract the large steel pins that supported the weight of the cage when at rest on the surface and down went the cage dropping the secondary safety gate as it passed below the rim of the brick lined shaft.

Gripping white knuckled to the overhead steady rail, Charles felt his stomach rising as the cage fell away in rapid descent to a speed where he experienced near weightlessness, the noise surrounding the cage was deafening and he wished he was anywhere but here!

After what seemed like half a lifetime plunging in blackness broken only by the dimmed Davy lamps carried by the team, the cage began to slow—at last they were approaching pit bottom. Charles' legs began to buckle as the engineman applied the brake on the winding drum, the arrival was the mirror of the pithead departure!

The team leader turned up his lamp followed by each of the other men with that of Charles being turned up for him by an obliging team member.

Even though there was no sign of continuing fire, there was still smoke and considerable heat in the gallery down here, it was creeping along the tunnel roof and curling away up the shaft and thus was no impediment to the rescuers. The heat and humidity was oppressive.

The pit bottom was deserted; men that had been stationed here to work the machinery had been ordered to evacuate the moment their lamps had flared indicating the presence of 'fire damp', explosive gases that accumulate and seep from exhausted and abandoned coal seams. Under normal circumstances, any kind of gas and foul air would be harmlessly scourged away by the powerful forced ventilation in the tunnels underground.

On this occasion however, the dangerous 'fire damp' had accumulated in a stagnant pocket formed in the roof of a distorted gallery and had been ignited by a spark from the wheel of a loaded coal tram on its way from the coal face to the pit bottom. The pony pulling the tram and the underground 'journeyman' tending it were killed in an instant but worse, the clouds of coal dust raised by the explosion was sucked into the ventilation shaft and ignited reversing the direction of normal draught and transporting a wave of searing fire deep into the working galleries. Almost a hundred men and boys toiled in these galleries at the exhausting business of cutting, extracting and conveying 'black gold'.

The rescue team made its way with extreme caution into the main tunnel following the tram rails and keeping below the escaping smoke. There were large rock and slag deposits strewn across the floor from the partial collapse of the tunnel and from the roof supports displaced by the blast but there was no evidence of flooding which gave the team leader confidence that they would be able to find some of the missing men. He was not at all confident that any might be found alive!

The rescuers pressed forward with caution replacing what they could of the fallen props as they went and watching their lamps for the tell tale 'flare'; each man knew that where rock falls had occurred, gas might be encountered. It was not long before the first casualty was found, the man stared up at the rescuers with wide expressionless eyes gazing from a coal blackened face that bore an expression of anguish and futility. 'I too was once beautiful,' it seemed to mock, he was dead!

They passed on, there was nothing that could be done here, they must seek the living.

A few hundred feet further their path was blocked by a heavy roof fall. How thick this barrier was they were unable to determine but it stood between them and the comrades that might still need them so they set about manhandling the debris away with a will for there was no other way of finding out whether there were survivors. The temperature in the tunnel was now all but unbearable, each man had removed his upper garments in an effort to keep cool. Perspiration stood out on their bodies as if they had just left the shower but each was reluctant to take water lest it should deprive those they sought to relieve.

"Form a chain lads," called the leader, "We're falling over each other here. We'll swap places at ten minute intervals so those at the head don't get too hot!"

They toiled on with assiduous and unreserved will using their hands where shovels wouldn't work, ripping flesh from bone as they passed rocks along the chain to leave a clear path for evacuees should they be fortunate enough to find any. Beneath the rock pile as it diminished lay another hapless miner, a boy of no more than 14 years of age. He had suffocated in wretched loneliness beneath that terrible compressing weight.

Each man among the colliers in the rescue team had known this boy yet not one amongst them spoke his name for he had been mate to one of them on first going underground and had served in their shift until redeployed.

The men shook their heads in silent sorrow and returned to the digging. It was then that they heard it— very faint but unmistakeable, a pick or something tapping against rock.

"Hush!" barked the team leader'. The men paused and listened with concentrated intent, yes—there it was again but this time there were *two* implements tapping together. A loud cheer split the gloom as the team realised that they had found *survivors!*

The men renewed their digging twofold spurred on by their will to get their comrades to safety, fresh air and comfort. A small hole appeared in the rock wall and fanning away the dust, the lead digger held up his lamp and peered into the abyss beyond.

"Strewth, it's young Harry Fortnum lads!" he announced.

"How many are you and are you all ok?"

"There's twenty two of us in here—we're trapped between two roof falls and apart from Wally Sadler we're all ok. Wally has a broken wrist and a bad sprain, he's in a lot of pain but at least he's lucky enough to be able to complain!"

"That's great news, we'll be through to you shortly boys! Are there any men beyond the next fall Harry?"

"I'm pretty sure there are, we were on the way to the face when the bang happened and there was a group in front of us. Mind you, the road divides a few hundred feet further up so maybe they got clear—got anything to drink"?

The rescuers passed drinking water through the fissure they had opened then returned to the task of clearing a man sized passage through the rubble. As soon as it was large enough, Charles crawled through the gap into the void beyond and immediately his Davy lamp flame began to curl sideways, was the hole letting firedamp in or was it letting it *out?*

He called to the team beyond, "Lamp's flaring lads— what's to do?"

"Ours are all ok came the reply—hang on a minute!"

The team leader held his lamp to the hole they had made in the rock fall and immediately it deflected giving the appearance of a flare.

"There's air passing out of the space you're in lad so we're getting air circulation from somewhere—that's bloody good news!"

"It's isn't firedamp so no need to worry, here, give my lamp to Harry and get him to take you to Wally."

Charles took the lamp and holding it up looked about him. What he saw was a sea of white eyes and grinning white teeth shining through coal black faces, each weary man expecting him to make the first move.

"Harry!" called Charles. He jumped as the reply came;

"Right beside you chum—this way." Harry took the lamp from Charles and motioned him to follow.

A few feet away at the far side of the fall a man lay half propped up against a large rock, his face distorted with pain.

"'Ow you doing Wally?" enquired Harry.

"Not good mate, not good at all—this the Doc?"

Charles knelt down and looked at the man's arm. From the strange angle that it formed it was obvious that it was badly broken, probably in more places than one! Charles was grateful that the gloom would hide his grimaces.

"I'm going to give you a shot of morphine Wally," he announced,

"It'll take a few moments to work but it will take away the pain until we get you to the surface."

"Come on lads, let's have you out one at a time," interrupted the rescue leader from deep within the darkness, the hole had been made wide enough for the trapped men to be safely released.

"One of the team will get you back to pit bottom where it's safer." Charles reassured his patient.

Wally made to nod. The pupils of his eyes, grown large from the constant darkness of his prison, were glazing. He was clearly falling under the effect of the morphine. Charles took the man's injured arm and placed it across his chest so that his outstretched fingers just touched his opposite shoulder and then bound the arm firmly to a splint. He secured the injured arm and splint to the man's chest with his remaining bandage so that it would not move as he was transported through the rubble to safety.

"OK men!" he called to the waiting team, "Ready to get the casualty out of here."

Two burly rescuers crawled through the enlarged hole carrying with them a small bolt of canvas and two poles. Rolling the canvas around each pole in turn they fashioned a makeshift stretcher onto which they placed the now semi-conscious Wally. Hoisting him to waist height with as much care as they could, they relayed him through the hole to the rescuers the other side.

"Right you two", the leader motioned to two the men waiting beyond the fall, "Get Wally and the others to pit bottom. If they can manage, tell the other survivors to get him to the medics at the pit head then come back as quick as you can—the rest of us will start digging the far fall to see if there are any survivors the other side. Catch up with us as soon as you can—we're going to need you!"

The men turned up their lamps and set off with the survivors close at heel, they had but two lamps between all of them and there were many stumbling blocks to negotiate along the treacherous way to the shaft bottom. Each of them knew they must make good progress for there would not be a lot of time before the injured man regained consciousness and it was a long journey to safety above ground.

The remaining men of the rescue team made their way through the passage that had been cut and set about removing the debris at the further rock fall.

"How long will these lamps last?" enquired Charles as much out of the need to communicate as the need for knowledge.

"At this brightness about six hours" replied the team leader, "thanks for the reminder," he turned to three of the others and instructed,

"We'll work by the light of two lamps, turn the others as low as you can to save fuel."

The others nodded their understanding then resumed the tiring business of digging, passing the rock and slag that those in front had cut away by handing it from one man to another in the chain piling it at the sides of the tunnel. Fingers were now raw from the chafing of the abrasive rock and many were bleeding but there was no slowing of effort, each man in the rescue team was driven by the need to find and bring to safety, as many of their stricken colleagues as they could. Physical discomfort was meaningless and had no influence in this God forsaken unholy cavern so close to hell and to the devil himself!

"GET BACK—GET OUT QUICK!" came a sudden urgent plea from one of the forward diggers,

"There's water coming through—there must be a flood at the other side of this fall—there'll be no-one to rescue in there!"

"Back beyond the next fall men"! barked the team leader, "While I check this myself."

Each man knew well enough what the presence of flood water meant, they each knew that the lads that had been removing the debris from the second fall had been doing so from the top down, that meant that a huge wall of water was dammed up beyond the fall. If the pressure this pent up water exerted started displacing the rock then the whole dam would give way and they would all be swept before the water and crushed as it tore back through the tunnel.

"Run you bastards—RUN!"

The steely edge in the team leader's voice spurred everyone to instant action as without a word they dropped everything and ran making their way quickly over the piles of rock that threatened to snare their ankles. Those who had abandoned their down-turned lamps in the scurry for safety now had to rely entirely on the lamps carried by the men who had taken lead of the fleeing column.

Charles realised that he still had his lamp although it was so dim as to be almost useless, he was not going to stop to turn it up now!

The bigger men had now overtaken him and he had truly become the 'tail-end Charlie' of the column. It was then that he heard the rumble of rocks moving accompanied by the roar of tumbling water.

'My God it's *happened,*' he thought and found himself shouting, "WATER LOOSE!"

They were almost at pit bottom, the two men who had taken Wally to the waiting cage had seen him to the surface and had only now returned to rejoin the team at pit bottom. They heard the fleeing men shouting and the water approaching in the distance and experience gave them the advantage of guessing what was happening; one of them held open the cage gate to get everyone in without delay. As Charles, the last man in the escaping column, passed through the man released the gate with an almighty bang. The other was already on the telephone that connected the banksmen at each end of the shaft, calling for a rapid emergency lift.

The noise in the tunnel had become ear splitting. The men now trapped in the motionless cage felt the pressure wave of the air that was being forced before the oncoming water and knew that time was running out.

Even in the poor light each could now see in the face of the others wretched expressions that told they were but seconds from death. Charles became aware of a peculiar sensation of uncharacteristic warmth from within his waist coat and in that instant recalled to mind the penny he had placed there on the day of his Sister's baptism.

He thrust two fingers into the tiny waist coat pocket and was astonished to find that the coin was *hot!* Brushing the incident from his mind and jerking himself back to the present, he realised with sickening horror that he was nearest the entrance to the cage and closest to the advancing wall of water. He knew without doubt that he would be the first to be struck and the knowledge of it caused him to recoil in terror. Then, as suddenly as the terror had come upon him, he became calm.

There was nothing that he, or any man, could do except brace for the inevitable impact, hold fast to the cage and wait and pray that the engineman above would start them up the shaft in time.

To his great relief, the cage began to move but Charles' heart sank in desperation, they were moving *downward;* every nerve in Charles' body screamed at this despicably unwelcome event. They were being lowered into the sump, the very *bottom* of the shaft that contained nothing but accumulated water drained from the tunnels and waiting to be pumped to the surface. His waistcoat pocket felt as if it was burning into his flesh and just as he was about to shriek in defiant disdain, he felt a firm reassuring hand grip his shoulder.

"Hold fast lad," came the steady voice of the imperturbable team leader, "The cage has to move down so that the retaining pins can be pulled from under the cage up top."

The man offered a brief smile then turned and looked calmly into the eyes of each of the others for a moment. One by one, he held their gaze instilling courage and fortitude where faith had begun to fade. He was a pinnacle of strength, inspiration and courage in this moment of great uncertainty—he was a natural leader.

The water struck them at the very moment the cage started its upward journey. It struck with such a force that every man within was propelled to the far end of the cage as if shot from a gun. The entire structure recoiled from the violent force of the irresistible wall of water and was sent smashing into the brick lined wall at the far side of the shaft severing two of the four guide wires as it went. The men couldn't breath. The water was without mercy, freezing cold to their hot, perspiration soaked bodies and thick black with coal dust collected as it coursed through the gallery.

Charles felt a searing pain to the side of his head and another to his cheek, his lungs were bursting from the lack of air and he felt sure his time had come. For the second time panic gave way to calmness as he accepted what must now be inevitable, he could hold his breath no longer, he had done his best, he would meet his maker in whatever manner was meant for him.

In that very second, that moment of desperate resignation, the cage rose above the swirling, blackened mass of crushing water accompanied by a noise resembling that of Niagara Falls as the weight of water it had ingested disgorged into the darkness below. There was nothing but absolute blackness surrounding the cage as it now ascended. The light of the lamps, every one, had been consumed by the deluge. Their tiny, life assuring lights that had cut so reassuring into the impenetrable darkness of the galleries below had been snuffed and would never be seen again.

How Charles had remained conscious he would never know, the pain in his cheek and head was excruciating and his stomach was retching as his lungs tried to clear the ingested soup of foul water and coal dust. Through this agony he could hear the groans of other men close by and was heartened that he was not the only man here living! The side of his head felt sticky and he knew that he was bleeding but not how badly, he felt around for the Doctor's bag with the intention of using a dressing pad from it to hold against the wound and stem the bleeding but it had gone.

There was no hope of light by which to find the bag so, tearing away the bottom of his water drenched shirt, he rolled it into a makeshift pad and applied that. Because of the lack of light and his own physical nausea he was unable to offer help to any of the other men so sat in silence as the cage wound its way onward.

The cage broke into the fresh air of the night and the piercing brilliant light at the pit head to the cheers of workers waiting on the surface. The searing light of the surrounding flood lamps stabbed into Charles' eyes like knives, driving him to raise one arm across them as a shield. As his eyes slowly re-adjusted, he looked around at the men in the cage and was horrified at the injuries that he could see. The stark realisation dawned upon him that these men, who had been behind him when the water struck, had acted as a cushion absorbing the massive force of the impact and had protected him from the injuries they themselves had sustained. The men had been swept against the far end of the metal cage compressed and crushed by both the water and the weight of Charles' body!

He was not aware that the injuries he had suffered had not been caused by the devastating pressure of the water nor by being flung across the cage, but by the liberated end of one of the severed guide wires as it sprang away from its pit bottom anchor and thrashed its way to freedom.

The gate was raised and Charles made his way unsteadily out of the cage supported by one of the surface workers. He turned and with saddened heart paused to watch the remainder of the team being borne out of the cage one by one. He was angry with himself, sickened and distressed that he had not been unable to offer them any kind of help or comfort in those long, agonizing moments that passed as they traversed their way up the shaft.

The injured men were placed on stretchers made ready by colliery medics and draped in blankets to ward off the cold and comfort them from the effects of shock and immersion, it was remarkable indeed that some of them found the strength to ask for water!

The blankets of two of the stretchers were pulled full length; these brave and indomitable souls had given all that there was to give for the love of their colleagues, they could no longer speak of their joys or disappointments, would no more pat the heads of their young—they had passed from the sight of man and would suffer no more!

Charles wept openly and without shame, he let the blood soaked shirt tail he had been clutching to his head fall into the mud at his feet, he had had enough, he felt he couldn't go on, didn't *want* to go on.

Thus it was she found him.

The nurse that had helped Charles during the earlier amputation was now at his other side, taking his free arm she draped it over her shoulder and gave an almighty shove propelling the trio towards the infirmary. Charles' head was bleeding again and he was experiencing waves of nausea as well as feeling light headed.

His mind began to drift and in his confusion he began singing, so soft it was barely audible, a Welsh song that his mother had taught him on her knee and although he had never understood the meaning of the words, he had always loved the feel of the song and its enchanting melody.

CHAPTER 5

Love Found

___

F OR TWO FULL DAYS Charles remained unconscious, unaware of the special care and constant attention that he was receiving nor to his surroundings. As he returned little by little from oblivion to the day around him; long before his eyes and his mind could determine where he was, he caught the sound of that same melody drifting to him from a distance.

The voice was as sweet and fresh as the crystal clear water of a bubbling mountain stream and fell on his ears as a fragrant bouquet of fresh sweet pea falls on the nose, lifting the spirits and bringing joy to the heart.

His mind cast back to the moment he had first heard his Mother sing that song, 'Myfanwy' it was called. He had loved it the first instant he had heard her sing it, it would be a song that he would love even to his grave.

But no, it *couldn't* be her, his mind may be confused still but he was certain that he was still at the colliery. He tried to prop himself up on one elbow to better see the source of the rendering but received a searing stab of pain from the side of his head for the effort and flopped back again.

"So you're awake at last?" The voice enquired.

"We were all worried about you—you've slept much longer than we were expecting"!

Charles' head cleared enough for him to enquire,

"How long have I been out then?"

"Two days and two hours just, I have been nursing you. Doctor Moody stitched your head. Nasty gash it was—seventeen stitches—you lost an awful lot of blood."

Charles looked at the nurse and actually *saw* her for the first time. With uncharacteristic boldness he ventured,

"You're very pretty nurse—what's your name?"

The girl blushed a little and with a feigned courtesy, tossed her long black tresses from her diamond bright eyes and countered,

"My name is Eira Stacey Sir!"

Charles grinned and felt his heart flutter, he found the mini exhibition endearing and in that instant he warmed to this young lady's pleasant personality.

"Oh it's grinning we are now is it?" teased the nurse,

"We must have you up and find something to do with those idle hands before the devil does"! she remonstrated.

"Can I call you Eira?" asked Charles.

"Only if you'll let me call you Charlie, Mr Charles!" she quipped returning the grin with a radiance that brought sunshine, trust and hope into that otherwise gloomy infirmary.

"Charlie it is then . . . . you know I'm not a Doctor don't you?" he ventured in a voice overshadowed by trepidation and half fears that she might treat him with indifference should she discover he was only a medical orderly.

"Of course I do silly, I had a long chat with Doctor Moody and he told me all about you—doesn't change anything for me—I think you're the bravest man I've ever met and after watching you using a surgeon's tools I think you'd make a really good Doctor!"

This time it was Charles that broke into a blush, light to begin with but deepening to an embarrassing crimson as it dawned on him that this angel in nursing white was impressed with him and may even be attracted by something more than his medical skills!

He was flattered, thrilled and confused beyond imagination all at the same time, he was conscious that he was experiencing feelings for this girl that he had never experienced before, feelings of spell binding charisma, a magic that he could not explain. He found it impossible to take his eyes from her.

This unexpected bombshell of a realisation set him stammering as his frozen mind quarried for something constructive to say.

"I-I-I!" he stammered but was mercifully interrupted by a familiar voice.

"Ah, the patient returns to the living, how are you m'lad?"

Charles tore his eyes from the girl to encounter those of Doctor Moody. Regaining some of his composure he responded.

"I'm feeling very much recovered Sir," and without so much as a hint of a stammer, "And you?"

"For an old man I am remarkably well," the Doctor paused for a moment before continuing,

"Three among your party of rescuers were lost Charles, two arrived dead at the pithead and it is believed that one, missing when you arrived at the surface, must have been washed out of the cage when the water engulfed you all!" Keeping his voice low he went on,

"The remarkable thing my lad, is that your party saved twenty two men directly from the first roof fall but by far the best, another forty six were able to be brought to safety via the emergency shaft once you had released the flood water that lay between them and their escape route. But for that action they would all have certainly perished!"

The Doctor searched Charles' face for signs of reaction to the information but was unable to glean any sense of the lad's innermost feelings. He was concerned about the blow Charles had received to the head and a little suspicious that concussion might be playing more than a small part here. He went on,

"You may not be aware of this yet my lad, but you and the rescue team that you were a part of are seen as heroes here. The Colliery owner, managers and workers and the families of those that were brought to safety regard you and the team you were a part of, in the highest esteem and you are going to find it hard to live this down!"

He looked deep into Charles' eyes searching for signs of the sadness he knew would manifest itself in the boy's mind sooner or later, if not now then in the very near future. The Doctor had always been sceptical about heroics and thought to himself that it was probably not a good thing to be admired as a hero at so early an age. He shook his head.

Charles had not been listening, he had let his concentration wander and his eyes return to follow the nurse, his expression softened as her gaze met his and again he felt his heart flutter deep within his breast.

The Doctor had not missed the smiles that were exchanged between these two young people. He felt gladdened that they had found each other but decided to be impish and play a little game with them.

"Nurse!" called the Doctor, adopting an official tone.

"You have not had proper rest since this nuisance of a lad got here, Perhaps it's time for you to go home!"

Eira's face fell, there was nothing she wanted in the world that would take her of her own accord from this place but she knew that one word from Doctor Moody to the Colliery medical Officer regarding her being on duty for two days would have her packed off home by order!

She stopped folding the fresh blanket she had been attending to and placed it on an unoccupied bed before making her way to the Doctor's side.

She looked at him through large clear eyes unbroken in steadiness and with a heart wrenching expression of irresistible appeal pleaded.

"I have taken frequent rest here in the infirmary Doctor whenever there has been time and I have looked after him personal—like. I would prefer to stay and complete that care until Mr Charles is well enough to leave of his own accord if that would not be inconvenient to you? I would consider it a favour indeed if you would not mention this to the Colliery M.O."

The Doctor laughed at the expression of consternation that this sweet girl bore and concluded.

"Don't worry my Lass, I can see why you want to stay and I can also see that it will benefit Charles' recovery in good measure to have you close by . . . . as a nurse that is"! He added not wanting to push this new relationship at too swift a pace.

"It's my opinion that he will be fit to leave very soon anyway. He will be fare better recovering at home though he will be in need of a good nursing attendant of course . . . . Hmmmm! Now I wonder where I might find such a nurse?"

"I am due a leave of absence Doctor and I would be more than happy to act as Mr Charles' nurse—if he will have me that is!"

"Hmm, I 'm not sure that would be at all wise," teased the Doctor stroking his chin in wistful thought and playing yet more games with these two.

"It might not be seen to be a model of propriety you know" he quipped.

"I believe you lodge with your parents in Pritchard Row near the colliery?" the Doctor raised one eyebrow as if to accentuate his query.

"Yes Doctor" replied the girl.

"That would make daily visits very difficult for you since it would involve covering a considerable distance on foot!"

"That is no matter to me, I am young and healthy and the walk will do me good," she retorted determined that the opportunity to look after Charles was what she wanted. She was well aware that on days when it rained the walk would be miserable; she would not only get wet but very muddy.

"I could ask my Mother to offer lodging," interrupted Charles, "After all, it would only be for a day or two until the wounds close and the dressings don't need changing so often."

Charles had the feeling that none of this was really necessary, he felt well enough in himself, just a little dizzy and lot of soreness but he was not about to pass up the opportunity to spend a few days in the company of this delightful girl.

He looked at the doctor with a plea that was impossible to reject.

"Very well—I will approach the colliery M.O. and the manager and see what can be done!" offered the Doctor,

"Perhaps you could ask your Mother about lodging when she visits today Charles, the colliery has arranged for a pony and trap to bring her." he turned on his heels and sensing there was nothing further to achieve here, strode from the ward.

Charles was delighted to hear about the Colliery sending for his Mother but at the same time more than a little surprised. Colliery owners always remained distant and aloof in their large houses and were seldom seen outside them except for frequent sojourns to more hospitable destinations abroad. They were as a norm, not nearly so considerate and that one had taken the trouble to become involved in the welfare of a subordinate was extraordinary, Charles was being privileged indeed!

Eira, who had been making like she was busy fussing around the other recovering men whilst the Doctor was present, made her way over to Charles.

"Now I've got you all to myself for a few moments," she enquired, "Do you think your Mother will help me with the lodging?" She hesitated before adding, "I know my Mum won't mind although my Dad might be a bit more difficult to persuade."

"It would mean Tom, my Brother, having to sleep downstairs, his room is the only one that would be suitable for you but I'm sure it will all work out." smiled Charles, smitten by this sweet natured lass.

It was mid afternoon before his Mother arrived. Eira had arranged a few screens around Charles' bed so that the family could be feel a little more private, she was sure that Charles' mother would like that. Sophie, Charles' baby sister, took and instant dislike to the enclosure however and furthermore was uneasy with the unfamiliar surroundings She communicated her dissatisfaction in the way that infants often do to the point where conversation became impossible. Eira smiled, she had brothers and sisters of her own and knew how difficult it was to placate an upset infant; she offered to take the child into the ward for a moment to give the adults a chance to catch up.

"Why, that would be wonderful young lady." thanked Mrs Jenkins handing over the infant. "If you find it hard to keep her quiet, bring her back at once and I'll take her outside!" she smiled.

Eira wrapped the infant in a shawl as her mother had so often done with her infant siblings, an action that had always imparted a sense of security and calmness to them in the same way that it had done for countless other families before. It had been done this way for centuries!

Rocking the infant gently back and forth she began humming 'myfanwy' as *her* mother had also done, until, through a lull in the conversation Charles caught her sweet tones.

"Listen!" he entreated his family, placing an index finger to his lips.

In the silence that followed a tear rose in the corner of his Mother's eye as the lilting melody brought back memories of her own upbringing in a Welsh valley surrounded by collieries. She had learned the Welsh tune whilst at infant school as all of the valley's maids had done for scores of years, hearing it now brought memories of those times flooding back. Memories of hardships and joys in equal measures that she had shared with her parents and her large family of brothers and sisters in those early days of industrial expansion and the never ending greed for good Welsh 'steam' coal referred to with pride as the best in the world!

It seemed that hardly a month would go by before yet another seam was found and yet another shaft sunk to chase it. The need for men to work these collieries was such that every day, strangers would come to take up employment and thus it was that the beautiful green fresh valleys that had once been the habitat of purely Welsh folk were diluted by Scots, Irish and English. Once, where only Welsh was spoken, English had become the common tongue.

If there was a denominator binding them all in friendship and accord, then it was the collieries, not in spite the sacrifice the work would demand of them but *because* of it!

The whole ward had fallen into a hush as the young nurse dispensed her infant serenade unaware that she had attracted an audience. Her eyes were engaged in unbroken faith with those of the child who returned the gaze with an expression of complete trust and contentment.

Eira knew in that moment what her future would be … or she *thought* she knew but the devil was watching!

She knew nothing of the existence of the penny nor the profound influence it would bring to bear on events and on people around her when its opportunity came!

It was almost as if Charles had no need to ask his Mother to lodge the nurse so engaged was she with this young lady who could take her daughter as a complete stranger yet have her so endeared in so short a time! She felt the urge to know her better.

"That's settled then!" announced Doctor Moody addressing Charles as the screens were removed.

"The colliery M.O. has agreed that the ambulance will take you and nurse Stacey home this afternoon and you will be pleased to learn that the horse is being hitched to the ambulance as we speak! I will call to see you this evening if I can remember how to hitch my *own* pony!"

"I'll give you a hand Doctor Moody Sir!" exclaimed Tom who had said very little until now, "I do it at the farm every day!"

"That would be greatly appreciated young man" the doctor replied, then added,

"I shall miss the benefit of your brother's services more keenly that he knows!"

He picked up his black bag from the bedside table and departed.

Pausing before the nurse he winked impishly, mischief was his mistress once more.

"I think you are both made for each other!" He remarked as he departed with Tom.

Eira stood motionless as she considered the doctor's parting comment, could it be so obvious? She had done her utmost to convey the impression that she was being nothing but professional, that all was normal and thought she had disguised her feelings for Charles very well.

She felt herself blushing. The timely arrival of the colliery M.O. provided a welcome interruption to what was becoming a confusing state of affairs.

"Nurse!"

He beckoned for Eira to approach him.

"As you are aware, it has been agreed that you will accompany Mr Jenkins to his home and to remain there as his attendant for a few days for which you are to be rewarded as if you were employed here. I have had his clothing laundered and bundled and you will find it in the ambulance. The infirmary porters will see that he is supported if he is able to walk, or will stretcher him to the ambulance if he is not, what do you advise?"

"Mr Jenkins?" enquired the nurse.

"Yes, yes, yes, girl . . . . You may know him better as Mr Charles!"

She had not thought to enquire after Charles' surname.

"I will ask him Sir." She replied with a dip and passed quickly to the bedside.

"Would you be well enough to walk Sir, or would you prefer to be taken to the ambulance by stretcher?" she asked Charles in a stiff professional manner.

"Sir?" enquired Charles thinking that their newly formed relationship was already cooling.

"Sorry Mr Jenkins!" she exclaimed then whispered under her breath,

"I can't call you Charles in front of the M.O.—he'd chastise me for not being professional and all nurse like!"

Charles chuckled and said for all to hear,

"You have tended me so well nurse that I feel strong enough to walk—as long as I can count on your support?"

"Good!" remarked the eavesdropping M.O.

"I will call the porters. Mrs Jenkins, may I escort you to your trap?"

"No porters if you please Sir" interrupted Charles,

"As long as the nurse will help me then that is all the support I will need!"

The thought of wrapping his arm about her waist filled his heart with joy.

"Very well young man, I will leave you to it . . . . Mrs Jenkins?"

He proffered his arm indicating he would escort Charles' mother to the waiting trap. Taking the arm she walked at the Doctor's side with the grace of a gentlewoman, she had not been escorted in such a manner in all her life and felt very proud of herself indeed!

Charles felt weak and a little dizzy as he was led to the waiting ambulance. The dressing gown he was wearing was much too long, so long indeed that he kept stepping on its hem as he and the nurse shuffled their way to the infirmary door beyond which the horse drawn ambulance had been reversed to await its patient. Arriving at the door, Charles made to step over the slightly raised ramp that bridged the sill of the opening into the rear of the ambulance. In doing so, he caught a full bight of the ill-fitting garment beneath his unsteady foot which propelled him and the nurse in an undignified bundle to the floor of the vehicle. She was thrown on top of him, her face now only fractions of an inch from his, he looked into her eyes and felt an overpowering urge to kiss her but as their eyes met they broke into simultaneous, raucous, belly wobbling laughter.

The porters viewed them both with scepticism, nodding their heads to each other as if to suggest something underhand was afoot. They helped the still giggling pair from the floor to the stretcher bench where they tucked Charles so secure into his stretcher that he was unable to move his arms!

Strolling to the crew seats high on the front of the ambulance, the porters were heard to mutter,

"Now he'll *have* to keep his hands to himself!"

Since the internals of the ambulance could be observed through a small window in the bulkhead behind the driving seat and between the two porters, the nurse set about taking Charles' temperature. She felt she should be seen to be doing *something* in a professional capacity to protect her reputation.

∇

Tom wasn't over keen to give up his room. Although it had never afforded anything but a modicum of comfort, it had always been his personal space and a place where he could be alone. Nonetheless he removed his personal things from the room without resentment and placed them in that of Charles so that he could dress or undress without the risk of compromising the modesty of the female members of the household (who now outnumbered the males!).

The next few days saw a turmoil of hustle and bustle about the cottage as everyone seemed to get under everyone else's feet. Charles refused to stay in bed claiming that he was more in need of exercise than rest and anyway, it was his head that had been injured, nothing else.

He and Eira spent long hours in the garden nurturing the few crops that there were and using the opportunity to chat and get to know each other better, it seemed to them that they had known each other for far longer than just a few days and each felt the bond between them growing as the moments together slipped by.

Charles' mother kept an attentive eye on them through her kitchen window, not so much out of propriety as pride in what she could see unfolding. The tenderness and sweet bliss of the developing relationship transported her back in time to those awkward moments those many years ago when on Sundays her husband-to-be had come calling. He would always fetch wild flowers from the hills surrounding their valley as he walked to meet her. She would greet him at the front door, her head lowered in shy innocence and would always notice his coarse, bedraggled trousers that never failed to sport large bulges where his knees reposed when sitting. No amount of ironing would remove them nor even influence their shape!

He had been shy and awkward by nature and had never received any formal education but was a man of steadfast honour and pride. The two would sit together in the dimness of the parlour of her parents home lit by a single oil lamp barely throwing enough light to see by yet it was somehow soothing as it sent out animated shadows on the whitewashed cobblestone walls. Large tin baths hung on the wall beside the lifeless range. On weekdays the baths would come down and the parlour would become a bathroom for the men of the family as they returned home coal blackened from their shifts underground. On those days the coal fired range would be blazing and upon it would be countless kettles steaming away singing different tunes, waiting for the moment they would be emptied into the baths.

After the preparations for the returning men were completed and the evening meal was satisfactorily bubbling away on the kitchen range in the adjoining room, the women folk would sit outside on the holystoned stoops of the colliery owned houses and a routine exchange of news (and gossip) would take place.

If you had never experienced this peculiar ritual it was said, you hadn't really lived! It was further claimed that it was from these occurrences that the notion of newspapers had begun!

"Did you know my girl" her grandfather had once said to her as they waited for the colliery siren to announce the discharge of the coal cutters from their subterranean halls, "Such was the honour of the folk here that a policeman was *never* needed in the valley!"

He had said it many times! She adored her Grand Father, he was always full of mischief and loved to play practical jokes on his grandchildren but to even think that he was anything but dedicated to them would have been sinful indeed!

"Any chance of a cup of tea Mother?"

Tom's question wrenched her thoughts back into the present.

"Sorry my Son, I must have been elsewhere" she apologised, reaching for the tea pot.

"I could do with one myself!" She muttered under her breath. The few moments she had spent in journeying to her youth had raised her spirits and gladdened her heart.

They lived in harmony for those few precious days and so much was there to do that no-one even mentioned Charles' recent experiences. His mother had wondered about that incident but had been reluctant to raise the subject for fear of raking over unwelcome echoes of a tragedy best left in its resting place.

They were sat in the living room discussing the ugly events that seemed to be unfolding in Europe and whether war was imminent when Charles became aware of the coin. He hadn't worn his waistcoat for some time and was surprised that the coin had not been lost or removed during the laundering after his escape from the flooding pit, but there it was!

He fingered it within the small pocket not wanting to remove it lest his mother should ask why he was carrying it.

Recollections of the way the coin had felt when death was about to strike rolled over him in waves of sickening veracity causing him to groan out loud.

He now saw unmistakably that a macabre connection existed between misfortune and this coin and swore in that moment that he would *never* let his infant sister have such a gift!

"What is it my Son?" his mother was quick to ask.

Mental pictures of the water crushing those men came back to him with a vividness so indelible, so moving that he was staggered; his head began to spin. The nurse rested her hand on his and patted it gently.

"Try not to dwell on it." She advised. She had been warned by Doctor Moody that something like this might happen.

Charles began to shake and beads of perspiration started down his temples even though his skin was cold to the touch. His eyes clouded as his mind plunged headlong down that God forsaken shaft to face again the thundering water and the screams of the dying men.

He was on the point of collapsing when the nurse took his shoulders and shook him.

The event had arisen with such suddenness that the others were overcome by the surprise of it and unable to properly comprehend what was taking place.

"CHARLES!" Eira cried shaking his shoulders again and searching deep into his un-seeing eyes.

Charles' fingers opened at once, relinquishing his fierce grip on the penny. His troubled mind came back to the room but the event was not over.

His mind still not fully recovered from the incident, he asked the question to which he did not want an answer, a question so dreadful that he had been trying hard to avoid asking it since regaining consciousness in the infirmary. A question which all his instincts told him to push away from his mind and out of his life.

He asked it with the utter resignation of a defeated man who already knew what the unwelcome answer would be.

"It was him wasn't it?"

He turned his head to look sidelong at his nurse; large tears were now coursing down his cheeks.

"It was the leader of my team that didn't come out of that shaft . . . . the man that had steadied me when all I wanted to do was run. It was *him* wasn't it?"

The room fell into utter silence. Neither Tom nor his Mother were aware of exactly what had taken place below ground on that fateful day. They only knew that Charles had been part of a group of brave volunteers in a rescue attempt deep beneath the earth and that he had had acted with courage and fortitude when his own life had been under grave threat.

The nurse *had* known. She had been told whilst she was searching for her new found acquaintance what had happened in those agonising moments after the cage had been struck as it began its journey upwards from the depths of living hell. She had made sure she would be there when the men were helped from their would-be tomb and knew well enough the names of those that had made the ultimate sacrifice and the manner of their passing.

Fighting back her own feelings of regret and dejection at the loss of such fine lives, she turned sharply on the self-pitying Charles and chided,

"You must get a grip on yourself Charles and accept what you are powerless to change, we will all help you face your burden when you feel your troubles are too much for you but *you* must *fight* your feelings and go forward. You have been given life that others have died to spare, you have to be strong and worthy of their gift to you!"

Tom shot a nervous glance at his mother, he badly wanted to help his unfortunate elder Brother through his misery but the lack of experience of his years denied him the means to accomplish his desire.

Charles felt a hand rest upon his other shoulder, his Mother had come to his side,

"Have courage my Son," she whispered, "The man that gave his life for you would have done so without question if there had been a choice for him to make. Learn from his example but don't take it upon yourself to try to bring him back by remorse. Nothing can be more futile than surrender to useless feelings!"

"I'll fetch water and logs!" announced Charles severing his mood. He hated himself for the weakness he had just displayed and felt the need for a few moments to himself. All eyes followed him as he strode from the room and made for the keen air of the early evening and the chance to clear his muddled head. He knew they were right.

It was in the solitude of the garden that he made what he would later come to regard as the best decision of his life!

He'd been outside a matter of a handful of minutes but that's all it took for him to realise that he had *another* question to ask. A far reaching question that would be pivotal to his life and to the future of the family.

Turning on his heels he made his way back into the cottage with a strong sense of purpose and wearing a grin akin to the Cheshire cat!

The hushed conversation ceased as the occupants focussed upon Charles' unexpected re-entry, they were bewildered and somewhat perplexed to find that Charles was now *grinning,*—had he become unhinged?

He marched resolutely to Eira and grasping both her hands in his wheeled her smartly around and placed her with an undignified thump into the fireside chair. He fell upon one knee and looking deep into her puzzled eyes blurted,

"Will you marry me?"

Stunned into silence, the atmosphere in the room turned from concern to astonishment. The air was full of unanswered questions. Expressions, first of amazement then of joy, crept over the occupants as the significance of what had just taken place sank home. The nurse was now beaming from ear to ear with her own Cheshire cat impersonation.

"Try and stop me!" she gushed.

Throwing her arms around Charles' neck she planted a resounding kiss on his forehead as if to seal the union but turned a beetroot red as she realised that this was perhaps a little forward in full view of her prospective family.

"What wonderful news, I think you two will be a very good match!" sighed Charles' Mother then added with a hint of caution,

"Congratulations to you both indeed, but I *do* think you should go to see Eira's folks as soon as you can and ask her Father's permission to be sure they are as happy about the match as I am!"

Charles rose from his knees, taking both Eira's hands again he hauled her to her feet and without taking his eyes from her, said to his mother.

"Thanks," he shifted his gaze to look at her then continued, "Hadn't thought of that—mind too full of myself to think properly I shouldn't wonder!"

Later that day when he was alone in the room, Charles removed the coin from his waistcoat pocket and returned it to the nook above the mantle shelf. It had been safe there before and there it must remain until he decided what best to do with it. It was fortunate indeed that his

Mother had not asked where the gift he had made had gone—perhaps she knew!

The walk to the rows of colliery houses where Eira lived passed by quick enough as Eira briefed Charles on the easy-going nature of her parents and what they would expect of him in the meeting that was to follow.

"Dad's a typical mining man, thick set and powerful but gentle with it," she said. "His hands are as big as the shovel he uses and although he's strong, he is very good natured but it's Mother that has the brains!"

She looked sidelong at Charles, a mischievous grin spreading across her countenance as she observed the obvious unease that was etched on his face!

"Don't worry silly!" she chided, "They are as good as gold and won't *eat* you!"

This was of small comfort to Charles and as each step drew them closer to the terraced, stone built houses he felt his stomach churning and an overpowering urge to turn on his heels and run. As they arrived at the railings that marked the start of her terrace and turned to make their way up the rough cobbled street, Eira drew her hand from his.

"Mustn't let the neighbours see us hand in hand or they will know before Mum and Dad and you can bet the news will arrive at my house before *we* do!"

There were ten large dwellings in this terrace, originally they had been twenty two for they were built into the side of a substantial hill and this allowed the colliery owners to configure the buildings as a house over a house the lower being accessed from another parallel road lower down the slope. These extra houses were necessary for the families of the additional labour that poured in when the pits in the valley were being sunk. There was an almost insatiable need for skilled men and labourers for the construction of the engine houses and many supporting buildings that were being erected and the rail and tramways that were being laid not to mention the deep shafts which were being hand dug. Once the pits were established much of this labour moved on and the lower houses were united with those above to become cellars for storage and for the children to play in.

On the opposite side of the lower service road was a row of brick built outside toilets with soil buckets that needed to be emptied daily for there was just one such toilet to serve each upper and lower storey! The last house in the row had been demolished to provide a link between upper and lower service roads to enable the local grocer family to get their horse drawn trade carts out of the street without the need to reverse the long very slippery slope of the road!

Every day such carts would arrive each plying a different commodity. Fish, fruit and vegetables, meat, bread, logs and kindling, pots and pans, tin baths and even second hand clothing for exchange. It was a much valued service but also provided a handsome income for the family of the traders that were engaged in the supply chain.

There were many children born to the families resident in these houses and, children being of an adventurous nature and ever resourceful, the cellars quickly became play areas with spooky nooks and crannies and cupboards that mustn't be opened for fear of releasing serpents that dwelled in the unknown depths beyond!

Whatever the age, if the toilet was needed after dark it would mean a lonesome trek through these forsaken, possessed, demonic spaces with flickering candle or lamp and frequent terrified glances over the shoulder into the blanket of darkness that concealed spectres, ghosts and goblins that formed a gauntlet lining the route to outside relief. Not surprising then that the youngest children would hold onto their water until breaking point. When, in the pitch blackness of a winter's evening, the children could hold themselves no longer and plucked up the courage to face the probability of a foreshortened future in the cellar of doom, the older ones would creep to the open doorway at the cellar stairs. Biding their time until it was certain the sojourner was at the point of no return, they would wail like banshees to make the journey that much more unbearable!

More than once a terrified, sobbing child would make his way back out of the stair well with dripping shorts not even having made the bottom of the clanky wooden steps! It was certain that if the transit was to be made by the light of a single candle, it couldn't be made quickly for fear of snuffing it out the thought of which drove stakes of mortal fear and impending peril into even the most hardy and apparently fearless of youngsters!

Over the years an embankment carrying the tramway to the distant spoil tip that now towered over the houses had encroached ever nearer the lower service road due to successive derailments and resultant shedding of tons and tons of coal spoil over what had once been vegetable allotments behind the toilet buildings. Despite all these discouragements, the families resident there were happy and mostly content and were always self reliant and fair.

Charles and his nurse made their way up the higher road and true to form, door after door opened as they passed, pleasantries proffered and reciprocated. The observers remained at their doorways after the couple had passed by watching them with open interest and darting inquisitive glances between each other seeking reasons for the appearance of this stranger in their midst.

Arriving at number seven, Eira paused at the door and looked briefly back at the folk they had just passed by. She knew well enough they would all stand there quite without shame waiting for news of what was transpiring, each believing they had a vested interest in the lives of the others in the terrace and each considered they had an irrefutable right to know what was going on.

It was not her custom in the normal sense, but because she was about to introduce a stranger to her Father's household, she knocked twice upon the door and waited. She could hear subdued voices approaching beyond and smiled, surely it was not possible that her parents knew they were coming?

The door creaked open revealing her Father unshaven and with open neck shirt without collar and braces dangling loosely at his sides.

"Dieu, dieu!" He exclaimed in complete surprise, "I wasn't expecting to see *you* girl!" He let go of the door and motioning with his hand said, "Come in, come *in* Carriad, why on earth are you knocking mun?"

Eira giggled and replied, "I've got someone to see you and Mam, scared to death he is so be gentle with him!"

Her Father turned and looked warmly at Charles thrusting out a giant calloused hand in genuine welcome.

"This man needs no introduction in *my* house, you are *very* welcome sir and do us an honour indeed!"

Charles took the hand and shook it firmly,

"It is a pleasure to meet you sir!" he replied. His eyes following Eira lest he should be left to fend for himself.

Releasing Charles' hand, Eira's Father brushed by them both to where his Wife had been patiently waiting and proudly announced.

"This is the young man we have all been talking about! Saved Dai's life and patched up several others underground he did! Dieu, dieu this is an *honour* to us all in this house indeed!"

Before Charles could grasp what was happening, the man made for the door and shouted the same up and down the road.

Charles paused before the lady of the house whilst Eira introduced him as her friend and then taking her hand, kissed her lightly on one cheek as he had been instructed.

"Very pleased to make your acquaintance Mrs Stacey and thank you for making me welcome in your home!"

"Hush lad," she smiled noticing his unease, she had anticipated the reason for this unexpected visit and knew that such encounters were uncomfortable for a young man. She added, "Would you like a cup of tea?"

"Thank you Mrs Stacey." He replied feeling a little awkward, "That would be very nice indeed!"

"Let us go into the living room then and make ourselves a little more comfortable. Eira, will you help me?" She winked at her husband, nodding toward Charles as she did so.

"This way," proffered Eira's father taking Charles by the elbow and easing him after the departed ladies, he was pretty sure now what the wink had meant and what this visit was in aid of.

The pair made their way into the living room and over to the range where Mr Stacey reached to the mantle shelf and took down his pipe and tobacco.

"Now young man, I have a feeling you may have something you want to ask me so out with it!" he said in an even voice. He raised an eyebrow and fixed Charles with a steady gaze.

Yes sir," Charles replied. Eira hadn't said that he would be alone when asking for her father's consent and he felt reluctant to make so bold.

He suddenly plucked up courage and blurted.

"I would like to marry your Daughter!"

The bluntness of the request took Eira's father by surprise, he had been expecting this young man to build up to the event but now that it was out in the open he pretended to be giving the matter some detailed consideration.

"Hmm". He ventured "and how do you propose to support her, I know that you are studying with Doctor Moody and I have seen first hand that you are a considerate and brave young man but will you be able to manage a family when it comes?"

"I shall ask the Doctor for a raise sir. I am sure he will oblige now that I am able to take on many of his smaller tasks!"

"What of my Daughter's nursing work at the colliery my boy, will she be able to carry on if you marry her . . . . until she is with child so to speak?"

"If that is her wish sir, I wouldn't want to take from her what I know is a good job and the chance to make something of her own life!"

"Well then," Eira's father paused, sniffed and shifted his gaze to the fire, taking several long pulls on his pipe from which issued dense clouds of throat tickling smoke.

"If you are both sure this is what you want and you feel you will be able to provide for my Daughter then let me be the first to welcome you into the family my lad!"

He extended his hand once more to shake that of Charles with a new vigour that went beyond friendship and warmed Charles' heart.

"One more thing though," added the man, "Have you given any thought to *when* you would both like to wed?" Now that September was almost out he thought it clearly unlikely to be *this* year.

"We haven't discussed final a date yet sir," Charles admitted, "But we thought October would be nice!"

"***October?***" Echoed the Father choking on his pipe. With a wide eyed expression of disbelief, he proceeded indignantly, "Good God Mun, that hardly gives any time at *all* to get ready!"

The misinterpretation struck Charles at once.

"October *next* year!" he affirmed, to the obvious relief of Mr Stacey. It was quite obvious that he had thought that his daughter must *already* be pregnant!

There came the sound of subdued giggles from beyond the kitchen door where the ladies had been eavesdropping eager to know how things were going.

"Dieu, *Dieu!*" he retorted with a sigh of relief, "You had me worried there for a bit butty!"

"Sorry!" replied a timid Charles kicking himself for his error, "Didn't mean to cause any worry!"

The misunderstanding and the obvious confusion of the two men presented itself as a comic relief to everyone and served to break the tension that Charles was feeling.

"May I tell the ladies?" he enquired.

"Certainly not my friend!" retorted the Father, "That is *my* job . . . . though I fancy they know already butt!" Turning toward the door he called loudly,

"Come on in you two . . . . there's no need to hide any more!"

They entered the room eager to rejoin the two men their faces radiant with joy and wearing broad smiles. They were thrilled that all had gone so well.

Eira looked deep into the eyes of her intended and raised a single slim finger to his cheek to lovingly brush away the tear of relief that had involuntarily risen there.

"Fetch beer Carriad," Mr Stacey instructed his wife, "we must seal this promise the Welsh way!"

It was late into the evening when the couple left the house and began their journey back to Charles' cottage. A light drizzle had formed cooling the evening air and bringing forth the fragrance of fern and pine though it must be said that the two of them had no notice of it as they walked hand in hand along the damp track that led to the cottage. Their only thought was to cover the ground quickly so as to break the good news to Charles' family fidgeting in anticipation. Both were keenly aware of the suspense such occasions can provoke!

Charles' spirits were soaring high above the drizzle and mist that was forming here and there in the lower pockets of the hillside, in part because of the elated feeling of success the day had brought, and part because of the fine old homebrew the Welsh were so good at making.

Yet again, without being aware of it, he began singing 'Myfanwy' beneath his breath but, soft as the singing was, it was quickly taken up by Eira who knew the song better than he did and whose sprits were flying high in close formation with his for she too was fond of a little Welsh nectar!

The journey seemed to fly by and almost before they knew it they were home and spreading the good news. Charles' family were delighted with the result but it must be understood that they had little doubt about the outcome from the start.

They talked long into the remains of the day as the where's why's and what have you's of the future were discussed one after another. There was much to be done even though the wedding was more than a year away!

Charles announced as they were all making ready to retire that he had rested long enough and declared to everyone that he intended to go back to work with Doctor Moody the next day. The decision would also mean that Eira would return to her parents and to her employment at the Colliery but as Charles reasoned, the act would give everyone chance to return to a normal life the better to prepare for the events ahead.

Rising bright and early, the couple set off together and walked the distance to the house of Doctor Moody almost in silence. Charles explained his reasoning carefully to the doctor expounding that he felt fit and ready to carry on where he had left off at the practise. The declaration was received with considerable relief by the old man who had been finding life more than a little strenuous during Charles' absence.

He examined Charles' wound and proclaimed his entire satisfaction with the speed and nature of its healing; turning to the nurse he remarked.

"You have done a fine job Miss Stacey, I presume that this fortunate young man will now take you back to the Colliery in the pony and trap?"

"First I must visit my parents Sir," she replied, "I have one or two things I must attend to before work and I need my colliery working uniform!"

"Yes of course," muttered the doctor, "I'm sure Charles will be good enough to run you home before starting his rounds!"

The pony seemed pleased to have Charles tending him again and enjoyed the exuberance of being put through his paces on the way to Eira's house. This was something his ageing master was now reluctant to do since he considered that a slow trot was much more comfortable and in keeping with the dignity of both his profession and his years.

Charles pitched himself into the practise with enthusiasm and renewed determination, he had decided to wait another week before announcing to the doctor and his good lady his betrothal, it seemed to him to be bordering on impropriety to be asking for a raise in salary so close on returning from absence.

There was so much to do and catch up on now that he was back that the days passed by such that Charles all but forgot that he had intended to ask the doctor for more money. Now that it had popped back to mind however, he decided he would do it right after the pony was stabled next day. Somehow, when the time came, he was unable to summon up the fortitude to make the request. He couldn't quite fathom the reason for his reluctance and lack of courage in being forthright with the doctor and make what should have been a simple request. The more he thought about it the more irritated and agitated he became, even those at home could see that he was not his usual confident self and that he was withdrawing behind some sort of obscure veil. He was becoming ever more short tempered and snapped at anyone who dared ask him what was troubling him. He could see for himself that he was creating bad feeling amongst those that he loved so dearly but, for reasons he was unable to comprehend, he was powerless to overcome whatever it was that had seized him.

For some while now he had been forcing the existence of the penny to the back of his mind but of late it had been pressing so strongly to the forefront of his thoughts, it had been difficult to ignore; impossible to repress. The more he had tried to thrust it away the more persistent it seemed to become. It seemed to be drawing him, pulling at his mind and twisting it this way and that until he felt that he *must* pick it up once more.

He made his way absently to the mantle shelf and unthinkingly took the penny down rolling it over and over in his fingers. He could feel it getting warmer and as it did so, he felt all the agitation of the last few days evaporating as if by magic; lifting from him to be replaced with an inner peace and tranquil calmness. His lost confidence came flooding back, he became his old self once more.

During the time that this was taking place Charles had been completely unaware of the loved ones about him but now he had come out of his dudgeon he was able to turn his mind to his surroundings, he became aware of the expressions of extreme concern on the faces of the others as they watched him fumbling with the coin.

"Is there something still troubling you my Son?" ventured Charles' mother.

"You appear to be completely lost in something . . . can we help in any way?"

For once Charles was able to reply without snapping at his mother.

"No Mother" he said evenly, "I'm sorry for the way I've been but I'm alright now!"

"Isn't that the coin you gave your Sister my Son?" she enquired.

The others looked on studying Charles in silence.

"Yes Mother," he replied and without meeting her gaze placed the coin deftly in his waistcoat pocket, "But I think I will find something more fitting for her in a day or two. This coin seems to have some something about it that might not be good for her!"

His mother nodded her acquiescence and brushed the incident aside, rising to her feet she declared,

"Time for some tea . . . . would you like a cup Charles?"

"Love some!" came the cheerful response and he smiled broadly for the first time in days.

Charles turned and looked apologetically into the eyes of his visiting sweetheart. He knew that she had frequently walked the distance between her house and his so that they could spend time together and yet he had been unforgivably unpleasant to her. He searched his brain in an effort to find words that would adequately describe the hurt and sorrow he deeply felt for the way he had been remorselessly abusing her good nature but could find none.

In sheer desperation he turned to face her thrusting out both his hands to her in a gesture of silent reconciliation and apology. She smiled the warm smile of someone greeting the return of a long absent and much loved dear one and moved swiftly and eagerly forward to take them in hers. This was a remarkable young woman indeed whose faith in and love for her man, could not be diminished nor yet faintly tarnished by the idiosyncrasies of whatever adversitys might befall them! She would need all the strength her faith in him could provide ere long in order to weather the approaching tempest that would push their relationship to the very brink of the abyss and into disparate abjection!

CHAPTER 6

The Penny Takes Hold

As Charles prepared the pony and trap for the day ahead he decided that he would tackle the doctor about the raise in salary as soon as possible. His strength of character having been restored he no longer felt reticent about asking and in fact was quite looking forward to getting it over with so that he could plan how best to save the money he would need for his share of the wedding. He didn't have to wait long, opportunity presented itself as he led the harnessed pony into the stable courtyard. The doctor was ambling toward him in the rolling gait that is so prevalent in the ageing, particularly those suffering from joint ailments.

He wore a smile that threatened to cut his face in two and waved a cheery good morning to Charles as he approached.

"My boy, my dear boy!" he blurted, "Is it true? Have you asked the colliery nurse to marry you?"

"I have indeed Sir," replied Charles, "I was about to bring the pony and trap to the house to tell you and Mrs Moody but you have beaten me to it!"

"Wonderful, wonderful!" enthused the doctor hardly able to conceal his absolute delight.

"You will be in need of a raise of course, will you not?"

"I had intended to ask you that question this very morning Sir," returned Charles wondering why on earth he had been so reluctant to broach the subject earlier.

"I have a proposition for you Charles that I think you will find to your entire advantage, no, no . . . . *better* than that, to your entire *satisfaction*!" enthused doctor Moody. "At dinner with the colliery owner Mr Grace-Williams last evening the conversation turned to you and the fine job of work you did during the recent emergency. He was very impressed with your skills and your attitude young man, and has offered to combine my practise with that of the colliery which means that you and your nurse can work together visiting my patients *and* the colliery sick at home where surgery or diagnosis is not needed. You are to be given free use of the infirmary pony and trap which you will keep at your home . . . . Now, what do you think of *that*?"

The proposition left Charles somewhat astonished, this was unbelievably wonderful news, almost too good to be true, he would be with his intended every day! They would be able to use the pony and trap to go *everywhere* even to visit Eira's parents. He almost didn't dare believe this stroke of good fortune, he wondered how on earth things could have changed for the better so quickly with so little influence from himself. He suddenly recalled why the conversation had been broached and re-affirmed anxiously.

"I take it from what you say sir, that the additional duties will bring a reasonable increase in salary, would that be right?"

"But of course my lad, of *course!*" replied the Doctor, "We didn't thrash out details of course, that is for the colliery pay clerks, but I *can* tell you that it will mean at least another *ten* shillings a week!"

"Ten shillings?" Charles repeated, hardly daring to believe this stroke of unprecedented good fortune, "That's generous indeed!"

"Now, be off with you lad and don't forget to call in at the colliery infirmary to collect their trap and for any instructions the medical officer may have for you! . . . . I take it you will lead my pony back and stable it before you go home!"

The kindly old Gent turned awkwardly and without waiting for affirmation began the walk back to the house. Charles called after him,

"Can I take you up to the house sir? Save your bones?"

"Must use these old muscles or seize up!" the doctor called over his shoulder without interrupting his stride.

Charles watched this wonderful and generous old soul as he waddled along the pathway to the house and blessed the day their paths had crossed, even *conjoined* to the immeasurable benefit of them both. Life could be blissful indeed!

The rounds that morning would bring Charles to the colliery at around noon if he were quick about them, he could then eat his lunch with Eira and tell her the astonishing good news. He set about the morning's tasks with high spirits and the dedication of one who loves his job, with relish almost, knowing that every house he visited brought him closer to the maid that had brought so much joy to his life! As he progressed between calls he used the time to go over in his mind how he would tell her. Should he tease her or play guessing games or should he come right out with it? My God!' the thought dawned, we could even get married *earlier*!

Arriving at the colliery a few minutes before noon, Charles took the pony and trap to the above ground stable. (Below ground pit ponies rarely came to the surface except when ill or at retirement!) Hitching the Doctor's pony to the ring set in the outside wall of the stable, Charles reported to the stable foreman who insisted in having the animal fed and cleaned as a mark of gratitude for the part Charles had played in the rescue drama.

"It's not often I get to return a favour for someone like you!" he had said bringing a flush to Charles' cheeks.

"Thank you, appreciate your help, I'll see you in about forty five minutes or so," said Charles and turned towards the infirmary. He stopped dead in his tracks as he came face to face with the pithead winding gear over that God forsaken colliery shaft. It was working again now and a hive of frenetic activity as tub after tub of coal and spoil came off the pit head and was manhandled to the screen for sorting. As Charles watched, each full tub pulled off was rapidly replaced by empties in a continuous chain fashioned to keep the monster pit fed, the men in gainful employment, and the masters in luxury.

Charles fingered the penny in his pocket, it somehow gave him the strength he needed to deal with the sight before him. It took away the harshness of the awful memories of that night and soothed his burning conscience that kept thrusting his thoughts into the bowels of hell to the silent screams of those wretched souls that had perished in that ill-fated incident. The foreman had been watching Charles and could see that his mind was troubled, he made to speak but Charles headed him off.

"Did they ever find the body of the man that was lost at the bottom of the shaft?" he asked trying to adopt an air of indifference.

As he uttered the words Charles could feel the coin warming in his fingers in response to the conversation and it was then that the realisation dawned upon him that somehow there was a connection between malevolence and the way this penny behaved. He had already realised that its presence imparted to him the confidence to do things that he had never been able to do or achieve before but now he was realising that it demanded a sickening reimbursement for those favours and some of that payment was to be of the mortal kind!

A shudder ran down his spine for he knew without doubt that he could no longer relinquish the formidable grip the coin had formed upon him. He had become the servant of something wielding an influence he could not comprehend and was seemingly powerless to resist!

"I'm sorry sir," the man replied sadly, "His body was never found. The pumps were running five days solid before the flood water was cleared enough for investigators to go down and search for him but nothing was ever found. They say he may have been forced into one of the abandoned areas that are still flooded. The chances of him being found now are very small because many of those places have since collapsed!"

"Pity!" said Charles pensively, "He was a good man, does he have family?"

"Yes, they live at the Scotch just up the hill. He has Brothers and a Son working here in the pit, they're taking care of the family."

Although the wind had been taken from his sails, Charles was not as despondent as he thought he would have been at hearing the news. The two stood quietly watching the pithead activity for a few moments longer before Charles broke the silence with a stifled sigh followed by just two words delivered flatly and without any sign of outward emotion.

"Thank you." he said, and continued his walk to the infirmary.

The foreman watched him for a few seconds longer then shrugged his shoulders and returned to his labours.

Charles had hardly passed through the door that led to the ward when Eira came sweeping toward him her face wreathed in smiles and her eyes bright and shining radiantly, it was obvious that she had already heard the good news so teasing her now would be fruitless.

She threw her arms around his neck and despatching caution and modesty to the wind planted a kiss on his cheek.

"Isn't it wonderful news Charlie? The M.O. told me about it not twenty minutes ago and I was so happy I just didn't know how I was going to wait until I saw you!" she gushed. "Have you seen him yet because he was expecting you to call to see him!"

"Not yet girl, I've just a few minutes ago got here myself!"

"He's away at lunch right now but he said to tell you he will be back by one o'clock, will you wait?"

"Yes of course . . . . it'll give me time to sit with you and try to cool your schoolgirl passion!" Charles chided playfully. "Away and make some tea for a hard working lad!"

"Cheeky devil you are Charles, I have as much if not *more* to do than you do!" She remonstrated mockingly, "I'll make your tea anyway."

She made her way between the rows of empty beds to the small staff room that abutted the end of the ward, Charles close upon her heels snack box in hand.

The meeting with the colliery medical officer went smoothly enough, it seemed Charles would be more of a chauffeur-cum-porter for Eira than the medical orderly he was expecting to be but it was of no concern to him given that he could be constantly at her side and was earning extra money into the bargain.

The daily rounds under this new system was proving a great success and it was an infrequent occasion indeed that required either of the Doctors to leave their respective surgeries. Quite commonly whole families would seize the opportunity to talk about *their* ailments and medicinal concerns when the pair made a home visit to a particular individual and it was a rare occasion indeed when they were stuck for the right solutions to problems. Everything seemed to be falling into place, the couple were happy and there is nothing so effective in medicine as a happy nurse. So engrossed were they both in their professional partnership that the days just flew by. Such was the hustle and bustle of their daily routine that they could find barely enough time to talk about the finer details of the approaching wedding!

Curiously, another event seemed to be developing in parallel with all of this, an event that was in itself surprising yet was not foreseen nor even noticed by Charles and the nurse.

A few weeks after the new medical arrangements had been put in place, the colliery M.O. became perturbed regarding the state of cleanliness of the infirmary ward. Previously the cleaning had been done by Eira in her free moments and when the ward was unoccupied there were plenty of those so the infirmary was always spick and span and ready for any medical eventuality. Now that she was frequently away however, there wasn't time for her to undertake this duty and in the realisation of this the M.O. enquired of his helpers if either of them knew of someone reliable who would be prepared to attend to the cleaning. He stressed strongly that the post must be treated as most urgent and needed to be filled without delay.

That evening over dinner, Charles mentioned the vacancy to his Mother wondering if the job would be of any interest to her.

"Yes," she replied eagerly, "It would help a great deal financially, especially when you leave the house! There is just one thing though, I shall have to take the infant with me, she'd be no trouble of course but how would the good Doctor feel about having a child around the ward?"

"Mostly the ward is empty now that folks have got used to having treatment in their own homes," Eira pointed out, "In any case, there's always the staff room . . . . she would be fine in there and because it has a glass door you would be able to keep an eye on her from the ward!"

"What would happen if there was another accident at the colliery Eira?" Enquired the Mother, her countenance clouded with doubt, "The cleaning would still need to be done, in fact it would be even more important but I couldn't allow the child to be around such misery and suffering!"

"Of course not Mam," Eira exclaimed smiling broadly as she went on, "Under those circumstances special rules are put into force and there is always extra medical staff brought in from the other collieries to tend to the injured as well as extra porters to help move the heavy men. The cleaning would need far more than one person could manage so everyone is expected to pitch in . . . . why girl," she added jokingly, "No one would even notice if you weren't there!"

The three of them chuckled at the thought of such a thing relieving the uncertainty that had pervaded the conversation.

"We would need to ride in the trap with you Charles . . . it's a long way to walk with a child!" entreated Charles' Mother.

"O' course," replied Charles, "The trap will take us all with a bit of a squeeze and it will be nice to have someone to talk to on the way for a change, especially when the weather is miserable; only thing is, I get delayed at the end of the day sometimes and may not leave the colliery early enough for you and the babe!"

Charles' mother gazed thoughtfully at her son as she took this in pausing briefly before announcing,

"Perhaps we'll cross that bridge when we come to it my son," she answered wistfully, "If needs be and the weather lets us, we can walk, God gave me sturdy legs and I'm sure we will manage."

"It's a little bit far for that Mum and you could never manage if you had to carry the babe all the way if the weather turns but don't worry, we'll think of something I'm sure."

So it was that Mrs Jenkins took up her new post, throwing herself into the task of getting the ward back into a state of thorough medical acceptibility. Her day was exacting when all was considered yet somehow she found more than ample time to see to her child giving her the love and commitment that only a good woman can confer and her diligence did not go un-noticed.

For a few days now the colliery medical officer, with little else to do, had been observing discreetly from his office adjoining the ward how this fine lady was able to fit in all that was asked of her yet produce a result which, when all was considered, greatly surpassed the expectations of even the most fastidious of masters.

He found himself strangely drawn by the manner in which she bustled swiftly about her work fleeting from chore to chore with the grace and carriage of a princess yet with the sense of purpose and thoroughness of a person dedicated to a life of toil. He decided that this was a remarkable person indeed, blessed with admirable intelligence and an attractive appearance, she possessed a most pleasing good nature. He found himself wondering how on earth she had allowed herself to be misled into forming a relationship with a man who clearly felt nothing for her and had ultimately reduced her to an existence of disgrace and misfortune. He had never married himself; it seemed to him that there had never been time for it and in any case there had never been a woman that he cared enough to strike up a relationship with. Now that he was in his middle years however, he had begun to yearn for the companionship of the fairer sex and was beginning to look upon the marital unions of his colleagues with a little envy. He had begun to notice how melodiously the fairer sex laughed and how dashed attractive they were when they spoke prettily and that a pair of fine eyes could melt a heart and send spirits soaring heavenward bringing a little tickle to the breast.

Without conscious intention, he had moved to the window overlooking the ward and with hands crossed behind his back so that his long black coat draped over them, he was openly studying the activity beyond.

A warm smile crossed his lips as he watched this woman. His mind drifted back to the day he had escorted her from the ward and how good it had felt to have a lady at his side her arm linked in his. For the first time he was aware of an empty, gnawing feeling in the pit of his stomach, could it be that he had feelings for her that were greater than compassion? He shook his head and moved away from the window afraid that he might be noticed and concerned that his actions might be mistaken for those of an untrusting master. As the days wore on however, he found himself thinking of her more and more and no matter how diligently he tried to push the thoughts from his mind they would return the stronger until it seemed that he could think of nothing else. The constant struggle with the urge to approach her and the need to preserve his dignity and good standing in the professional community by not becoming involved with a fallen woman was beginning to tear at his composure. The result of this inner conflict made him impart an attitude of complete indifference, even hostility, towards Charles' mother whenever they encountered each other.

She accepted this with equanimity as the customary master/servant relationship that was the norm for those days and dismissed the situation as unimportant little knowing that it was affection drowning in protocol that was at the heart of it all!

Oddly enough, she admired the colliery doctor much more than she wanted to admit believing him to be a fine example of a man. She considered him to be honest and forthright and fair and considerate both as an employer and as a person, in fact she had become enamoured of him ever since the moment he had shown her such kindness when leaving the ward after visiting Charles all those weeks ago. It was something of a sadness to her that he could be so curt with her at times but under the present circumstances she simply attributed his distant attitude to the need of propriety.

Like all good employers, on regular occasion the colliery doctor would summon his staff to his office to discuss the day to day running of the facility they managed and to give praise where praise was due for good work or to remonstrate if things had not gone as well as expected. It was on just such an occasion that Mrs Jenkins found herself before the doctor. She had been suffering several sleepless nights for one reason or another, nothing she could pinpoint as a single reason but rather a collection of things that were troubling her mind that seemed only to occur in the middle of the night and as such seemed to take on an unprecedented significance that was disturbing enough to deny her the relaxing and refreshing rest that she so badly needed.

Thus it was she now faced her employer in a delicate state of mind and her resistance to misfortune seriously depleted.

The medical officer instructed her to be seated and paused for what seemed like an eternity before speaking. He had pushed his oak chair back from his desk and sat sternly with his arms folded across his chest in an attitude of superiority that was immediately daunting to his employee. Her mind raced for she could sense that something was not as it should be, had she done something wrong or perhaps was it to do with her child?

"Mrs Jenkins!" he began. "It is some weeks now since you came to work here and I have nothing but praise for the way in which you have conducted yourself and performed your duties."

The words were encouraging but the manner of their delivery suggested that there was more to come and that they would be less than praiseworthy.

"However, I am concerned that you have not been so diligent of late and feel that you may be having second thoughts about your duties here!"

He unfolded his arms and leaning forward placed his elbows upon the desk with the fingers of both hands pressed against each other in the form of a church steeple. Looking down at his fingers he went on haughtily,

"I refer to the matter of the chamber pot your child used that remained un-emptied in the staff room when you left for home last evening, this is just *not* acceptable!"

He looked up at his employee and his heart sank for tears were rolling freely down her cheeks, her shoulders heaved silently as she fought to control the unwelcome emotional breakdown that had seized her. The doctor rose hurriedly to his feet in reaction to the distress he had caused propelling his chair backward as he did so. Moving quickly he fell on one knees before her and grasped her hands in his.

"My dear lady," he said remorsefully, "I meant you no harm, I meant only to make mild rebuke and get to the bottom of what has been troubling you, I meant to *help* not to hurt, *please* believe me!"

His own eyes clouded as he tried to find words to make amends for his diffident behaviour whilst at the same time thrusting away an overwhelming urge to take her in his arms and hug her tightly.

She looked deep into his troubled eyes and could see the guilt that was in them but behind the guilt she could see compassion and longing and unexpectedly felt as if she somehow belonged to him.

She couldn't understand this feeling but somehow she *knew* that something life changing was about to transpire. She smiled weakly at him through tears that were still clouding her eyes; it seemed to her that the sun had suddenly broken cover to shine thinly through rain that was yet gently falling!

For some time they remained with their hands locked passionately together in their own solitary world as the enchantment of their feelings for each other passed wordlessly between them. It was as if they had been sweethearts all their lives and had at this moment re-discovered each other after a lengthy parting impressed on them by ill chance and cruel misfortune.

The Doctor severed the moment by releasing her hand to reach for his handkerchief. Taking it from his jacket upper pocket he reached to her cheek and caringly dabbed away the moisture.

"Will you forgive me my dear?" He whispered disengaging his eyes from hers in an act of humility.

"Away with you man!" She scoffed playfully, "You have done nothing but properly apply your authority!"

The Doctor released her other hand and rose uneasily to his feet wincing as he did so from the pain of having held for some time a position that his lifestyle had long since ceased to be accustomed to.

"My word," he exclaimed, "I'm not as young as I used to be!"

The statement was superfluous to say the least but it brought a wry smile to the lips of his employee. She watched him closely as he made his way back to the displaced chair behind his desk a little uncertain of what had just taken place. One thing was certain, she knew now that she had real feelings for this man that were far deeper than respect but was not at all sure what she should do about it! She decided she would play a waiting game and allow things to develop in their own good time if that was to be the way of things.

"Mrs Jenkins,—Violet—you don't mind if I call you by your first name I trust?" He enquired, "You know that the colliery provides a house for me adjoining the hospital." He paused briefly before continuing, "It is much too large for me and I have been too long alone in it. You see, I have never married thinking myself to be without need of the encumbrance of a companion but of late I have come to realize that I have real and genuine feelings of affection for you and the child and would ask you to be my wife if you would be good enough to consider me!"

He added, "I realize that this will be very sudden and unexpected for you but perhaps you would do me the honour of considering my offer and in due course let me know your answer?"

"This is indeed unexpected Sir," she went on, "Though we have been in each other's company daily, I don't even know your first name but one thing I *do* know is that if your offer of marriage is genuine then I will have no hesitation in accepting at once!"

The Doctor rose energetically to his feet his countenance openly reflecting the joy that was in his heart.

"My dear Girl!" he exclaimed, "This is wonderful news indeed and with your forbearance I will take steps to make the necessary arrangements. Do you have any preference for the date of the event?"

She looked at him and raising one eyebrow quizzically replied,

"I will leave that entirely to you though I do think that we should wait at least three months so that everyone will have time enough to realize that the wedding is nothing to do with the unnatural order of things!"

The Doctor laughed heartily as he caught the significance of the statement.

"I see your point clearly my dear and will take action accordingly. Oh, and by the way my first name is Ernest!"

The most extraordinary of events can have the most ordinary of effects on some folk for when the news was broken to her family, there seemed little to be surprised about!

"You seem to be the only one that couldn't see the Doctor's liking for you Mother!" Remarked Charles without emotion, his Mother raised her eyes from her ironing in plain astonishment.

"Why Charles, do you mean to say that you have noticed this and have said nothing to me?"

"Wasn't any point," Charles remarked, "I guessed that you'd find out sooner or later!"

He smiled impishly and returned to the newspaper he had been reading.

'Funny how things turn out!' he mumbled.

The days passed by for Charles with no conscious regard given to the existence of the sleeping penny that he now carried everywhere and was afraid to be without. There had been little opportunity for the devil to work his tricks so the coin had bided its time awaiting the opportunity it knew would sooner or later present itself—and so it did!

Charles was by no means a habitual drinker. There was enough for him to do without finding the time to frequent ale houses but journeying home one evening in piercing, driving rain had left him feeling miserable and somewhat 'out of sorts'. The last time he had visited the Six Bells public house had been whilst he was still working for the mint and before his Sister had been born so this was a rare occasion indeed! As he opened the large rough door and stepped down into the bar beyond the rain seemed to follow him, swept in almost horizontal waves on the biting wind. The occupants of the bar turned as he was closing the door to see what was disturbing the warmth and serenity of the company assembled in this den of kindred spirits. All but one face brightened as Charles was recognised. He was seized at once and propelled to the bar amidst numerous offers to 'stand him a drink!' Most of the occupants were colliers whetting their whistles after completing a hard afternoon shift before going home to their baths and families. White teeth stood out like beacons from coal black faces as they beamed their approval of the visit of this remarkable young man who had risked his own life to help save the lives of their comrades and had come to mean so much to their band of Brothers.

They slapped him on the back and shook his hand so vigorously that Charles thought it was going to fall off! He was overcome by his reception for now that so many days had passed since that fateful incident the recollection of it had faded in his own mind and he had relegated it to the annals of history as far as he was concerned.

All in the bar that is except one!

This man had somehow never liked Charles nor any of his family for that matter. There had never been any contact between them and it must be said that Charles had never even met this person but some animal instinct buried deep within the man had caused him to harbour openly resentful and hostile feelings toward Charles and his kin to the point that whenever Charles' name had been mention he would spit upon the floor in undisguised hatred.

It was unfortunate indeed that the company within that room should be tarnished by the presence of such a troublemaker; it would have been to the good of all if the dissenter had had the courage to take his malevolence home and leave the company be, but no—he was determined that spite should strike a blow to the armour of this young man who had been raised to a position of hero worship among his contemporaries just by being at the right place at the right time!

He listened to the sickening praises being offered to Charles and grew ever more belligerent as red hot pokers of hate probed his poisoned mind.

"You are one of the finest, most honest and upright men I have ever had the pleasure to shake the hand of!" remarked one of the miners.

"Pity you can't say the same for his Mother!" blurted the dissenter so loudly that it stopped all conversation stone dead!

The penny in Charles' waistcoat pocket had suddenly sprung to life. Charles could feel it even through the layers of rough serge of his suit and through the wool of his underclothing. He turned his face from the men to stare at his own reflection in the ornately engraved glass mirror that formed the backdrop to the bottles of ale and spirits lining the back of the bar not wanting to spoil the atmosphere that had previously brought conviviality to the room. The assembled men looked from one to the other not knowing how best to deal with this development for the dissident that had spoken was a huge man towering above all of the others and was well known for being someone best not engaged with physically.

"There's no call for that sort of talk Idris, leave the man be. Don't you think he's been through enough for us?" spoke up one of the more forthright of the men.

Idris raised himself from his rough wooden bar chair to stand his full six feet 3 inches and rolled up his sleeves revealing forearms the size of an average person's legs. He spat into the palms of both hands and rubbed them gleefully together. The penny was glowing, it would have flesh this night!

"His mother is no good—she gave herself to Williams-the-pit and has carried the price of it. Now, do *you* want to make something of it?"

He snarled the words through clenched teeth in a manner that was intended to intimidate all that heard them and having laid down his challenge was grinning in the knowledge that there was *no one* here that would want to take him on. The incident was sheer pleasure to his twisted mind!

The assembled miners closed ranks and formed a half-circle that would prevent Charles from taking arms against this giant of a man who would make mincemeat of him. The atmosphere in the bar was so heavy it could have cut with a knife yet the miner that had spoken out, small as he was, had hurled his ale at Idris drenching him from the neck up.

The look of sheer surprise that now replaced that of snarling scorn on the countenance of the giant caused the assembled company to break into uncontrolled laughter and it was to be hoped that this would be the end of a nasty affair but the penny needed its conquest and was not yet done!

Idris shook the droplets from his face and his expression darkened. His eyes narrowed to piercing slits, drawing back one huge arm he made to strike his challenger but the man was far too nimble for him and quickly side-stepped the blow.

The sheer force of delivery and the missed contact sent the giant reeling in a half circle as he toppled forward under the action of his own weight, he crashed into the other men sending them scattering like nine pins spilling ale in all directions. He drew himself up again and grabbed his challenger by the loose folds of his working jacket. Throwing him effortlessly over his shoulder he turned to make for the door with the intention of pulverising his opponent outside, Charles continued to stare into the mirror, he could feel the penny tying to burn its way through the serge of his waistcoat pocket but no longer cared, his mind had retreated into itself as he contemplated what had been said about his mother. He now *knew* the name of her undoer.

It has been said many times and has always proved to be truthful that it is never the size of the dog in the fight but the size of the fight in the dog that matters and what was about to transpire would be faithful to that simile!

The smaller man, draped ignominiously over the back of the giant reached down with extended arm and thrusting his hand between the crotch of the giant grabbed his testicles and squeezed murderously hard. The shriek of anguish that followed is said to echo around the valley to this day when rain falls on a blustery south westerly wind.

The giant fell as if pole-axed striking his head against a chair as he went laying him out cold and so ended what might have been a very nasty affair indeed! The penny cooled in Charles' pocket as all hint of further conflict receded; the men filed out of the bar one by one thrusting Charles before them. There wasn't a single man who wanted to be there when Idris came to!

The pony turned its head to watch Charles as he wearily mounted the trap by the single extended step, the expression of indifference the pony sported resembled for all the world that wonderful quotation from Shakespeare's 'A Midsummer Night's Dream'

'Oh Lord what fools these mortals be!'

The rain had eased a little but it was small comfort to Charles as he made his way home, he pulled his oilskin coat tighter about his neck to keep out the wind and the trickles of water that were trying to find refuge closer to his body but it was what was going on in his mind that was the real adversary. The more he dwelt on what he had discovered the more irrational he became about it. That the loving mother he so adored could be cheated by a man who was supposed to be a pinnacle of virtue and a man of property ate into his mind like a cancerous canker penetrating and contorting his every thought.

Thomas Grace-Williams had inherited the colliery from his Uncle whose family had been granted mineral rights to all the land in and surrounding the valley in return for services to a prominent and influential member of the aristocracy during the Napoleonic war. Exactly what those services were had never been made clear, after all, that was how favours were rewarded and none could question it.

Holding such a position Mr Grace-Williams was automatically entitled to the dignity and respect of all those that served and dwelt in the community; he held the lives of ordinary folk in the palm of his hand to mould and shape as he saw fit—at least that's how *he* saw it!

Such folk were so engrossed in their own arrogance that they paid scant regard for anything or anyone outside their acquaintance or their circle of influence. Little wonder then that the attention and interest Grace-Williams had shown in Charles' attractive mother when she was working as a domestic at his mansion had turned her head. Wealth and position had afforded him good food and fine clothing with all the trappings of a luxurious way of life. If those weren't blessings enough, he was ruggedly handsome for his years and blessed with an appealing outward personality which was perhaps more cultivated than natural! He was nothing if not persuasive and persistent in his encounters with the fairer sex and was known as a person who always got what he sought however long it might take.

Visions of the conquest rolled over and over in Charles' mind until he could think of nothing else. Blind anger fortified by alcohol had risen in his breast, knuckles, deathly white from the pressure with which he gripped the reins were now balling into fists.

Wrenching the reins he drew the pony to a halt and sat as if set in stone in the rain which had gathered momentum once more. Rivulets formed beneath his oiled hat coursing to fall on his already cold hands numbing them further.

"You Bastard!" He yelled.

"You miserable, cheating **Bastard!"**

Anger had given way to rage and the penny boiled its approval in his pocket.

"Bastard, Bastard, BASTARD!" He screamed loosing spittle from the corners of his contorted mouth.

In a single movement he wrenched violently on the reins and wheeled the pony back in the direction of the colliery, towards the mansion of its owner. A painful whinny of protest broke from the animal, it was not accustomed to being treated in such an objectionable manner from a master it had grown to love but it obeyed just the same.

Trot became canter became gallop as the fearsome grip of irrationality drove Charles relentlessly on. He had no notion of what he was about to do but knew that justice must be meted out to this horror of a person who had defiled his mother. If he had not discovered who the man was, Charles would have reasoned that his Mother was about to find the happiness she sought in the company of a professional and honourable man and that justice was not his to administer. Rage and revenge heightened by alcohol is a mistress that cannot easily be placated however, Charles was seeing red. He didn't stop to reason that the action he was embarked upon would jeopardise his Family's hopes and aspirations for a secure future. ***He didn't stop!"***

The pony could no longer gallop and had slowed to a weary trot, it could give no more, it forced itself onward as best it could responding to the whip-like snaps of the heavy reins on its aching back from a master it no longer knew but its heart was broken. It had not eaten nor taken drink since long before Charles had finished his day at the colliery. It was now ventilating heavily and coughing in searing rasps but still Charles drove it on relentlessly, a strength of purpose compelling him that was blinding in its nature and overpowering in every sense of reason.

The stricken pony staggered, its forelegs gave bringing its mouth heavily into contact with the ground. It tried its best to rise as it slid through the saturated mud but there was nothing left to give, it sank again, steam rising from its broken body. It made one last Herculean struggle to get to its feet but sank exhausted. It would never move again.

Charles was enraged even further by this new encumbrance, this added barrier to the task he had wholly committed himself to, blind to his situation he vowed to have justice this day!

As he looked down at the battered form of Grace-Williams laying motionless before him, he was overcome by remorse. He knew at once that he had been wrong to perpetrate this idiotic and unnecessary act of violence and knew also that he had been in the grip of the object in his pocket. His knuckles were dripping a mixture of his own and his adversary's blood, the flesh torn and lacerated as if he had put his fist through glass.

His senses retuning, he became aware of the housekeeper screaming for help in the back-ground but he no longer cared. The deed was done and could now not be undone.

Charles turned leaving the unconscious Grace-Williams in the open doorway and began a journey that would change the wonderful life that he had first fashioned then destroyed by his own efforts.

CHAPTER 7

Retribution

C HARLES ARRIVED AT THE house of the only Constable in the area completely exhausted, devoid of remorse for the silly action he had taken and drained entirely by it!

He knew that the only course of action was to surrender himself to proper justice and accept whatever his fate would now bring, however distasteful that might be. He knew that if he had killed the man he would surely hang for it and hoped above all that he had not gone that far though his subconscious was telling him that the worst must indeed have taken place.

He had no clear recollection of the meeting with Grace-Williams nor the moment that had sparked his vicious onslaught on the fellow but seemed to remember dimly the man saying "She deserved it!"

Perhaps that had been the catalyst?

"The Constable has been called to the mansion Mr Charles." The Constable's Wife informed him.

"I've no idea how long he will be but I know it's very serious, Perhaps you could call back."

"No, I don't think so, it would be better for me to wait if that's alright?"

"Certainly Mr Charles. You are welcome to wait in the interview room but you must understand it's a little cold and not well furnished!"

She opened the door for him.

"Don't worry, I'll be alright." Mumbled Charles as he made for one of the plain wooden seats that adjoined the stark plank table.

As he sat there Charles fingered the coin in his pocket and wondered what the future would hold for him. For all he knew he could soon find himself being presented hoodwinked to the hangman, a disgrace upon his family that would be un-surmountable and would ruin everyone's chances of any kind of future happiness. He crossed his arms before him on the table and lowered his head dejectedly into them no longer able to fight back the fatigue that recent events had placed upon him. His last recollection was the sound of the Constable's Wife making a whispered telephone call before drifting deep into a troubled slumber.

He awoke with a start at the sound of a door slamming and was at once confused by where he found himself, he was sweating profusely and felt nauseous but had little recollection about where he was nor how he came to be there. The room was lighted by a single electric lamp suspended from the ceiling above the table on a long cord wire, something most houses had yet to experience. The light it gave flickered frequently and was without passion or appeal, in fact it had nothing but convenience to recommend it for it showed everything in the room to be plain and unappealing. It was without the softness of an oil lamp or the character of a single candle. Charles decided he did'nt like this new facility and was about to lower his head again when the Constable entered the room accompanied by and unknown Gentleman dressed in a tightly buckled rain coat and trilby hat. Both men eyed him with caution and appeared to be reluctant to approach too closely. The two exchanged knowing glances before trilby instructed,

"Carry on Constable—you know what must be done!"

The constable removed his black hard covered notebook drawing the pencil from the pouch that bordered its side and turned to Charles.

"You are Mr Charles Jenkins of the cottage at Dell's meadow?"

"I am Sir." said Charles his memory now beginning to clear.

"Then I must inform you that I am arresting you on suspicion of causing grievous bodily harm to one Mr Thomas Grace-Williams of the Mansion, Colliery Acres.

I must further inform you that you may say nothing but that anything you do say will be taken down and may be used in evidence against you during any further proceedings!"

The constable looked up from his notebook with an expression of genuine sadness and wished he were not the one having to detain this brave if foolish young man. The things that Charles had done for the mining community would count for nothing in the harsh environment of a court of law, he would receive no favour, no consideration, no pity. The act that caused this crime to be perpetrated would not be taken into account for that would bring into doubt the character of an important and highly influential person. Such things were unthinkable. Charles would receive whatever justice the friends of the colliery owner felt fit to dispense for the influence of Grace-Williams had penetrated all facets of local society!

The charge read and the arrest made, Charles was transferred to the solitary cell within the Constables domicile, it was dank and cold and smelled strongly of urine for the only use it had previously been put to was holding 'drunk and disorderly' colliers following an overdone night out!

The cell was a mere seven feet by five feet and contained a tiny window too high to look out of and a long bare wooden bench upon which Charles would sleep that night. The Constable handed over a single very coarse serge blanket and relieved Charles of his boots, braces and belt before turning to leave. He paused at the door and whispered over his shoulder with genuine sadness.

"Sorry lad, I wish it had been anybody but you—the bugger deserved it!"

The constable thought of his own Daughter and how she had almost become victim to the same man!

Standing before the Judge Charles was expecting no mercy, he had made no plea.

"Before I pass sentence on this man," enquired the Judge, "Is there anyone in this Courtroom who is prepared to speak in his favour?"

He paused and stared defiantly into the Courtroom over his pince-nez glasses his gaze sweeping around in due order. He was convinced that a sound birching followed by transportation to the Colonies until death was the only solution in this case. He raised his gavel in anticipation of the sentence when, to his entire chagrin, an unexpected voice spoke up. It was a voice that in the moments shortly before had been condemning this young man roundly.

A voice that came from a still scarred face. The voice of Grace—Williams himself!

The Judge, gavel suspended in mid air, was so taken aback he was at a loss as to what to do next for the plaintiff could not be denied the right to comment especially when it was a man whose influence had helped him on his journey to the bench itself!

He lowered the gavel slowly and laid it to rest on the pad to which it belonged. He stared almost vacantly at the bench, he was most reluctant to continue for he had the feeling that some form of compassion was about to be applied, that the authority of his conclusion and considered sentence was about to be diluted. He wasn't wrong.

"The Court recognises the Plaintiff—Mr Thomas Grace-Williams, you may speak Sir but you must bear in mind that sentence has not yet been passed and that this Court has examined the case against the accused and on the evidence you yourself have presented have found him guilty as charged!"

"Very good your honour, I am cognisant of the situation and aware that sentence is yet to be passed and it is on that account that I now speak!"

The Courtroom had fallen silent, Grace-Williams was not known for any sense of compassion, understanding or regard for those beneath him. What was he up to, what new game was this he was playing? It would be sure to be to the detriment of the accused.

The Courtroom was packed with Colliers and their families who had arrived in support of the young man who had sacrificed so much to do his duty to them when *they* most needed it. Now it was *their* turn to show gratitude and support even though they knew they would not be able to speak in favour of their friend. On more than one occasion the Judge had been forced to call them to order as they chided 'shame' at the evidence being presented. Grace-Williams now stood before them again in the witness box, he was up to no good for sure!

"Your Honour," he went on, "I must make the Court aware that this young man is normally very rational and that there were extenuating circumstances that forced him from the path of propriety on this occasion. I will not here relate those circumstances as it could result in the breakdown of good order and discipline within the community at large."

He was thinking of his own skin and how it could likely be flayed from his bones if the miners present really knew what had happened.

"I must further point out that the accused displayed courage and fortitude during an unfortunate colliery event a while ago. In view of the points I have presented to this Court in mitigation I would consider justice to have been served if the accused would agree to serve his Country in the forces of His Majesty King George in the conflict with the forces of Imperial Germany which now appears to be inevitable. I leave the Court to consider my suggestion and the length of time he would be required to serve!"

A loud cheer shattered the dignity of the Courtroom, a cheer that rattled the very rafters and which showed no sign of abatement as the Judge slammed his gavel against the block time after time In an attempt to restore dignity and good order to the proceedings. Hats were being thrown into the air and the more enthusiastic had left their seats and were shaking hands with joy and approval in the aisles!

"Bailiff, *bailiff*!" shrieked the powerless Judge, "Clear the Courtroom, clear the Courtroom AT ONCE!"

But the Bailiff was just one man and the din within the room was drowning out the pleas of the Judge even though it was plain to the smiling bailiff what was being asked of him.

"Bugger off!" muttered the Bailiff under his breath. He too was in surreptitious support of Charles. He remained rock still within the entrance to the Court eyes fixed steadfastly on the ceiling and pretended he couldn't hear. In any case he thought the crowd might tear him to shreds!

The Judge gave up and seated himself until the uproar finally worked itself out. He waited for the appropriate moment to present itself and struck his gavel hard on its block once more. This time the unruly mob responded and the Courtroom once again became a paragon of virtue.

"This Court finds the accused guilty as charged and in view of the plea for leniency made by the Plaintiff and the suggestion put forward by him I sentence you, Charles Jenkins to serve a term of not less that five years in gaol or as an alternative, five years in the army of His Majesty King George or until death in that capacity—there is to be no remission and appeal is denied—do you have anything to say?"

"Only that I am sorry for what I have done and the grief I have caused others and to thank Mr Grace-Williams for his generosity in speaking for me!"

"So be it!" barked the Judge banging his gavel with far more energy than was needed, he was glad to be rid of this case!

"All rise!" exclaimed the Bailiff finding his voice again.

Charles was retained in custody at the Police House pending collection by the Army and was treated with the respect and admiration he was used to. A comfortable horse hair mattress had been found for him and he was treated to meals with the family who turned out to be very friendly and not at all officious. Charles was visited by Eira every day, she was devastated that she would be losing him to the Army but swore that she would wait forever for him if that were needed. The red rings that bordered her eyes told of the tears she had shed and was still shedding for the way their lives had been shattered, for the way their dreams had turned to ash and for the desolation that she would yet face knowing that her treasured Charles would be forced to take up arms in conflict even though his nature was to heal and to save!

She told him of the decision of his Mother to no longer marry the colliery Medical Officer because of his relationship as a paid servant of Grace-Williams. His Mother would not come out of the house since the incident at the Mansion no matter how Eira pleaded with her so there would be no opportunity for Charles to take his leave of her.

It was almost two weeks before the Army sent an escort to collect Charles. Britain was now at war with Germany but it was said that it would all be over in six months, the opinion was that few in Germany had the stomach for prolonged conflict and did we not have the mightiest Armed forces in the world?

The utilicon vehicle that arrived at the Police House had certainly seen better days. The wooden spoked front wheels with their solid rubber tyres leaned miserably inward at their tops and the radiator was gently boiling sending curved trails of water vapour into the air to be caught up and swirled by the breeze. The canvas top sagged sadly, was shredded with age and had been repaired time and again, the chains that drove the rear wheels had stretched so much that the catenary formed by the excess material almost drooped to the ground. The driver, an ageing Lance Corporal, appeared to mirror the impression the vehicle made and had clearly been in the Army for most of his weary years. He climbed down from the cab by reversing to face the vehicle and holding the steering wheel whilst lowering himself painfully stern first to the plank running board and thence with a 'clump' to the ground.

Two younger and more energetic soldiers alighted from the rear of the truck and moved sharply around to stand in formation before the Corporal who, with an attitude of almost complete indifference ordered,

"Escort party 'Ten-*shun*!'"

The lads snapped their booted heels together and threw out their chests as the Corporal turned to face the Constable who had arrived to see what all the fuss was about.

"'Morning Guv." The Corporal addressed the Law as he now addressed all officialdom—with his customary well practised indifference! He was of the unshakeable opinion that he now *owned* the British Army.

The utilicon tender trundled its way wearily whence it came with the two young soldiers sat either side of Charles. The air that leaked in through the holes in the canvas cover proved beneficial to Charles in that it diluted the stale odour of perspiration; it seemed that his escort must be overdue a visit to the ablution block or had been working too hard for too long!

The solid tyres did nothing to ameliorate the discomfort that the myriad of potholes in the road were causing, the vehicle bounced and clattered its way toward the camp where Charles would begin the process of induction and training as a soldier. His escort related stories of what was to come, stories that were quite clearly intended to un-nerve, stories which seemed to imply that no one ever got to the end of the training period without dying or being seriously disfigured! Not once did they enquire of Charles what he had done to be ordered to join the Army. It appeared to Charles that once minds had been indoctrinated by Army thinking and accustomed to the Army lifestyle, nothing outside of that sphere was worthy of any consideration! He thought how very strange that was, he had a lot to learn.

The next three months were living hell! The escort soldiers had relayed some elements of truth in their assessment of the training process but Charles was determined to see it through and had made up his mind from the outset that he would be the best at whatever he was given to do. The time that he had spent in the company of Doctor Moody and the Colliery surgeon had stood him in good stead imparting knowledge and wisdom and a logical way of assessing things and situations, these were elements that had always been missing from the short and very limited education that folks got in those days and thus set him above the others in the esteem of his superiors. It did him no favours in the eyes of his contemporaries however, nor with the non Commissioned Officers to whom he was subordinate. He frequently found himself singled out for extra drill and physical punishment but this only served to harden his resolve and his muscles for he had developed a good strong frame and a mind to match, there was little that could be thrown at him that he could not master quickly and efficiently.

His progress and his ability had not gone un-noticed by the Training Officer.

Summoning him into the office towards the end of training, the Training Officer, Major Thisltlewick-Smythe sat him down and asked what it was that Charles felt he was best suited to do in the Army—did Charles not feel he was perhaps a little too academic to be a combat Soldier?

"It was always my intention to join the Medical Corps Sir!" Charles exclaimed.

"I have already had considerable experience in this field and would really be grateful for the opportunity to serve as a medical orderly."

"Yes, I see from the report that your local Police submitted to the Army that you are well suited to this task—you were most respected in your former place of work it seems." The Major continued.

"I will see to it that you are transferred to a medical training unit without delay, it is nothing if not certain that they are in need of you though I must tell you I am reluctant to lose someone with so bright a future!" The Officer shuffled the papers on the desk before him and with nothing further to add declared.

"That's all Jenkins, you may return to your duties!"

Charles rose quickly to his feet and saluted the Major. Turning on his heels he marched from the office into the sunshine outside feeling an overwhelming sense of relief for he had never seen himself as a person that could aim a gun at another human with intent to kill. The tickling in his breast told him that he was far more excited about the prospect of returning to medicine than he had realised.

Needless to say, the news that Charles was being transferred to a 'cushy' job was treated with rancour among his contemporaries who immediately branded him a coward and closed ranks upon him. Few would take the trouble to reply to his daily greetings and life seemed to be reduced to misery once more. To say that his immediate superiors in the training camp viewed things differently would be foolish for nothing that Charles now did would meet with their approval. His boots were never clean, his rifle always soiled and he was accused of being 'too slow' to respond to the tasks he was allotted.

Charles bore the resentment with equanimity and bided his time, no-one was going to goad him into the fight that some of the men were spoiling for, if there was one thing he had learned and learned well it was that he *never* wanted to cause physical injury to anyone ever again!

It was indeed fortunate for everyone that the transfer came through quickly, Charles was to entrain for a new establishment that had been recently built near one of England's greatest Cities, why, the Cathedral that the City was so proud of was said to be among the finest in the world boasting architecture surpassed by no other.

The war in France was not going well and casualties were mounting daily, the need for medics was acute and it seemed that the number needed were not being trained quickly enough. The training and experience that Charles had received before joining the army now stood him in excellent stead for he was allowed to take up the medical orderly's course more than half way through and quickly accelerated through the rest passing out with strong distinction.

Much good his ability had done him though for now found himself sea-sick. The crossing to France in that coal driven tramp steamer was not a desired introduction to the high seas. The ship reeked of fish and there were far too many men packed into that dingy unlit and unventilated hold. It appeared that the motion of the ship was at the instigation of the Neptune himself and was never constant. Just when Charles thought the ship was about to plunge and braced himself to weather it, it would screw sideways and roll instead. He cursed the ship, the sea and the fish in it, his life, the Army, the men around him, the war, the bloody priest that was saying something about 'These see the works of the Lord and his wonders in the deep.' He cursed the day he was born, his stomach and himself!

To remark that he was unhappy with his lot at that time might be viewed as a gross understatement. The confinement of that crowded hold was no place to vomit but his eyes were swimming and his head so light it might have been a balloon, his stomach was lurching and churning and he was under enormous abdominal pressure but somehow he held on.

Finally the motion eased and then at last ceased. Mercifully that accursed floating nightmare had brought them to the safety of a haven but also closer to death, destruction and the heart wrenching anguish that is the battlefield.

The planks and canvass of the hold covers were rolled back one at a time to reveal a bright summer's day. The fresh air that sank into the hold was as sweet as any Charles had ever had the pleasure of remembering and was as reviving as it was welcome. The stomach turmoil had faded into the past now that they were alongside and disembarking to the jetty; there they were to await transport or marching orders.

For Charles Lady luck was smiling benignly for he was to ride to the field hospital at Verdun by train courtesy of the French railway network which was very advanced for its time. It was usual for personnel to travel in box cars often with equipment or stores to guard but on this occasion Charles was to ride with a group of Army Officers and NCO's bound for the front and so would be travelling in the relative luxury of proper carriages with plush upholstered seats and toilets—yes, *toilets!*

The carriages turned out to be of the long open omnibus type without corridors or compartments and were very crowded indeed with at least two persons allocated to each single seat. The seats were primarily taken by Officers who boarded the train first in order of seniority so when Charles finally mounted the steps there was nothing but standing room and very little of that! From where he was stood Charles could see that many of the Officers had removed their top coats and that more than a few of them were flyers, pilots and observers of the Royal Flying Corps. One Officer stood out from all the others by nature of his uniform; it was dark blue with two gold rings on each sleeve and a beautiful pair of woven gold thread pilot's wings above the rings of his left sleeve. He was chatting amiably with the flying Corps chaps.

What on earth is the Royal Navy doing travelling to Verdun? mused Charles recognising the uniform. Little did he know that the Navy had despatched a number of pilots to assist in replacing the numbers of RFC pilots not only shot down by Germans but lost in flying accidents due to weather and mechanical failure. The RFC were not just running short of pilots but also aeroplanes so as many as the Navy could spare were being despatched to fight at the front.

The future for Charles seemed cloudy and uncertain to say the least but he resolved to deal with it a step at a time. The men around him seemed jovial enough, perhaps they were unaware of the carnage ahead. Charles shrugged, there were so many men in this train he was sure he would never see any of them again, fate is fickle however for it would not be very long before he would meet some of these men again away from the relative safety of a rail car and close to the battle front under heavy fire!

The journey was long, slow and uncomfortable. The toilet had long since run out of flushing water and it was impossible to catch a wink of sleep standing up the way he was. There had been nothing to eat or drink during the trip save for the sandwiches they had all been issued at the start of the journey, everyone was famished and becoming a little irritable. The water stops they made for the engine now and then provided welcome respite from the continuous clanking of the wheels riding the rail joints and allowed the men to relieve themselves without having to fight through crowds of reluctant, disgruntled standing soldiers to an overflowing urinal in a grossly unpleasant cubicle where paper was strewn all over a floor saturated by 'spills'.

The Officers had somehow procured wine and from the comfort of their plush seats were enjoying life to the full in party mood. One of them must have been a magician in a former occupation for he suddenly produced a live chicken to the joy of his fellows who applauded boisterously in raucous appreciation of the diversion. The chicken was not so enthralled and clucked its way loudly to the overhead luggage rack amidst flying feathers and grasping hands trying to haul it down. There it remained in relative safety its procurer having lost interest in it! It would not have lasted long had there been any cooking facilities available on the train.

CHAPTER 8

The Front

THE OCCUPANTS OF THE train could not only hear the gunfire as they drew nearer the front, they could *feel* it! Minute pressure in the inner ear and behind the eyes resulted in a 'puffy' feeling in their ears as they reacted to the percussion caused by the exploding shells.

As the train came to a halt the men looked from one to the other as if to say 'Here we go!' There was nothing to see that resembled a station or a platform yet Military Police personnel were passing along the outside of the train bellowing orders for its occupants to get out.

"Why are we getting off here?" an Officer demanded of one of the red capped MP's.

"Front's moved Sir, we are in retreat again—get your men out as quickly as you can there are lorries to get them to the battle line to try to hold the Huns!"

He returned to his bellowing and the marshalling of those that were not accompanied by Officers.

How on earth will they know what regiments to send these men to Charles wondered as he viewed the bedlam around him, 'Where on earth am *I* supposed to go?'

"YOU!" barked one of the red caps gesticulating in Charles' direction, "In that lorry over there!"

"What unit am I going to?" asked the confused Charles.

"Don't matter mate—your going to the front with everyone else—you'll be told where to go when you get there—don't matter where you were *supposed* to be going—now, in the lorry before I lose my patience!"

He jabbed a thumb in the direction of the truck and started bellowing again.

Charles climbed aboard as instructed and was surprised to find several of the flyers from the train in there, it was unusual indeed for Officers to be sharing transport with other ranks but these were desperate times and there was a panic on!

The noise of gunfire was horrendous as they trundled closer to the front and so was the mud. Successive movements of horse drawn and motor vehicles had churned the surface into a giant mud pie making progress difficult and unpleasant. There were motor vehicles bogged down everywhere Charles looked and the irony was that teams of horses were trying to pull them out.

Within a few minutes the vehicle they were riding in also bogged down, its heavy narrow wheels losing grip and sinking into the quagmire. The flyers had been spared the mud having been dropped of well before the front at a makeshift airfield beautifully situated in a green valley surrounded by trees. All around the stranded lorry wounded men were being brought back from the front to a makeshift canvass hospital erected at the rear of the camp on duck boards in an attempt to keep the mud back. The notion may have been sound but the practicality of it appeared to be doubtful. Now and then the odd shell, wrongly fused, would explode close to the camp scattering mud everywhere, this was the last straw—mud coming from the air!

Charles reported to the field hospital and was promptly provided with a bag of field dressings, morphine in a dirty bottle with a matching syringe, a steel helmet marked with a red cross and two arm bands likewise embellished.

"Grab that young 'un over there and this 'ere stretcher," instructed the Corporal orderly pointing to a waif of a boy shaking from head to toe.

"There's loads of wounded coming in—the huns are pushin' forward again—do what you can for the lads yourself and get the worst ones to any of the Surgeon's willing to take 'em."

Charles nodded and approached the shaking youth, one look at him as he got closer told him that the lad was probably suffering the after effects of some sort of shock.

"You alright chum?" he enquired.

Looking into the boy's oversized darting eyes Charles was even more convinced that there was shock at work here for they were wild and in constant motion almost as if the effect of keeping them open was agonizing.

"T—T—T TTTT", He stammered.

Charles was unable to make out what the lad was trying to say but could see that the attempted response was more than the boy could manage. He stretched out a hand resting it on the boy's shoulder,

"No need to talk lad," he said quietly, "I can see that you are in trouble and I'll do all I can to help you!"

The lad looked at Charles through large fear filled eyes, eyes that carried just a glimmer of trust, then lowered them to the ground again.

"I need help moving the wounded lad, are you able to manage that? If I don't get help then more of them will die!"

The youth nodded his head briskly as if glad to be asked to do something useful.

The two of them trudged off through the mud with the stretcher held between them, the going demanding even though they were carrying little weight. Ridges thrown up in the mud by the constant movement of vehicles were treacherously slippery, the pair would need to take care not to lose footing on the return journey with the wounded. Gunfire noise was continuous and had become so much a part of the background that Charles realised he was becoming accustomed to it. The frenetic movement of vehicles carrying troops was as ceaseless as the gunfire, drivers seemed not to see the two men as they negotiated the ruts and made no allowance for them.

"*Orderly!*"

The shout came from a horse drawn wagon just ahead of the two men. They made their way quickly to it where they found three badly wounded foot soldiers.

"Unroll the stretcher Tommy." Instructed Charles as he set about examining the men. The first was already dead from a dreadful head wound, he moved to the next, a man barely conscious. One look at his leg told Charles that it was very badly smashed by a bullet in the lower bone that had shattered it beyond help—the leg would have to come off!

Visions of the colliery incident came flooding back to him and his blood ran cold before realising that now he was able to call upon the field hospital to do the tricky bit. He swung his field medical bag before him taking out the morphine bottle and syringe. Filling the syringe he plunged the needle through what was left of the fellow's trousers into his upper thigh before Pulling the tourniquet from the bag. This he wrapped tight above the torn skin winding the stick attached until the blood ceased to flow, it occurred to him that there seemed to be remarkably little blood in evidence considering the severity of the wound. He used a little of what there was to mark a large M on the man's forehead to let the surgeons know that morphine had been used. The third soldier had also been shot and although unable to move his right arm he was able to walk. Charles immobilised the arm securing it across the man's chest in a sling, although painful to the poor soul it was not serious enough to merit the use of drugs. The colour had drained from the man's face and he was clearly shaken by his demise but nonetheless confirmed he would walk to the hospital with the medics.

"Come on Tommy," Charles called, "Lets get the unconscious man on the stretcher!"

He had kept the penny constantly hidden on his person from the day he had come to realise that it gave him powers that were not naturally present in him and without which he would degenerate into a fumbling, indecisive dreamer. Charles could feel the coin beginning to grow hot in anticipation of claiming a victim.

"No you bloody don't!" spat Charles directing his attention to the coin, "You'll take no-one on *my* watch!"

Tommy faltered unsure what his companion had said and was about to stammer again when Charles added,

"Not you old son—come on," he grinned, "Let's get them to safety."

They made their way well enough through the thickening mud considering the weight they were now carrying and delivered the casualties to the makeshift field hospital.

"Over there!" barked the field surgeon they encountered, "Get to him soon as I can."

The two men left the unconscious man in the hands of the nurses but before leaving again marked his forehead to show that morphine and a tourniquet had been applied and the time of doing it.

"Well done Tommy," Charles chirped, "Can't do without you now. You did a great job there and those men will live thanks to you!"

The lad beamed from ear to ear displaying a set of badly damaged teeth, it was some time since anyone had shown any interest in him and even longer since he had been told he'd done a good job!.

"TTTTT." he started again but couldn't complete the word.

"I think you mean thanks Tom, right?"

The lad nodded in agreement. The interest and kindness Charles had shown him and the feeling of usefulness that he had just experienced working in a team had given a real boost to his self esteem.

He had placed his complete trust in Charles and would have followed him into the jaws death itself had he been asked.

They worked long into the night transporting casualty after casualty to the field hospital, they did it without rest, without food and without complaint stopping only for a drink or to relieve themselves.

The 'push' had fizzled out, the advance halted by the Germans just six hundred yards inside what had been German territory the day before; the human cost to both sides was appalling. Charles allowed his thoughts to dwell on all those poor souls who would never see the beauty of a new dawn nor the smiling faces of those they loved and his heart became heavy. He shook himself and redirected his attention to the injured men they had rescued from the jaws of death and the many more that had been dealt with by other teams like themselves consoling his misery with the knowledge that he and others around him had striven without respite to bring relief and comfort to so many unknown faces.

All this carnage for so little gain! He felt sickened by the senseless futility of it all.

The next day seemed quiet by comparison, gunfire had temporarily ceased and the myriad of trucks, troops and ammunition movements had ground to a halt as each side licked their wounds and buried their dead. Vast acres of graveyard were beginning to creep over France.

Both men had slept in acute discomfort upon the damp, mud covered planks that bordered the side of the field hospital marquee and awoke feeling cold and very hungry. Charles woke first, his first thought was of the wretched 'Tommy'. He propped himself up on one elbow and looked across at him. The lad had stopped shaking but looked devastatingly tired, Charles reached over and shook him gently.

He leaped to his feet with a look of sheer terror in his eyes, Charles reached out and steadied him.

"It's alright Tommy—nothing to be scared of." he whispered, "Time to get something to eat and a good wash if we can find somewhere."

They walked together to the rough and ready ablution block where lines of near naked men were doing their best to rid their aching bodies of the smell of battle and the lingering stink of oil and munitions tainted mud. Those soldiers would wear again their rough serge uniforms muddy as they were, but their bodies would be clean—such was the pride of ordinary men!

Tommy and Charles walked the lines until they found unoccupied 'sinks'. These were galvanised water pails lashed between long stretches of timber hoisted to waist height on similarly makeshift trestles but it was not so much the manner of the facility as the facility the manner offered!

It was sheer heaven to sluice away the layers of blood contaminated caked mud and Charles found his spirits lifted by the doing of it. Tommy had not washed for days, such was the depths to which his morale had sunk. He had been treated badly by his NCO's and his comrades alike because he was a little slow by nature and not naturally able to undertake any but the more simple of tasks. He had been chided constantly for his slowness and had become the unwitting butt of everyone's jokes; his teeth had been broken by a bully of a man without either understanding or compassion who had beaten the lad senseless for spilling the tea he had demanded. Tommy had become so confused and demented that he had deliberately wandered into 'no man's land' in the hope of being shot and by this means bring to an end the torture that his life had become. In full view of his contemporaries and the enemy alike he stood on the parapet of what had once been an occupied trench now isolated between the two opposing battle lines and waited for the blow that would end this misery. Fate is a fickle master however and the peculiarity of his action had raised nothing but a diverting curiosity in the Germans who watched him closely wondering what this lunatic would do next. What could one man do anyway—wasn't worth expending a round on him!

Tommy had stood there motionless for some considerable time whilst the German curiosity turned into indifference then irritation, what was this bloody fool doing? A feldwebel (corporal) decided he would have a little fun with this annoying Englander and instructed his two bombardiers to lay a mortar as close to Tommy as they could to bowl him over but without killing him Men being what they are a book was opened with bets being laid on how far they could blow him and whether he would die or not. The boredom and daily routine of trench warfare could twist the minds of even the most understanding of souls! Bets were already running on the English side as to how long the lad would survive and how many pieces of him would be left to collect.

Lucifer is more fickle than fate it would seem!

It was the mortar that had caused Tommy to shake for it exploded some distance from him sending earth and stones smashing into him with such force that he was knocked off his feet and sent sprawling headlong into the abandoned trench where he lay unconscious convulsing violently in the mud and water.

Two days he laid there, no longer unconscious but too terrified to vacate the trench even under cover of darkness. There he remained until a 'push' by the allied forces re-took the trench and liberated him. Considered to be demented, he was sent behind his own lines to the field hospital which was where Charles had found him, he had been declared unfit for further front line duties and more or less abandoned.

Tommy had milled around the field hospital for days and had been pushed away by everyone he had tried to engage with so it was little wonder that his self-esteem had now completely deserted him!

The arrival of Charles and the interest he had taken in him had been profound, he had found somebody who actually *needed* him. He had begun to believe in himself again and was heartily embracing the new friend he had found and the day that stood before him.

He pitched into the cleansing as if it were the maintenance of his soul he was attending to, he would emerge a new man.

Charles couldn't help but notice that Tommy's shaking had now ceased and with the mud washed from his face and from his caked hair he took on a completely new appearance, he looked much younger than he had the day before.

"Do you know Tommy?" he mused, "I don't even know your proper name?"

Tommy turned and gazed unblinking at Charles pausing to take in the face of his benefactor then said clearly and without hesitation,

"Tommy will do fine—Tommy Atkins, the faceless British soldier!" He ventured.

"How old are Tommy?" enquired the curious Charles.

"Just eighteen by two days." he replied without emotion, the birthday had meant nothing to him—there had never been anyone to share it with since the date of his birth in the workhouse which was also the date of the death of his Mother!

He had been born into and always lived a life of extreme poverty, he had received no formal education but rather the streetwise education of an individual fleeing from one punishment to another. He had lied about his age to get into the Army where he had hoped to be taught useful skills and find a life of acceptance among his comrades but his inability to read or write or make clever conversation had relegated him to the status of the runt of the litter, he had sought but found no friend!

Cleaned and fed, the two returned to the field hospital and were set to work cleaning away the blood and mud of the previous day. Tommy worked like a demon but would not leave Charles' side, he followed his every move like a puppy seeking the affection of a displeased master.

Just before mid morning there came the staccato rattle of machine gun fire from somewhere above the hospital which sent everyone outside to better see what the commotion was all about. There above them was a stricken three winged aeroplane buff coloured and sporting large allied roundels. Its engine had stopped and was pouring smoke as it weaved and jinked losing height the whole while. The onlookers could see it was being chased by a German aeroplane and it was from this that the machine gun fire was emanating as it followed the stricken craft hell-bent on destroying it and the young man inside. The staccato rattle was joined by more as the troops on the ground opened fire on the German with their small arms.

"Cocky bastard!" someone remarked, "Give it to 'im lads!"

Charles was aware that the coin in his tunic was burning hot—something dreadful was about to happen!

Bang! with an almighty roar the front of the German craft disintegrated in a ball of flame as a lucky shot penetrated the fuel tank. The aeroplane rolled over on its back its nose rising high in the air as if in final salute to the victor before the whole thing looped onto its back and plunged headlong into the earth. A resounding cheer rang out from the watching crowd but that was not how Charles was feeling about the incident.

"Come on Tommy!" he yelled and grabbed a stretcher from the stack leaning against the hospital tent. He ran at full pelt dragging the stretcher in the direction of the crash with young Tommy hard on his heels trying to reach down and pick up the trailing edge of the stretcher but missing at every attempt! That they were the only ones attempting assistance for the stricken German pilot was both a measure of their diligence and the disregard in which the other onlookers held the enemy.

Charles halted dejectedly some distance from the downed 'plane and let the stretcher slip from his grasp, the wreck was the right way up and still smoking but there was no fire. The wings had collapsed and were burnt out as was the sides of the fuselage, the pilot sat upright in the wreckage and was himself smoking but not a cigarette. What remained of his scorched goggles was still in place over his unseeing eyes for he had passed beyond the help of man, he had been burned to death. Charles shuddered involuntarily and began to approach the 'plane slowly with Tommy at his heels, not a word was exchanged as they took in the sight before them. The pilot appeared to be smiling broadly, almost manically, his right arm raised above his head seemed to be pointing to the sky that he had given his life for.

As they drew closer they could see that the pilot wasn't smiling at all but had lost much of the soft flesh of the lower jaw to fire from hell.

They stood and looked in disbelief at the wretched apparition before them, could this have once been a vibrant, happy young Mother's Son full of life and eager to get on with it? Charles felt physically sick but contained himself as he broke away the burned wood frame that surrounded the pilot. For dignity's sake this once fine man must be laid to rest properly and in a manner suited to a fallen warrior.

There were no cheers or claps as they passed through the camp on their way to the mortuary, just silent bystanders staring at the blanket covered corpse with arm still raised in defiance.

"C.O. wants to see you chum—you're for it I reckon!" the mortuary orderly informed Charles.

"Daft bugger—should have let 'im be, the lads would 'ave buried 'im out there." He jerked a soiled thumb in the direction of the crash site.

"Now we've got bloody paperwork to do and the Gerries will 'ave to be told!"

Charles didn't grace the comments with any kind of reply, just turned on his heels and made for the Commandant's office.

"The Major does indeed want to see you private Jenkins." imparted the adjutant as Charles reported to the Office, "You may go straight in."

Charles removed his helmet and brushed the mud from it as best he could, he had cleared the mud from his boots on the boot scraper at the entrance to the office before reporting. He made to move in the direction of the C.O.'s Office when the Adjutant barked,

"Where the hell do you think you're going?"

Charles turned sheepishly and ventured,

"To see the C.O. Sir!"

"Not *you*, bloody fool—your *mate!*"

Charles swung around to find young Tommy hard on his heels and couldn't help but releasing a little giggle.

"Sorry Sir," he replied, "Tommy, will you wait outside for me? I won't be long!"

"Wouldn't count on it." The Adjutant muttered under his breath.

It was customary for a drill Sergeant to march men in and out of the Commandant's office and Charles found it odd that this was not happening on this occasion, if there was temporarily no Sergeant available the next subordinate would do the job but this time he was marching in alone.

There were far too many imponderables about life in his Majesty's Army for ordinary folk to bother their heads with so Charles just put it to the back of his mind and rapped smartly on the door.

"COME"

Charles opened the door and stepped inside, his helmet tucked neatly under his left arm, he closed the door and marched stiffly forward halted at the desk bringing his heels together and saluted.

"SIR!" he reported and then almost dropped dead from shock for the Commandant was no other than Thomas Grace-Williams!

Charles' heart sank, of all the rotten luck, of all the people in all the world that could have been sat before him it had to *this* man—now Charles could see the reason for this man's request in Court. Revenge can be administered in many ways and the clever bide their time and engineer fate to get the right opportunity at the right time entirely on *their* terms!

"Stand easy Jenkins." the Major instructed,

"I came across your name in the Adjutant's personnel portfolio and wondered whether it was yourself so called for your record. I cannot say that I was delighted to find that it was indeed the same person who had caused me so much pain the scars of which I still bear."

He turned his cheek to display the evidence of the surgeon's repair.

"I have asked you to come in to clear up a few things us for although we have this unfortunate history between us I see that you continue to execute outstanding service to medicine and to the Army. In view of this I am prepared to let the past remain in the past so that we may go forward in harmony to the greater good of King and Country. Are you willing to start afresh?"

Charles was astonished, this was not the man he had always believed to be a vindictive waster, this was a man with a conscience and the will to forgive.

"Yes *Sir*!" Charles replied preferring to keep his distance until he was sure this was not a ruse.

"Very good Jenkins. That said I must inform you that it is my intention to recommend you for early promotion to Lance Corporal Medical Orderly!

By the way, I consider the humane act that you and your assistant have just carried out to be of the highest order and in keeping with the best traditions of the Service—you may leave."

"Yes Sir thank you Sir!" Replied Charles.

He saluted the Major, turned service style and marched swiftly from the office closing the door as he departed.

The Adjutant smiled benignly,

"Bet that's not what you were expecting *corporal* was it?"

"No Sir, I'm a bit overcome with it all. Will that be all Sir?"

"Call in at the clothing store and give them this lad, it's authorisation for you to draw your stripes" He went on jokingly. "Next time I see you, if you are not wearing them, I will put you on jankers for being improperly dressed!"

Charles stepped out of the Adjutant's office into the sunshine of a lovely afternoon to find a minor commotion unfolding. It seems the Allied pilot that was being pursued earlier had made a successful forced landing not far away but rather than walk to the camp he had waited for the squadron tender to pick him up. This was often the case with downed pilots for they rarely flew alone preferring to have a distant wing man that would report incidents such as this one and note the exact position of the 'plane's landing (or crash!) The tender was always dispatched to retrieve the crew or their remains if the landing was inside our own lines. If the pilot was known to have survived, his squadron always bundled into the small truck with as many bottles of champagne as they could lay hands on to pick him up and accompany him back. The idea was to sink as many bottles of champagne as possible on the outward journey and encourage the survivor to do the same during his return.

On collecting this particular pilot however and after pouring the first bottle of champagne down his not unwilling throat, the pilot insisted on visiting the camp to find out where his adversary had come to earth. He was not aware of the misfortune that the man had suffered, only that he had been shot down and himself spared.

Thus it was that the unruly bunch of over-exuberant youths had burst into the camp and were demanding to see the duty Officer (or Occifer as they put it!). It was a strange coincidence that all were Captains bar one, that was Lieutenant Skinner Royal Navy late of His Majesty's Ship Amiable. He was not only the pilot who had been pursued by the German and shot down but also the Officer Charles had encountered from the train journey to the front!

Charles looked at him in amazement for the man was covered from head to toe in dirty oil, his face coal black from the same except where his goggles had been which in stark contrast looked un-naturally clean. From his behaviour and jovial attitude one would never have suspected he had just brushed with death!

The duty Officer stepped down from the elevated guardroom boardwalk and approached the group.

"What can I do for you louts? If it's more champagne you need then sod off!"

"What sort of way is that to greet folk who keep mambie-pambies like you safe from the skies?" asked one of the pilots, "what we want to know Occifer is where the bloody Gerry crashed!"

"He's dead—now go away you clots!" retorted the duty officer.

"Ooooooooo—oooh!" they all cried in unison feigning mock indignity.

"Bet you he's an Eton chap!" said someone "Toffee nosed buggers!"

"What do you want with the crash site anyway? the 'plane is burned out." The duty officer informed them, now getting fed-up with this unruly bunch of half-officers. Should Court Martial the bloody lot of them he thought ungenerously.

"I would like a trophy—something from the 'plane to hang with the other trophies on the squadron mess wall—no, no, wait a minute—I DEMAND a bloody trophy, so there!" announced the peeved Lieutenant.

"Oh very well." the duty officer was growing tired of this encounter and decided the only way to get rid of this lot was to send them off on a wild goose chase in the hope they would run out of champagne and get sore heads.

"Corporal!" he signalled for Charles to approach him.

"Sir?" said Charles hesitantly.

"Take this lot to the crash site!"

He winked at Charles for he had no idea that Charles had actually been there.

"Very good Sir." said Charles and went off with the group in search of 'trophies for the mess'.

All that was left of the downed 'plane that could be recognised as such was the tail fin and the rudder still bearing German markings.

"That'll do *splendidly*!" announced the Lieutenant jubilantly

"Who's got a hacksaw?"

They looked from one to the other turning out their pockets lest they should perchance find what they needed. It was no surprise to Charles that no employable implement was forthcoming and the sight of these supposedly respectable officers turning out their pockets in search of something much too large to fit into them evoked a laugh from him.

"I bet *He's* got it!" bawled one of the group, "De-bag the bugger!"

"Bet he's a bloody Eton chap." came the remark again, "They only know one bloody song anyway"

They looked at each other again, then as one they charged at Charles.

"De-bag the bugger!" they shrieked, they had forgotten what they had come for!

Charles, sober and fleet as he was, departed the scene with all haste trousers intact. His pursuers were no match for him and one by one they fell inebriated and out of breath to the ground. What the purpose of all this effort was bewildered Charles beyond belief.

He walked briskly back to the camp to find Tommy fretting.

"I-I-I-I-.I thought you had been kidnapped" he stammered.

"Calm down Tommy—I'm fine, just had a walk that's all."

They made their way to the field kitchen like two famished mongrels just in time to catch the last of the rations. The food, although plain and simple, was sustaining enough if tasteless, complaint would bring no improvement anyway so, like so many other things in the Army it was just accepted.

Dusk was approaching swiftly now bringing a weak but pleasant enough sunset to close what had been a very quiet day as far as warfare was concerned, there were always few casualties in times of a stalemate.

It wouldn't be long however before the Generals would be greedy for territory again!

Strains of 'My Bonny Lies Over the Ocean' came floating into the camp on the evening air. Faintly at first but gaining in volume as a single vehicle approached from the North East. Charles strained to catch the lyrics for the words that he could distinguish were not those he was accustomed to hearing. Now they were close enough to catch over the sound of the labouring lorry engine they became clear,

"I have landed my plane rather badly
From my bravery I contemplate fame
But there's only one thing that I want now
To be flying the bugger again!"

Oh God—it was the bloody flyers again! Charles hid in the mess tent reluctant to offer himself of service to them a second time.

The song grew louder and louder until the vehicle drew to a halt outside the guardroom. This time only one flyer stepped down from the tender, it was the Navy Lieutenant once more.

The guard Sergeant stepped out to the edge of the raised boardwalk and standing stiffly hands crossed behind his back leaned forward and said benignly.

"Now come on kind Sir, we don't want to be a nuisance now do we?"

The officer was having a job standing upright, his balance organs having been consumed completely by copious drafts of bubbly.

"Where am I?" he asked sheepishly, "I was on my way to find a bloody gerryplane to get a bloody troofy but some bloody General ran off with it!"

He bent almost double backwards, nimbly turned a half circle and came upright again facing away from the sergeant.

"Where did the bloody Sergeant go?" he enquired of himself.

"Bet he's a bloody Eton chap!" came weakly from somewhere inside the truck.

"Now come on silly Gentleman," The Sergeant took the unsteady Officer by the elbow and led him benevolently to the rear of the tender.

"We don't want to cause trouble and draw attention to ourselves Sir now do we? It will only mean lots more paperwork for us all!"

Drawing back the canvas curtain he lifted the Lieutenant and almost effortlessly hauled his posterior onto the sill and rolled him in to join his fellow inebriates.

"Don'wan' any poor maperwork!" The Officer mumbled and joined his fellow revellers in the trouble free land of nonsense nod.

The Sergeant closed the curtain and secured it by its laces with triple granny knots. 'They'll be too far gone to work out how to get *that* undone' he mused.

He made his way around to the driver, a simple private soldier.

"Now listen to me lad," he stabbed a finger at the driver, "Take this lot back to their quarters and get their batman to turn them in. If I so much as *hear* this bloody truck again tonight I'll have your wedding tackle for a necktie—got it?"

"Got it Sarge!" the driver replied.

"Have *you* been drinking lad?" retorted the NCO, "It's *Sergeant* to you—and don't you forget it!"

"Sorry Sergeant!"

The driver apologised as he made his way to the front of the tender to crank the engine into life.

The camp returned to an uneasy silence.

CHAPTER 9

The Foxhole

"WIPE THAT SMILE OFF your face Jenkins—you are about to meet your maker!"

Charles looked steadily at the major and kept his silence, the expression he bore was one of 'do your worst, you'll get nothing from me.'

The coin in Charles' pocket grew unbearably hot, stark terror gripped his mind as he thought My God, it's going to take *me!*

It was clear to Charles that the Major really was about to pull the trigger when fate took a hand, perhaps influenced by the power of the penny itself.

High above the foxhole a rogue mortar exploded prematurely, discharging its metal fragments in tiny pieces. One such fragment, so small it was barely noticeable, but which was travelling at very, very high speed and spinning like a miniature circular saw, penetrated the soft under flesh beneath the rear of the Major's skull and sliced its way through the spinal cord into the main blood artery which it machined its way into as it expended the last of its satanic energy.

From where Charles sat it was as if nothing had happened, he had heard the mortar explode and was aware of the fragments hitting the earth around him but there was no *visible* evidence of the action that had claimed the Major. Almost imperceptible at first, the hatred that had blazed in the Major's eyes as he triumphed in his revenge, dulled to a glazed emptiness. His stare continued to hold Charles as his pistol arm fell, fingers relaxed releasing the weapon to fall harmlessly at Charles' feet.

He watched the Major in disbelief not knowing quite what had caused the man to suffer what appeared to be some form of seizure. Even though he thought himself still under threat he started forward to give help but halted himself as the realisation dawned on him that the man was dead, there was nothing that could be done for him.

There came another loud 'crump' from a mortar exploding close by followed by more showers of flying earth amidst which a breathless Tommy came tumbling on his backside down the side of the foxhole clutching a couple of canvas covered water canteens.

As he caught his breath he proffered one of the canteens to Charles stammering,

"WWWhat's the boss doing here?"

Receiving no reply from his preoccupied mentor he shrugged and made to offer the Major a drink. As Tommy sat there holding out the canteen the realisation struck home that 'the boss' was dead!

This spectacle of sheer irony was one too many shocks for Charles. He burst into raucous belly wobbling laughter causing a perplexed Tommy to wonder whether his mate had become unhinged!

"What happened to the boss?" blurted Tommy, repeating his earlier enquiry in a timid attempt at seizing

Charles' attention and so divert him from whatever insanity was troubling him.

"Copped some shrapnel I think, must be pretty small though because there's no sign of any bleeding!"

Tommy sidled over to the dead Major being careful to keep his head down and not make a target for the sharpshooters.

"Christ!" he exclaimed, "You should take a look at the back of him, there's a stomping great wound in his neck and all the blood you couldn't see is filling his bloody tunic!"

They both fell silent as they drank from the canteens, the freshness of the cool liquid proving sweet as well as reviving.

The pair waited for dusk and a suitable lull in the shooting before crawling out of the foxhole on their bellies dragging the remains of the Major between them. Bullets were striking the earth all around them as the sharp sighted enemy observed their attempt at escape but somehow they got back to the Allied trenches without being hit. Rolling themselves over the edge of the parapet to the infantrymen waiting in reserve below, they left the Major lying above with his arms dangling forlornly into the trench his head deep in the mud. Without a word of enquiry the disinterested trench soldiers tugged on these until the hapless Major tumbled into the space between them.

The sector watch Officer, a Lieutenant, stepped forward and listened to Charles' account of the Major's demise and the manner of his return to allied territory but said little. He fixed Charles' eyes with a steady sympathetic gaze, instructed him to get the body out of the way and departed no longer concerned with matters beyond his influence.

Loading the body onto a stretcher the two carried him from the front through the myriad of trenches that linked with the transport sector where they hoped to find an easier means of getting their charge to the field hospital. Charles tagged the dead man with a rough account of his demise and the names of the retrieval orderlies, (himself and Tommy) and left the body for transport to deliver to the mortuary. Much good his wealth was to him now!

The two arrived back at the front in time to go over the top with the reserve battalion. Bullets didn't seem to matter any more, if they were going to be hit then that was that. In a place like this Lady fate would manoeuvre you wherever her fickle will chose and if she had decreed there was a bullet with your name on it then no amount of dodging was going to change the outcome!

This last assault turned out to be a particularly bloody affair as fellow after fellow fell, wounded or dead. There were so many casualties that the orderly teams were forced to leave the dead and too far gone where they fell and focus all their effort on helping those that had a chance of survival. This was unpalatable in the extreme to Charles but there was nothing for it but to put all their effort into saving those that could best be helped. Morphine was running low, next time back he would send Tommy for more.

The two of them lifted a groaning semi-conscious man from the quagmire and did what they could for the wretch. He was in dreadful pain and strapping him into the blood and earth contaminated stretcher was made the more difficult by his cataclysmic convulsions. The tourniquet and several field dressings they had applied to the man's mangled leg would need to be released in the next twenty minutes to prevent the onset of mortification and they were a long way from safety. They would need to crawl at a superhuman pace if they were to drag this man to safety before death took him. Tiredness gnawed at their muscles as they set out to get the man to the help he needed, darkness was almost upon the field now cloaking them in half light making it more difficult for the enemy to pinpoint the pair as they made their way, inch by inch, toward the safety of their own lines. How they achieved what they did is a reflection of the determination and tenacity of the folk of their island race, they had covered the distance cut and bleeding, in seventeen minutes.

It was as they were lowering the casualty to safety that the mortar bomb exploded. In a blinding flash it released its bone smashing, flesh shredding energy that lifted Tommy like a rag doll sending him crashing across the open trench to the ramparts on the far side. The blast propelled Charles sideways in a barrage of flying earth and stones. that snatched him up and was tossing him across the ground.

Charles regained partial consciousness in the field hospital casualty ward. The clothing had all but been ripped from his aching body by the blast and both his legs had been lacerated above and below two fractured bones. He felt no pain, indeed he felt quite calm and very relaxed and thought of silly little things from his childhood.

Now and again he would laugh audibly through his stupor as something comical brushed through his fuddled mind. During the course of that day Charles had dispensed many shots of morphine to ease suffering, now the tables were turned, he was at the receiving end and was experiencing the effects as his patients had done. As time passed, waves of alternating confusion and cohesive thoughts passed in and out of Charles' waking moments until the moment that he recalled to mind the vision of his closest friend being torn from him.

A reaction of overwhelming loss burned through his mind and tore into his heart as images of how, like a discarded leaf, Tommy had been snatched up by and hurled through the air. Tears flooded his eyes, muddled as he was he couldn't bear the thought of losing the only true friend he had made in the Army; he couldn't bear to lose the boy that had become his shadow, his right arm, his example of courage when all around was failing him, he couldn't let Tommy go!

His heart felt heavy as his mind embraced the stark reality that he *must* have lost this young spirit to whom he had shown just a modicum of compassion and understanding but had in return received limitless gifts of devotion, unswerving loyalty and true dedication.

Though his eyes were still closed tears streamed in rivulets down his face and if the choice had been his to make he would have let life slip from him to take his place in whatever kingdom there was intended for him.

"Daft bugger—what's wrong with your eyes?"

The simple enquiry snatched Charles' mind from its nightmare wanderings into lucidity. The words from such a simple yet gratifyingly welcome plain and unequivocal voice sent Charles' spirits soaring. Even through the mist of confusion that was Charles' present state of being he embraced the words and adored the voice that delivered them. Overcome by feelings of innate confusion he was unable to utter a sound, not a single word that would express his relief and gratitude in that moment for the sparing of his friend but if God in his wisdom measures feelings, then he would ask no reward for granting continued life to this simple but so loyal a soul.

"Tommy?" whispered Charles, "Tommy?"

His face radiated a smile of heartfelt gratitude out of sheer delight for just a split second before his eyes clouded and he transcended once more into the elevated, serene and trouble free chambers of oblivion that is the kingdom of Morpheus.

The following day Charles had come out of his stupor and for the first time experienced the full measure of pain from his injuries.

The broken bones were painful to make little of it but the agony they radiated paled into insignificance by comparison with the searing hot burning of the ripped and scorched skin that the blast had claimed.

By his own choice Charles had declined the offer of further doses of morphine to ease his discomfort, he knew that if he didn't resist the drug it would inculcate an overpowering desire for more. He knew instinctively that the drug could lead to a dependence on the blissful relief that it brought from the horrors of a war that had ensnared and was ever engulfing him.

He bore his agony as best he could, for the most part in silence allowing only his eyes to communicate the true nature of the torment within.

Tommy had gone when Charles awoke from oblivion yet he remained a constant in his mind, not a day had slipped by when he had not wondered where his assistant had been redeployed. He knew full well that if Tommy was recovered from their ordeal he would be needed on the battlefield; the call for medics was acute since so many of them, like Charles himself, had been injured or had given their lives in the course of trying to save others.

Charles was irritated by the lack of any kind of information in the field hospital about the day to day conduct of the war and how it was going, it was even worse that no-one knew what had become of his friend!

He had tried with scant success to tackle the ward attendants, pleading with them to ask among the constantly incoming medical orderlies as they arrived with casualties whether any of them had heard any news of Tommy but no-one had heard anything of him.

Two weeks merged into three; Charles hobbled around the recovery ward on crutches in a constant effort to exercise his repairing body and work back the strength of his scarred and torn muscles. The effort proved exacting and dreadfully painful but he knew that if he was to re-kindle his friendship with his absent mate he would have to prove that he was able to return to active service, that he was physically and mentally capable of going on.

During his amblings on the boardwalks surrounding the hospital Charles had discovered that there had been several minor skirmishes along the front during his inactivity and a single hard 'push' from the Germans which had not resulted in the exchange of a single inch of territory but had marked the planting of many more wooden crosses in those far off fields!

The limited activity of the recuperation process, which was restricted to the confines of the R and R marquee and its surrounds, and the isolation from proper detailed information was driving Charles mad. He longed to be out of that place and back where he was needed on the field but, although he was healing speedily he was still seriously restricted in mobility hobbling as he was with his leg supported in splints. He had been told to his vexation that he would need to keep the splints in place for at least another week; that it would be many more weeks before he would be able to walk without the aid of crutches and that it would be very likely that he would be shortly repatriated to complete his recovery in England.

The information mortified him, it was far more important to him to know of the fate of his friend than it was to make a comfortable recovery in England and the thought of returning to the land where he was still branded a felon was unbearable—something would have to be done!

Charles made up his mind that he would visit the Adjutant who had shown compassion and understanding toward him when he had been summoned by Major Grace-Williams before his promotion. That he would relate in the strictest confidence to him the occurrence in the foxhole and ask for his assistance in remaining at the camp to serve in whatever capacity he could, anything other than being sent home!

Getting permission to leave the marquee proved to be an impossibility,

"Go for a walk outside?" the R and R orderly scoffed, "You must be bloody joking mate. With all the mud out there and you with splints and crutches you'd bog down before you got a hunnerd feet!"

"I'll find someone to help me!" bleated Charles but he could see he was getting nowhere. He was about to make another plea when all hell broke loose.

The big guns on both sides had opened up again filling the air with the smell of cordite and pounding the ears with wave after wave of crushing percussive pressure. It sounded to Charles like the incoming shells were very close indeed to the marquee and he began to fear for the wounded that couldn't be moved. He cowered involuntarily as a single shell exploded, he could hear the earth it had raised smattering against the thick canvass sides of the marquee to all the world like rain falling rhythmically on a tin roof.

The wounded started arriving almost at once.

"They're after the bloody ammo dump again!"

Charles heard one of the stretcher bearers remark to the reception orderly,

"If they hit *that* lot we'll *all* be bloody gonners!"

Charles slipped out of the marquee amid the diversion this new wave of arriving injured had presented, it would be 'all hands to the pumps' for the next couple of hours so no-one was going to miss him!

The orderly had been right about the mud, the going was extremely difficult his crutches sank deep into the quagmire affording him little in the way of support and twice he had been almost unable to free them from the suction that threatened to hold them captive. He was perspiring freely and feeling very feeble, he knew that he must rest or pass out.

"Damn!" he cursed roundly as yet again the suction embedded one of his crutches and this time it seemed the mud was not going to relinquish it under his power alone. Charles let go of the free crutch to concentrate his entire effort on freeing the other, he hauled for all he was worth.

"SOD and bloody DAMN!" he cursed, this was becoming too much for him.

"Jeeze Charlie—what in hell's name do you think your'e doin'?" came a familiar voice.

Charles swung around in surprise and succeeded in bowling himself flat out in the mud. He put his hands to his eyes to clear the splattered mud but only succeeded in rubbing more on to his face. He took on the appearance of a commando about to embark on a night raid or perhaps something from the old musical 'Mammy'!

Tommy burst into laughter.

"Daft bugger!" He quipped chidingly.

He helped Charles to his feet and pulled out the embedded crutch almost without effort which he thrust under one arm whilst he retrieved the other. He handed them over.

"Well?" he enquired again.

"Trying to get to the Adjutant's office—where the hell have *you* been anyway? I've been asking all over for you!"

"Yes I heard Charlie, guys kept asking if I knew of any Tommy—they didn't recognise it was me because my real name is *George*. Couldn't get here before because I've been on rear operations stretcher party detail getting the injured and the shell-shocked onto trains for blighty. I've walked ten bloody miles to find you—daft bugger!"

"It looks as if you've walked slap bang into another push and more work at the front old chum!" observed Charles.

"Not me mate," replied Tommy, "I've been sent from rear ops with a message for the Adjutant himself, got it here look."

He displayed a sealed leather pouch strapped to his midriff beneath his rough serge tunic.

"What d'you think of *that* then?" he announced with an obvious display of pride in himself that he'd been chosen to relay dispatches.

"Blimey old Son, you really have gone up in the world." remarked Charles astonished at the confidence his young friend now had.

"Come on." he instructed Charles, "Put your arm around my shoulder and we'll hobble there together." He suddenly looked at Charles with genuine consternation and added sheepishly.

"That's if you still want to go and if you think you'll be able to make it!"

"Course I can, what are we waiting for?"

The two made their way very slowly through the bog that was had once been a road and were passed every few minutes by horse drawn ammunition carts trundling their way from the dump to the artillery line. The Scammel transport lorries had long since given up and the ammunition they would normally have transported was now being delivered by horse and cart once more! It was little wonder that the army was sending teams around England scouring the country for and commandeering horses to serve at the front. Few of the promissory notes they used to pay for them would ever be honoured!

By the time they had struggled their way to the Adjutant's office the pair were just about exhausted. They were saturated with mud and looking completely dishevelled as if they had walked all the way from the front itself.

They were greeted at the entrance by the Sergeant.

"Wot do you waifs want?" He enquired gruffly.

"Like to see the Adjutant Sir!" stated Charles unequivocally.

"Wot *for* may I make so bold to enquire?"

"Personal reasons Sergeant." said Charles

"What 'appened to you lad, you been at the front?" asked the Sergeant seemingly noticing for the first time the trappings of injury.

"Yes Sergeant, that's what I want to talk to the adjutant about if that's alright and my mate here has a dispatch pouch for him!"

Charles signalled to Tommy to hand over the pouch.

"Name?"

"Jenkins sergeant, corporal Jenkins!"

The Sergeant eyed him carefully before asking,

"Aren't you the lad that tried to 'elp the downed Gerry pilot? Wait a jiff—it was the *two* of you wasn't it?"

"Yes Sergeant."

Charles almost swallowed the words the recollection of the sight of that poor unfortunate wretch laying lifeless in the wreck of what had been a few moments before an aeroplane about to taste the spoils of victory still brought intense sadness to his heart. He had always wished that things had turned out differently and that the flier had survived to live out the war in the relative safety of a prisoner of war camp. He shook himself free of these morbid thoughts and forced his mind back to the task in hand.

"'Ang on there a minit lad." Instructed the Sergeant as he stepped through the heavy canvas that formed the entrance to the field office. He was gone only a few moments but it seemed much longer to Charles who was now so tired he was finding it difficult to remain upright and longed above all for the chance to take the weight off his painful legs.

"In you go lads, both of you, the Adjutant wanted to see you anyway!" the sergeant informed them casually.

What was about to unfold would turn all of Charles' intentions upside down; would tear at his heart and his mind and make him wonder what his future *really* had in store for him!

The Captain was now a Major and was temporarily filling the dual roles of Adjutant and Officer Commanding. He had received a field promotion following the demise of Major Grace-Williams and given command of the post pending the arrival of a replacement when he was to be posted to command a forward battalion further to the West of the lines.

The pair, dishevelled as they were, stepped as smartly as they could before the Major and saluted as Army regulations required.

"Most fortuitous indeed that you should show up together just as I was about to issue orders to have you brought here." smiled the Major. He eyed the discomfort with which Charles stood before him and waved to a couple of folding chairs.

"Sit down both of you and tell me why you have come."

Taking the weight from his injured legs was as blissful to Charles as the moment he had first held his baby Sister though it was more a physical bliss than an emotional one.

"I thought I had better let someone know about the circumstances in which Major Grace-Williams met his death Sir."Ventured Charles glancing reluctantly at Tommy and wondering whether he should suggest to the Major that Tommy should leave.

"Good God!" exclaimed the Major in obvious astonishment overlaid with genuine delight,

"That is *precisely* the reason I have sent for you both—what a curious quirk of fate!"

"Yes Sir." Charles continued, "But you may . . . ."

"Before you go on lad," the Major cut in, "I have something very important I wish to tell you both about that incident and since I am able to exercise the privileges of rank then I feel I must relate *my* information first."

He paused whilst he removed a sheaf of papers from the dispatch pouch; reading quickly through the first two pages his eyes settled upon the paragraph he had been seeking.

"Ah!" he glanced up from his reading.

"I would normally instruct you both to be standing for what I am about to read to you as it embraces the very essence of Army discipline and the good conduct of the regiment but in view of your obvious injury Jenkins I will allow you to be seated. Your companion . . . ?"

The major severed his delivery to raise an eyebrow at Tommy.

"Infantryman First Class Fredericks Sir!" Stated Tommy snapping to his feet and saluting.

"Your companion Infantryman Fredericks must remain at attention!"

My God, this has the makings of Court Martial about it—they already *know!* Thought Charles, his spirits flagging.

The Major raised his eyes and took in the expressions of consternation that were clouding the faces of his subordinates and satisfying himself that the dignity of the event about to unfold was properly established he continued to quote from the dispatch.

"By order of the General Officer Commanding Second Brigade, Eighth Regiment of Field Medicine of the Royal Medical Corps it is hereby ordered that Infantryman George Fredericks and Corporal Medical Orderly Charles Jenkins, whilst serving in the second battalion Royal Medical Corps as field medical assistants, be each awarded the Military Medal for devotion to duty above and beyond the call of that duty in that they did jointly and without regard to their own safety attempt to preserve the life of Major Thomas Grace-Williams and whilst under fire themselves and suffering personal injury did recover the body of that Officer to be interred with dignity within the confines of his own lines which act is considered to be of the highest order and commensurate with the finest traditions of the British Army!"

The Major looked up from the manuscript with moist eyes.

"Well done both of you—you are among the first to receive this prestigious decoration instigated only recently by King George himself, you are both a credit and an inspiration to us all!"

This was not what Charles had been expecting and as his mind raced to try to take in the enormity of this new development the Major went on;

"There will be a formal presentation of the medals themselves by General Staff in due course but in the meantime you are to sew these medal ribbons to your tunics—wear them with the pride they deserve!"

The Major handed over the red, white and blue medal ribbons and drawing himself to his full height saluted the pair with genuine pride before continuing his official delivery.

"I hereby grant you both three weeks survivor's leave to be taken in the United Kingdom effective immediate." He relaxed and made to turn when he suddenly remembered an oversight.

Oh! before I forget Jenkins, I have a small package for you from home."

He handed Charles a small rectangular cardboard box the size of a deck of playing cards.

"As your censoring Officer I was obliged to open it and read the accompanying letter. From it I feel that the leave I have just granted will be entirely appropriate."

Charles gingerly took the package from the Major's outstretched hand. As he unfolded the letter a small card slipped from it coming to rest on his thigh. Charles retrieved it without taking his attention from the Major.

"I would entreat you to read it here in privacy whilst you are still seated, your companion and I will leave you to yourself and I will see that some tea is sent in to you!"

The Major signalled to Tommy to follow him from the office.

The room lapsed into silence as Charles closed his mind to the gunfire and began reading.

'My dearest, dearest Charles.

Let me begin by saying Happy Birthday to you my love. I hope you like the card I have enclosed. (Charles paused to look at the card and was taken aback by the beauty of the needlework embroidered inside arranged in the form of a faithful full colour Union flag surrounded by crimson hearts).

Wherever you are I know you will be working hard so the little piece of cake I have sent might help to bring you comfort and remind you of us all.

Life has not been the same since we said goodbye but nothing has changed for me, I will wait for you to come home to me until God calls me and I will pray to him every day that he returns you safely to us all, we love you more than you can ever know.

The Colliery Doctor calls on your Mother every day but she continues to refuse to leave the house until the day you come back to us. I have moved in to be with her since we both share our devotion for you and because I can help with teaching your Sister as well as the housework.

I am now driving the pony and trap and helping Doctor Moody myself and I have found I like doing it.

Tom is running the farm now that the farmer has had a stroke and he is making a good name for himself. It was hard at first but people are now talking to us again. Mr Grace-Williams has been killed in action somewhere in France and the Colliery is now owned by his half-Brother Iaian Evans. He is very kind and my Father says he is a much better boss. Mam and Dad both send their love and say don't worry, everyone in the valley still admire and respect you. Your Sister is coming on fine and is very good with her ABC and her numbers, you would be proud of her.

I can't get much paper in this box so I will sign off now. Remember we all love you my dearest but most of all don't forget me for you are my sun and my moon and my only reason for living. Hurry back safely to us all.

Forever Your Eira.

∇

The paper was slowly crinkling as it absorbed the tears that fell freely from this brave and caring young man, he folded it, then folded it again before placing it with the treasured card inside his tunic next to his heart. He was sniffling as he turned his attention to the box; lifting the already open flap at one end he shook out a collection of crumbs that had once been a slice of cherry cake.

He separated out a half of it and devoured it eagerly, the other half he saved for Tommy, he had forgotten that he had had a birthday!

His mind turned to Eira and his family, conjuring up pictures of how they had all looked when he had last seen them—was that years ago?

As fleeting recollections of how wonderful things had been passed drowsily through his weary mind the relief from the doubts he had suffered through the preceding weeks brought his head gently to his chest and he drifted into the welcome oblivion of sleep.

The protracted silence caused Tommy to worry about Charles, he had no idea as the major did, what the contents of the letter conveyed and he feared that there may have been something in it that had brought his friend grief. He could bear it no longer.

"Sir." He addressed the Major, "Can I go and check on my mate, p'raps take 'im that cuppa you mentioned?"

"Sorry old bean, I'd completely forgotten that, yes nip over to the table there and sort that out would you? There's a good chap!"

Tommy made the brew in lightning quick time and made his way back into the office. Charles was snoring gently, his relaxed lips beating out a trembling tattoo as the snoring came and went in time with the rise and fall of his chest. Tommy just stood there with an enormous grin on his face, here was a man who had just been decorated with one of the highest accolades that an ordinary soldier can win and he was so enthused by the event he was fast a bloody sleep!

The grin developed into laughter as the enormity of the sight before him sank in but even this didn't wake the slumbering soldier.

Curiosity got the better of the Major, the laughter drawing him to his office like a magnet.

"Good God!" He exclaimed sardonically as he took in the spectacle, "Who'd have thought my news would have been so thought provoking!"

The two men laughed conjointly and now it was the Sergeant's turn to bow to the force of curiosity as he too advanced to see what all the fuss was about.

CHAPTER 10

The Return Home

B EFORE PRESENTING HIMSELF AT the adjutant's Office the prospect of a spot of leave at home had been so remote and unreal to Charles that he didn't even dare to think seriously about it yet here he was with Tommy climbing aboard the French Railways hospital train for the journey back up through France to Boulogne. As the steam engine hissed, barked and clanked its way out of the camp Charles couldn't help wondering how this turn of events had managed to develop to his favour.

Just yesterday he was going to ask to be retained at the front and all his efforts to find his friend had failed and now, with a complete reversal of fortunes he was going home with his friend at his side.

Tommy had confessed to Charles that he had no-one waiting for him back home and no place that he wanted to return to so without hesitation Charles had insisted he accompany him to meet his folk and stay with them.

"They would be proud and pleased to have you under our roof and don't forget—you're a bloody hero now, Infantrymen Georgie Freddericks MM!"

He feigned a mock court bow.

"Bugger off!" said Tommy gruffly.

They were singled out for special treatment on the train, the nurses made a fuss of them and they were never without someone to talk to, the ribbons on their smart clean tunics had given them new status and placed them in awe in the eyes of their fellow travellers. In the light of what had really transpired in that foxhole it is no surprise that when approached to relate the tale of their achievement on the many occasions that arose during the journey, neither of them wanted to talk about the incident preferring to shrug it off. Perhaps for Charles it was because he knew the *real* circumstances and the incident that had motivated the Major to enter the foxhole!

▽

With his spirits now lifted by the thought of what lie in store for him at home, Charles' injuries were healing swiftly and he could even manage a few steps without crutches as long as he used the support of a cane. Away from the mud and horror of the front and with a reasonable wholesome diet his physique was returning to its previous muscular, well formed appearance. Indeed, he was filling out so quickly that he was getting concerned about arriving home to greet his folk with a tunic that wouldn't button up!

Every few minutes a troop train or an ammunition train would clatter by in the opposite direction and now and then a flatbed train would go past carrying peculiar looking armoured vehicles with tracks instead of wheels and bristling with guns, objects more akin to ships than any of the vehicles that the lads had seen in the Army!

The existence of such weapons was the subject of much animated discussion and rife speculation amongst the ordinary soldiers the more imaginative of which invented incredible stories to account for their being.

The days rolled past with only the occasional allied aircraft to buzz the train as they made their way South to provide reinforcement to the squadrons at the front. Sometimes they came so close they could see the pilots grinning like Cheshire cats as they enjoyed the exuberance and made the most of the exhilaration of what they regarded as their 'sport'.

The train journey was long and slow but with each moment that passed it brought the men inevitably closer to reunion and real recuperation in the confines of the comfort of a welcoming home and a loving family.

One day, just after Dawn there came the unmistakeable sound of an aircraft engine, spluttering and popping it could be heard even above the rattle and clank of the carriage wheels click-clacking over gaps in the iron rails. Heads were thrust out of windows in an attempt to identify this new diversion.

"There he is!" called several voices at once, "He's going to buzz us!"

To the admiration of the onlookers, the pilot wheeled his machine skilfully around following the direction of the train to parallel the moving carriages. He maintained position for a while before creeping slowly sideways closing the gap between him and the train.

"Silly bugger's going to hit us!" shrieked one of the onlookers and started trying to wave him off.

The others, those that were able, hundreds of them, were now leaning out of the windows taking up the challenge and joining in the waving which the pilot gleefully accepted to be an act of applause. Encouraged by what he obviously thought was enthusiasm the pilot puffed out his chest and set about giving his audience something to write home about.

Inexorably the craft drew steadily closer to the carriages until, with a skilful movement of the control column, the pilot raised the steed a few feet, slipped deftly sideways and deposited its wheels on the carriage roof with a solid thud that was audible to those inside even over the hysterical shrieks of trepidation!

He kept the flimsy aeroplane there blipping the throttle for a full minute before opening wide and flying off to the side again to salute his audience, the gold of a single ring on a dark blue sleeve could not be mistaken. Waggling his wings in triumph he wheeled the aircraft steeply through a half circle and was gone!

"Did you see that?" asked Charles.

"Couldn't miss it—daft bugger!" retorted Tommy though he was secretly thrilled with the short lived entertainment.

"Bet he's a bloody Eton chap!" remarked a familiar voice somewhere along the carriage!

The harbour at Boulogne was a hive of frenetic activity as the train pulled into the goods siding. Makeshift wooden steps were brought to at each of the carriage exits and the 'walking wounded' were disgorged to wait in the open on the dockside. It was drizzling now so capes were unrolled and quickly donned to keep out the inhospitable element. Military Police were marching stiffly along the lines of men shouting directions for them to form up and make their way to one of the several ships that were unloading stores, equipment and ton upon ton of high explosive ammunition. The lesser able hospital carriage wounded were taken by stretcher into waiting ambulances which departed grossly over occupied for the short journey to the waiting merchantmen that would return them to the land they so adored and would soon lay foot upon once more—those that still had them!

The sea crossing was supposed to be short and probably would have been but for the sea state. The wind had got up and was driving relentlessly against the single funnelled steamship as it tossed and rolled its way towards Southampton on the turbulent sea. Its occupants, cock-a-hoop about going home before departure, were now groaning as their constitutions did their best to part company with the nourishment they had been given as they set sail. Mercifully, when the ship entered the Solent the cruel sea relinquished its torment calming the confounding motion the ship had been imparting and settling the stomachs of its passengers once more.

The scene at Southampton docks was a mirror image of Boulogne as the Military Police Marshalls assisted by conscripted ordinary soldiers, tried to get the slow and battle worn repatriated troops from the ship to Southampton terminus station whilst at the same time get replacement new troops out of arriving trains and onto the same ship. Many of the returning troops had suffered injury and all were mentally exhausted and thus were understandably slow and unresponsive to the needs of the well fed and well rested M.P's who were keen to march men in well ordered easily controlled groups that could be manoeuvred to avoid those travelling in opposite directions. Men with sticks and crutches do not feel the same however and the transit on foot between the two points was just added inconvenience and misery so they tended to lapse into long straggling lines. Obstacles to good order seen through the eyes of the marshalls!

∇

The carriage was cold and damp and smelled of a mixture of human sweat and stale body odours but at least they could console themselves with the knowledge that with each jerk of the couplings and each screech of tortured metal they were inches closer to a warm bed and good food in company of *their* choosing.

As the journey progressed, Charles took time to describe his family and his beautiful home to an attentive Tommy, the gunfire, mud and squalor of the battlefield became so remote it was almost as if it had never existed. Visions that passed in pleasant indelibility through Charles' memory were translated into vivid words that painted tantalising pictures, captivated and held the spell bound Tommy prisoner.

He clung on to each and every new description translating them into pictures to store in his own mind. He was experiencing the life in which Charles had grown up and mentally substituting it for the misery and subjugation that had been his own upbringing.

For the very first time in his life he was experiencing in surrogacy a loving Mother, Brothers and Sisters, friends, relatives and people who really cared about you, actually cared whether you existed or not. He was captivated by it all!

Charles told him of the mint but not of the penny. He could *never* tell anyone about the penny. He told him about the Doctor and how he had been drawn into surroundings of such kindness as Tommy had never known. About how he had come into medicine and about how he had first applied it to injury in the shadow of death at the colliery. About how he had gone underground with that team of unwaveringly faithful men and how they had been overcome by the deluge.

He left out the part he had played because he was still haunted by memories of the fear of wanting to run when things had got bad in that underground prison and they had come face to face with what might have been their own deaths!

Tommy listened in silence but as each new episode in Charles' story unfolded he felt more strongly bonded to this man who had achieved so much from such small beginnings.

Tommy recalled to mind the progress he himself had made since Charles had miraculously extracted him from that dark, vacant and crushingly oppressive period that had led to his attempt to take his own life at the front.

He warmly embraced the recollection that the confidence and belief he now had in himself was entirely due to a few moments of compassion, trust and belief placed in him by this man he was so proud to call his friend.

Charles continued for hours, he had hardly given the folks at home a thought since his separation from them and his ignominious departure from his place of birth and upbringing.

Pangs of guilt passed through him as he recalled how close they had all been and how he had somehow never managed to write home. Time had flown so swiftly since his departure and his self-dedication to saving life had consumed all of his waking moments such that opportunity and fatigue had prevented him from putting pen to paper. Neither had he written to say that he was returning.

As he talked, he felt the shadow of shame returning to haunt his conscious thoughts. Not enough time had placed itself between the action that had brought him to disgrace the good name of his family and his return home to allow folks memories to dim sufficiently to forgive.

What would folks think of him, what would they say? Would his appearance now resurrect the past and would they resume the shunning of his family as pariahs, would they shun him and shut him out of society, would he be able to face them and accept the innuendos that would inevitably be whispered covertly behind backs of hands?

The intrusion of these unpleasant thoughts had halted Charles' narrative but Tommy said nothing. He could see that something in Charles' recollections had triggered an unpleasant reaction but, loyal to his character and his respect for his friend, he held back the urge to enquire what was bothering him. Instead he looked unblinking into his eyes, his own moistening in empathy. Reaching across the gap between them he placed a hand gently on Charles' knee, a hand extended that said without words,

'I'll share your sorrows, whatever they are!'

The journey drew them inexorably onward, to a homecoming and reunion for Charles, to a new beginning for Tommy.

∇

At Bristol the train was marshalled into a little used platform in the old Brunel building for the occupants to get out and stretch their legs. A row portable field latrines had been erected to one side of the small goods yard that opened out beyond the station wall and between those and the platform a field kitchen was busy preparing meals for the ravenous soldiers.

"'Bout bloody time!" exclaimed Tommy, "My stomach thinks my bloody throat's been cut!"

The remark evoked a ripple of laughter from the men close around him, the humorous exclamation was something of a welcome relief from the sheer boredom of the train journey.

Whilst they were eating, the train was divided into two sections for the onward journey comprising of nine carriages and three carriages. Nine carriages would continue northwards through the midlands with the remainder travelling west through the Severn tunnel into South Wales. Charles and Tommy would take the northern route as far as Gloucester where they would change trains and travel west towards Monmouthshire where they would change again to the single carriage train that would take them past the mint almost to the Welsh border to the tiny single platform station where the passenger line terminated. (The line actually continued up the valley on a busy goods spur which served the colliery that Charles knew so well.) The two lads would have to find their own way from here to Charles' homestead some five miles distant.

Charles had been giving this last phase of the journey some careful deliberation. Although he was now able to get around quite well, the thought of a five mile hike on crutches was not appealing and would mean making frequent stops to recover his strength.

Charles began to wish he had written to announce his homecoming, had he done so he felt sure that his betrothed would have met them with the pony and trap, what a relief that would have been. He dismissed the thought and took pleasure from the image of surprise and delight that his sudden and unexpected arrival would evoke in the faces of those he loved.

∇

Several whistles began shrilling at once wrenching Charles' mind back into the present and signalling the end of the recreational break, it was time to entrain for the journey onward.

During the break each man had been given a sheet of paper marked with a large letter and a number and a pin with which to secure it to his tunic. The letter was to indicate which section of the train he was to travel in and the number the designated station at which he would leave the train. The marshalling teams now used these to direct the men to their appropriate platform, a process which was both noisy and boisterous as the more mischievous attempted to confound the perplexed marshals by constantly changing positions.

It seemed like hours before the provost marshal was finally satisfied that everyone was where they should be, the process had consumed far more time than had been allotted to it and had left the organising teams exhausted both physically and of patience!

To the relief of all, the two steam engines clanked and grunted their way out of the subsidiary platforms and were despatched to their respective routes. The support teams at the station felt a strong sense of relief at having successfully fed and sent the soldiers on their way and were themselves enjoying a break but it was to be short lived for trains were even now clanking their way into the Army platforms bringing hundreds of replacement troops for the war in France. The activity would begin all over again!

The refreshment of food and a little exercise had produced a soporific effect on the two men relaxed in the comfort of the rug covered seats for they now slept deeply to the hypnotic background of the continuous clickety clack of wheels passing over rail joints. So deeply did they drift that they were astonished to be woken by one of the other soldiers in the compartment.

"This is Gloucester mate—your stop!"

The soldier urged Charles, "Better be quick 'cos the train won't hang around long!"

Tommy leapt into action and grabbed both his and Charles' kit bags, opening the door he threw them onto the platform before turning to help his chum negotiate the not inconsiderable step down from the compartment.

Although the guard was already blowing his whistle and waving his green flag the train remained at a standstill until Charles was clear but even as Tommy slammed the door it lurched into motion and was quickly on its way!

The lads stood there a few seconds enveloped in swirling wisps of steam listening to the echo of the engine barking its way out of the lofty hall of the station canopy, darkness had fallen and but for them the station seemed to be deserted. Neither of them had been told where they would find the connecting train that would take them to their next destination in Monmouthshire and this was a vast station with dozens of platforms. They looked at each other both feeling a little isolated having lost the company of hundreds of their fellow soldiers; they felt more than a little lost. Neither man had ever experienced railway travel before the army and were a little perplexed regarding what they should do next. Tommy picked up the kitbags throwing one over each shoulder.

"Come on Charlie!" He exclaimed, "Let's find someone to ask!"

He ushered Charles to a dimly lit, unheated waiting room and set the luggage down.

"No sense in both of us going on this trek Charlie, sit yourself down and I'll have a scout 'round!"

The quest brought him to the only place he could hear life, the staff rest room where languished two elderly Porters comprising the night duty team and supposedly in charge of the entire complex.

"'Torr mate?" responded one to Tommy's question. "Connection left forty minutes ago, not another one now until seven thirty tomorrow morning! 'Ow many of you are there?"

"Just the two of us." replied a subdued Tommy, thinking, 'how in hell did we miss the connection?' He became irritated as he realised that the lost time at Bristol had cost them a night of their leave and there was nowhere for them to sleep. He felt disturbed by the thought of Charles having to sleep on a cold station platform.

"Bring your mate in here, we can stoke up the fire and tea's already brewed. Chuck down a few coats to sleep on and you'll be snug as bugs in a rug!" Suggested one of the benevolent Porters with a warm smile.

"We've only got a few more trains to tend to then things will quiet down till around six tomorrow."

Tommy left to fetch Charles, explaining the missed connection and the proposed arrangements as they made their way back to the Porter's rest room. The long day and the tiring effect it had had on Charles was now showing in his face, his eyes had receded and his lids drooped heavily lending him the appearance and pallor of an ageing, sick man.

They made their way through the door closing it firmly behind them, the night outside was becoming inhospitably cold and the pair were grateful for the heat emanating from the single, pot belly stove to one side of the room.

"Come on in lads." The porters chorused, thrusting out two mugs of steaming hot tea. "Either of you hungry?"

"Bloody starving!" quipped Tommy, famished as ever.

The porters nodded to each other as if to say, 'Thought as much'.

Within minutes they had stoked up the stove and were cooking bacon and eggs on a small coal shovel. They had learned this from the engine crews who frequently did the same using the fireman's shovel heated by inserting it, eggs and bacon cupped in its spoon, into the firebox.

It made a superb, nutritious and very welcome repast accompanied as it was by doorstep sized chunks of grain bread. The porters helped the two to lay a dozen or so thick serge coats belonging to the off-duty staff onto the wide wooden benches that surround the four sides of the large square table in the centre of the room and then left to attend to an incoming train. When they returned twenty minutes later they found the worn out soldiers, barely visible in the pile of coats, soundly in the land of nod!

They were woken by the porters at six-thirty. The large blackened kettle was singing on the stove and the white enamelled jugs that would be used to make a brew were already charged with dry tea.

"Breakfast will have to be the same as supper lads."

The information seemed apologetic but neither soldier was going to complain. In their esteem forged out of gratitude, the meal the night before would have been worthy of a jolly good hotel!

Charles was feeling better. His pallor had returned to a normal rosy glow and his eyes were bright and attentive,

"Any chance I could nick a little of that water for a wash mate?" he enquired of one of the porters.

"Help yourself chum—there's an enamel bowl and stuff over there!"

He jerked a thumb in the direction of one corner. Both soldiers grasped the offer with relish and took the opportunity to rid themselves of two days of accumulated dust following which all four sat down to another slap-up shovel fry!

"Neither of you guys told us you're war heroes." Remarked one of the porters as they finished mopping their plates.

Tommy and Charles looked at each other, neither one of them had given their decoration a second thought and really didn't think it was anything you should mention to decent, honest, hard working railway folk anyway.

The porter went on,

"The stationmaster came looking for you last night, he'd had a telegram asking where you were and was really put out that you had been forced to sleep in here. Seems to think you should have stayed in his house, he told us you both got the Military Medal for bravery."

Lost for an appropriate comment and a trifle embarrassed Charles haltingly replied.

"I slept like a baby .... wouldn't have slept any better anywhere else!"

"That goes for me too." Added Tommy,

"Thanks to the two of you we didn't have to sleep on the platform and we got some great food into the bargain."

The porters grinned broadly, they were glad that they'd had the opportunity to meet some real war heroes and honoured that they had played a small part in helping them to enjoy a little comfort in that cold and draughty station.

"Better get out to platform seven lads." suggested one of the porters.

"Your connecting train will be pulling in about now and we need to get to platform two to meet the seven-twenty-five from Bristol. There'll be quite a few passengers making for your train from the seven-twenty-five so go get some good seats now."

They group shook hands and went their separate ways.

'Strange how our lives are touched by others' Charles mused as they made their way to the waiting train, 'Ships that pass in the night!'

Platform seven appeared to be deserted but for a solitary porter as the soldiers stepped from the footbridge and made their way to the miniscule combination of a small steam engine drawing two carriages that was to convey them onwards. The lofty, cavernous station burst into life from the din of an arriving express from Bristol thundering along a distant platform and screeching to a protracted, agonised halt. Echoes of doors banging, trolleys transferring parcels and luggage, shouts of distant greetings, the roar of steam blasting from the engine's safety valve and the flapping of wings from disturbed pigeons all combined to produce a bizarre blend of symphony in railway flat major!

The lads made their way toward the branch-line train keen to be on their way when, as if from nowhere, the lone railwayman was joined by a second. Charles reasoned from the man's bearing and manner of dress, that the newcomer was the more senior of the two which proved to be an accurate assumption for he was now gesticulating to the porter to take the baggage from the soldiers. He turned out to be the stationmaster who, stepping forward to greet them, took their hands in turn and shook them with considerable vigour and welcomed them on behalf of the Great Western Railway Company to Gloucester City Station.

There followed a profuse apology for not knowing they had been stranded by their missed connection and for not offering them the hospitality of his own home. To make up for it, he had been authorised to offer the soldiers onward transportation in the first class carriage closest to the engine and in a compartment reserved entirely for *them!* The stationmaster's chest swelled visibly with pride at the generosity of his Company's offer; sporting a broad smile he ushered Charles and Tommy through the compartment door being held open for them by the porter the window of which was emblazoned by a large piece of white paper announcing RESERVED. Charles and Tommy looked at each other in astonishment bewildered by this peculiar treatment but said nothing more than a simple 'Thank you' to the dignitary and made themselves comfortable.

The compartment was spick and span and smelled of fresh lavender which was a very welcome change indeed from the odours they had endured from previous trains. Tommy repositioned the kitbags furthest away from the door to give themselves the benefit of the space they could now enjoy and both sat facing the way the engine would go to better catch scenery that neither of them had ever seen before. The two felt mutually excited about the fairly short journey to come, from their privileged position they would be able to see without the obstruction of crowding soldiers what was passing by outside and because the train would progress at a far more leisurely pace they would have time to take it in!

The night porters had been right—within a few seconds of settling down the platform came alive with the arrival of a small assortment of impatient travellers all scurrying for the best seats. The first class passengers were few and thus had no need of haste for there was no competition for seats in their elevated world.

None of the embarking first class travellers would have chosen to join the lads even if the compartment had not been reserved for class distinction was very much the order of the day and eminent souls like first class folk would *never* be seen to be travelling in the company of ordinary soldiers. They could not have known and probably would not have cared that these two soldiers were *extra*ordinary!

As the diminutive train began to move out of the station, a troop train thundered South through the centre track at high speed, whistle screaming 'right of way' and packed to capacity with more Khaki clad young men bound for the killing fields of far off France. The penny in Charles' inner pocket grew warm then just as suddenly cooled again as potential victims swept by—it was biding its time but it was still seeking.

Charles was dismayed by the stark reminder, he hadn't fetched the penny to mind since the ordeal in the foxhole and had quite overlooked his possession of it. He shuddered in dread at the recollection and forced the devil's trinket to the back of his mind.

The journey was quicker than the lads were expecting, perhaps because of the comfort they found themselves in and perhaps because of the distraction that some of the most beautiful scenery in Great Britain provided, perhaps even because of a combination of the happy effects of both.

Here they were about to arrive at Torr with the same feeling they had experienced when alighting at Gloucester station, what to do, which way to go?

There was just one more short train journey remaining and they would be almost home! Charles' spirits soared in excitement as he thought of those he loved and how close they now were.

The train drew to a halt and before either of the lads had even left their seats the carriage door was opened and beyond it the Torr stationmaster stood smiling.

"Welcome home lads!" he greeted and motioned an attendant to collect the kitbags which Tommy had made to pick up.

The stationmaster helped Charles from the train to a wicker bath chair that had clearly seen better days, Charles would much prefer to have walked but saw at once that this would have been a snub to the station staff who had put themselves out to look after him. The group set off amid turned heads and inquisitive glances from folk on the platforms curious to know what the cause of this fuss might be. Charles felt himself flushing with embarrassment as the party made their way to the final link in the railway chain that was to take him to the final station in the branch line. A station that was far more accustomed to the through passage of coal trains on the way to Cardiff docks and long lines of empties in the return direction than to passenger carrying.

Although this station was the nearest to Charles' home, it was actually just over the border into Wales and was still a full five miles from the cottage at Dell's Meadow. The thought of this walk was daunting but thrust to the back of Charles' mind by the stronger more pleasant ones of re-unions to come!

The train comprised a single black GWR pannier tank gleaming from a recent overhaul and an obvious careful polishing and a single brown and cream first class coach similarly well polished. Charles recalled to mind that this was somewhat unusual because the soot and smoke that was constantly being belched out by the collieries and the railway engines themselves, combined with the lack of young male help conscripted into the war, had left engines and carriages alike in a state of perpetual grime.

The stationmaster proved to be something of a chatterbox which was fortunate for the lads because neither of them were now in a very talkative mood and even though they had eaten a good breakfast just a couple of hours ago, their stomachs were insisting on being fed again.

The imminent homecoming had pervaded every thought in the lad's minds and all but a few of the words the stationmaster had uttered sailed completely over their heads. That word of words, that *special* word that would forever unlock doors to new friendships for Tommy came out of the fog of conversation.

'Hungry?'

Tommy's eyes lit up.

"Starving!" he uttered beseechingly.

The stationmaster redirected the party to the cafeteria, he had been expecting this reply and had planned for it accordingly.

"What about our train; what time does it leave?" enquired Charles, concerned that he might miss yet another connection.

"Don't worry about that lad," replied the stationmaster, The driver has instructions to have you at Guilloshen station at *precisely* mid-day, not a minute before, not a minute after. You have time enough to enjoy some light refreshment."

Charles nodded his understanding but thought the reply strange, he couldn't ever remember there being more than two passenger trains a day, one in the morning and the other very late afternoon.

He reasoned that perhaps the service had been reduced to one train a day now that there's a war on,

Both men were grateful to be on their way on this final leg at last. To their irritation the chatty stationmaster had opted to accompany them to Guilloshen and to return with the train at the end of the day. (The engine lived in the locomotive sheds at Torr). They had hoped for a little solace and the chance to take in the rolling hills and lush green fields that were all around them, non stop chatter wasn't really needed. Soon they would be approaching coal country and following the valley floors where the land had been forever scarred by towering tips of black coal spoil and trees had been turned brown or buried by the encroachment of the tips or contamination of the nutrients they needed. Rivers and streams that had once been crystal clear with tints of red infused by natural iron oxides were now black and lifeless.

Once again, the journey was providentially short, a mere eight miles and even at the not much greater than walking pace of the engine they were soon creeping into the approaches of the station. Motivated by the prospect of arrival the two had forsaken the company of the stationmaster and had taken position at the window closest to where Charles knew the single platform would be, which act didn't deter the chatterbox in the slightest, his liturgy describing his family, his house, his garden, his pets etc. etc. etc.

There were children. Lots of children waving little paper Welsh Dragon flags and Union flags on short wooden sticks—no wonder the train had slowed to a snail's pace!

Charles unhooked the thick leather strap from its securing knob and let the window down with a thump. Thrusting his head through the window he was truly amazed at the spectacle there before him. The track was lined with hundreds of people all with the same little flags, there was bunting and full size Union flags draped *everywhere*, People were cheering and so tightly packed on the platform that the colliery brass band that was playing marshal music at the far end were all but drowned out! Draped full across the approach end of the station canopy was a huge banner with the words, 'Welcome home to our heroes'

Charles pulled his head back in, his mouth wide open in astonishment and was at once replaced by a curious Tommy who quickly ducked back in saying,

"Bugger me—they must be expecting someone special!"

The stationmaster laughed engagingly, he had been in constant touch with the stationmaster at Guilloshen since they had heard that the two men had left Bristol. To the disappointment of everyone in the valley the whole thing had needed to be put back a day when the men had failed to meet their connection from Gloucester, but here they *were*.

The train drew to a halt in the middle of the platform. The band was redeployed to stand astride the path the soldiers would have to take to meet the Mayor and his dignitaries and, of all things, a red carpet had been unrolled for them to walk upon.

"The reception is for the two of *you!*" announced their companion with genuine delight. He had come to admire these men not just for their achievement as soldiers but because of their complete lack of corruption by the award they had received and the acknowledgment of it they were now receiving.

The lads, dishevelled and unkempt in appearance from days of travel and sleeping rough now brushed themselves down as best they could. Charles strained and strained to catch a glimpse of his beloved fiancé whom he realised he had missed desperately and with whom he needed to meet and hold and kiss above all else. There were so many people, so many faces he didn't know, so much movement that, skin his eyes as he might, he was unable to see her. His heart sank in despair as thoughts of her being pushed to the back by the eager and more boisterous colliery hands dashed through his anxious mind.

'Where *is* she?'

Perhaps she hadn't come at all, perhaps she was at home with his mother, perhaps she was tending the sick and unable to free herself!

Charles stepped from the carriage first but all that followed meant nothing to him, he got through it all as best he could and thanked everyone for their kindness and for making this a very special day. He had never had to speak in public before and found it daunting and hard going but even that was as nothing in comparison with the difficulty he was having in fighting back his disappointment that his intended was not there. A lump was welling up in his throat.

The Mayor called for three cheers for the heroes and the response all but brought down the station canopy and there she was!

A prettier picture Charles had never witnessed. She was a vision of sheer beauty radiant in an all white gown with posy and parasol. The skirt was full from her tiny waist and the shoulders raised in white lace around her slender neck. Her complexion was as pure as pure can be resembling hues of honey, peaches and cream. Her eyes, oh her eyes, clear as a cool mountain stream and gazing steadily at him with smiles creasing their corners and a promise of love so divine that his heart fluttered, jumped and bounced with joy in his breast. His grip on himself he could sustain no longer. The suspense and excitement of the journey and the long anticipated meeting with his love overcame him in a single un-resistible flood of overpowering, debilitating emotion.

Before all those people assembled in his honour his resolution collapsed and he gave way to the tears that he had been forcing from himself for so long.

The assembled company fell silent, not in embarrassment but in sympathy for the stress they knew this man must have suffered and in acknowledgement of the enormity of the emotions his homecoming had subjected him to.

Eira stepped forward and took Charles' hand and guided him into the privacy of the stationmaster's office. Doctor Moody had told the family he would need to be treated with great care. The doctor had been right about Charles following the colliery incident and he was right now, thanks to him Eira had been able to prepare for this moment.

Eira shut the frosted half-glazed door and the couple embraced for the first time since those dismal days before their parting. They embraced tightly, so tightly, tightly enough to intimate to each other that nothing would ever come between them again.

Not a word was exchanged. Charles' rested his head lightly on the crisp frill that encompassed Eira's neck not wanting to crush it but at the same time wanting to snuggle as close to her as he could. He could smell the sweet smell of rose water and soap on her soft skin and the hint of perfume in her hair and the fragrances sent his mind reeling with pleasure.

They remained locked in each others arms for a full three minutes whilst Charles fought to control his emotions and work the pools of heartache from his soul.

Finally, he eased her to arm's length and with all the strength and determination he could gather said.

"I asked you before but now I ask you again with all my heart—will you marry me?"

"I told you before and I say it again—try and stop me!" she responded with a smile that radiated across her entire countenance. Her eyes had widened and Charles noticed for the first time how long and curled her eyelashes were. His heart fluttered and he wondered how on earth he had ever been so stupid as to jeopardize their future by committing that stupid act of violence against another being. An act that had almost cost him his life.

They kissed for the first time since Charles' departure and from the kiss sprang hope and happiness, Eira brushed away the moisture from her cheeks, sparkling jewels, tears of sheer joy!

They stepped outside arms linked, faces bearing expressions of dazzling bliss and it was clear to all that they were one in spirit.

The colliery, closed for the day for the miners to attend the welcome party and the reception, was staffed only by the boiler man and pump hand who now struck up the pit head whistle in harmony with the railway engine. Cheers such had never been heard before in Wales rang the length and breadth of the valley—there would be celebration this night!

As the cheering subsided, Eira turned to Charles and said,

"I have a shock for you."

The joy in her smile suggested to Charles that this was not so much of a shock as a surprise.

"The Magistrate and the Minister are here and I have obtained a special licence for us to marry. I can't wait any longer for you to set a date so what about *right now!*"

She had been right, it was indeed a shock and the last thing Charles had been contemplating but *yes* he *would* marry her right here and right *now!*

He hesitated as he remembered he had a duty to his family as well as to his intended and asked uncertainly.

"What of Mam Eira? I can't wed without her blessing but most of all her *presence!*"

"Your Mam, my Mam and Dad and *all* our family are waiting fully dressed for this very moment in the parcels office. We have talked about nothing else since we had the telegram from the War Office to say you were coming home." She paused awaiting his reaction then, tapping one foot lightly on the flagstones added in feigned indignity,

"Well—are you going to stand here all day and keep us from our marriage bower and our company from their celebrations—or *what?*"

"I am ready girl, it's *you* who's doing all the talking—lead me to it!"

They both laughed in unison as they called for the rest of the wedding party.

There were to be two best men, Tom, Charles' Brother and Tommy his friend who would now have to use the name given to him by the orphanage, something he would have preferred to avoid but things had to be conducted officially for the sake of propriety and good order.

As he stood beside this vision of loveliness in her crisp white dress (which Charles now saw was always intended to be a wedding gown) in his dishevelled uniform bearing its bright new medal ribbon, Charles felt a hundred feet tall. Just yesterday he was dreaming about *meeting* his love, today, in a few moments, they would join as one and seal their bond for eternity before their God and their kin!

The ceremony was conducted in true Welsh tradition by the minister that had served Eira and her family and *all* the families in the mining community for longer than anyone dared remember. Instead of Mendelssohn's wedding march the colliery brass played Eira's request for 'Myfanwy' the song being rendered by the assembled colliery male voice choir in such close harmony as to melt your heart!

The couple were whisked from the station to the workmen's Hall, just up from the station and adjacent almost to the colliery, in the Rolls Royce that had once been the property of Thomas Grace-Williams. It had passed with all his other property to Iaian Evans as part of the colliery sale. Almost the first person after the family to greet and congratulate the couple in the hall was Iaian Evans himself, his predecessor would never have considered lowering himself to mingle with his employees no matter *what* the occasion but that was of no concern to anyone now!

The hall was *packed,* granted there was free ale in 50 gallon wooden casks and no sane Welshman would turn *that* down, but folk were there to celebrate the return of two heroes, the wedding, the day absent from the colliery, the dog with the white spots and anything else that could be toasted or held in celebration. Ale flowed freely, rivers of it and the brass band played throughout the evening though it must be admitted that many of the notes were becoming fluffy as lips lost their resolve.

In later years, so distant from that terrible war, Tommy was to recall to his children and grand-children alike how he had seen a cornet player trying to play and laugh at the same time and the peculiar sounds that came from the trying of it!

"Ahhh *that* was a day to remember!" he would sigh pensively before lapsing into silence as his mind's eye carried him back to those wonderful, carefree, joyous days spent with his chum!

Life at the cottage was crowded even though the newlyweds were living with Eira's parents at Pritchard Row. Tommy and Charles would meet up daily at the six bells for a few drinks (which they rarely had to pay for) and carry on lively conversation with the off-duty colliers. The two were treated with nothing short of reverence by all and the experience of having folk around him who truly wanted to be his friends saw Tommy emerging as a confident and intelligent adult with a puckish sense of humour that kept the colliers in fits. His impersonations of local dignitaries and the colliery officials was truly remarkable and he was able to produce them in a passable Welsh accent drawing loud applause from those around him.

The days drew by so quickly that Charles suddenly realised that he had spent far too little time with his

Mother, he had meant to ask her about Doctor Williams the colliery MO, but somehow time had flown by and the opportunity had never really come about. He decided he would put this right and see his Mother at once.

Eira drove him to the cottage in the colliery trap before continuing with her daily rounds of the local and colliery sick. The practise had expanded considerably in Charles' absence and was thriving admirably so she was not able to stay long.

"I'm going to stay long enough to see that your Mother comes to her senses!" She announced as Charles hitched the reins to the cottage front fence. The act took his mind back to that day when he had been dismissed from the mint and his Sister had been born. He smiled at the recollection of it and all that had taken place since!

"Well, well, *well!*" exclaimed a smiling Mrs Jenkins, "Look what the cat's brought in! How is married life treating the two of you Carriad?"

"Well enough Mother," said Charles, "Sorry we've been such strangers but we're here *now*!"

"No matter my Son," his Mother smiled, "Tommy Bowser has been keeping me up to date and I've been to the shop once or twice—Mrs Freeborn has all the gossip and has been telling me all about how proud everyone is of you!"

"Good!" said Charles, "That makes what I have to say easier!"

"How are things between you and Doctor Williams Mother? I know you refused to leave the cottage and to take up his offer of marriage because of the shame I brought upon you and family but surely, now that things are different, will you not re-consider?"

His mother smiled even more broadly and blushed a little at this mild embarrassment.

"Funny you should bring that up *now* of all times! I saw him yesterday and he has asked me again. It was never him that held up our wedding Charles, even after what happened with Mr Grace-Williams, it was *me*. He has pointed out to me that if you two can be so brave in these bad times then *I* should show a little courage and copy your example!"

She looked at them both and giggled coyly like a self-conscious schoolgirl,

"We are to be wed the day after tomorrow in St Barnabas' Church in the village so that you can return to your Army knowing that your Sister and I will be well provided for!"

"This is *wonderful* news." Chorused Eira and Charles.

"Wonderful, wonderful, *wonderful!*" Repeated Charles grabbing Eira and dancing around like a fool. It came to him from what his Mother had just said that his days in the peace and tranquillity of this heaven he had always known as home were drawing to a close. He brushed the thought aside to be dealt with later.

"Who is to be your best man and who will give you away?" asked Charles anxious that all should be concluded as swiftly as possible.

"Iaian Evans is to give me away and I have asked your Brother to be best man so that you and Eira can be free to enjoy from a distance what you have recently done yourselves. That way you can be together at my wedding feast and we can all be happy!"

CHAPTER II

The War Goes On

Tommy was getting restless, the enjoyment of being in the company of so many friends and the knowledge that he now had family even though not blood related, had led him to wish the war a million miles away to be fought by any other Nation other than his. He had heard countless stories among the colliery and valley folk about Dads, Uncles, Sons and friends whose lives had been shattered by injury or loss and was feeling guilty that he had enjoyed so much leave whilst the war raged on and good men continued to be maimed or lost. He was almost *glad* when the telegram arrived.

It arrived in the familiar small brown envelope broad printed along the top 'ON HIS MAJESTY'S SERVICE', and contained a single sheet of thin message paper with lines of characters printed on thick paper tape stuck to its surface. It read:

'BY COMMAND OF HIS BRITANNIC MAJESTY KING GEORGE V

Infantryman 1st class GEORGE FREDERICKS MM kps264214332 of 2nd Rifle brigade 4th regiment of foot.

YOU ARE TO REPORT TO THE PROVOST MARSHALL'S OFFICE GLOUCESTER STATION BY 1500 5 JUNE 1916. YOU ARE TO PRODUCE THIS INSTRUCTION AS PROOF OF ENTITLEMENT TO TRAVEL AT CROWN EXPENSE.

The order was duly ratified and given under the hand of some bigwig in the war office.

∇

Now that it was in his hand, he hated it, it made the future uncertain all over again and brought a sinking feeling to the pit of his stomach.

The thought of returning to the carnage of the battlefield sent shivers rattling down his spine. He inwardly cursed the Politicians for bringing the war about and the Generals for the manner in which they so willingly implemented their 'duty' in casually sending young men to face certain death, often for no material gain!

He fingered the other brown envelope addressed to Charles and plunged into a melancholy mood as he thought of the partings that were to come and the worry that Charles' new bride would have to carry daily not knowing whether or not she still had a husband!

The war had been supposed to be 'all over by Christmas'—Christmas *last* year! The newspapers were now suggesting that perhaps it would be over by Christmas *this* year instead.

Tommy knew better, he had seen first hand how men were fighting day after day, week after week, month after month and simply see-sawing over the same neck of land leaving their blood as they fell to lay nutrient to future generations of nature's vegetation. He felt tempted to throw the envelope away but sense prevailed as he reasoned that the action wouldn't do Charlie any good—they'd just come and cart him off and anyway, once I go he'll *know* something's wrong.'

He set off for the six bells on what would be his last sojourn for there would be no time for visiting tomorrow, he would have to start preparing his kit. He hadn't touched his uniform or his boots or webbing since discarding them for the more casual togs of a Welsh working lad on arrival in this Arcadian paradise, now he would have to see that it was all brought up to Army inspection standard before returning to his Regiment.

He hated the thought of handing over that horrid order to his friend and hated even more the prospect that he would probably be returned to the infantry to fight out the war in the trenches to whatever outcome fate had decreed him. He would be forced to part company with Charles who would rightly continue with his service in the medical corps—that was his proper calling, whereas Tommy had only temporarily become a medical orderly because of Charles' faith and trust in him at a time when his own kind had regarded him as an outcast and treated him with contempt and disdain!

The walk to the six bells was less pleasant than any of his previous journeys, dark clouds were already gathering. Even the sound of the Cuckoo calling for a prospective mate and the myriad of other birdcalls that provided the usual pleasant accompaniment to his walk did not penetrate the outer shrouds of the dark, depressive mood that was accumulating and threatening to engulf his buoyant spirit.

His pace slowed to a crawl then halted abrupt. He sat himself on a tump of grass bordering the track that had been worn into the hard soil by the passage of countless carts and buried his face in his hands. How would he manage without the friendship and encouragement of his mate?

Visions of the treatment he had received in the infantry came flooding back to him in an overwhelming torrent of dread. For the first time since being befriended by Charles, Tommy was experiencing self-doubt and sinister forebodings that he would be unable to cope with life without his mentor.

A voice somewhere deep in his subconscious told him to get off his backside and prove he was worthy of the trust and admiration he had *already* earned! To prove to Charles that he was everything that Charles had believed him to be. He gritted his teeth and determined that he would *never* allow himself to be lowered to the standard he had once been reduced to. He would prove once and for all that he was a man!

To say that Charles was thrilled about returning to France would be ridiculous in the extreme but it must be said that he had been expecting the mobilisation telegram and was more than well aware that the time for him to return to the Army was approaching. He slit the envelope open with his little finger and took out the instruction; it read much as Tommy's had done except that it additionally instructed him to report as 'Corporal Medical Orderly to 46 Squadron His Majesty's Royal Flying Corps'. Charles had no idea where this squadron was based nor even where in all of France it was but no doubt he would be told in due course.

Neither of the lads were in good humour and left the Six Bells earlier than usual making their way back to Dell's Meadow in almost complete silence as their thoughts wandered together the paths of uncertainty.

"I've enjoyed my leave so much I never gave a thought to having to return."

Tommy broke the silence wistfully, "It's come as a bit of a blow to have to think about the Army and the bloody war again!"

"mmmm," mumbled Charles in reply, reluctant to engage in conversation.

"I've got to report to the Provost Marshall's Office at Gloucester Station on 5[th]June—what about you?" Ventured Tommy afraid that Charles might be travelling on a different day.

"Same!" quipped Charles. His thoughts were with Eira, how he wished he didn't have to break the news to her.

"Oh well," replied a slightly more cheerful Tommy, "At least we'll be travelling together!"

The pair continued in silence once more as Charles tried work out how to tell Eira of his impending return to France and the war without distressing her too deeply.

The whole family had been following events along the Western front in France and had frequently commented on how, try as they might, the Germans had been unable to bring about the fall of Verdun. The City had come to represent the determination and resolve of the French in their resistance to attempts at subjugation by the Imperial German boot.

The family, indeed, everyone in the valley knew that the two had been at Verdun during the earlier gory conflicts and that it was here that both men had been decorated and here that Charles had received his injuries They knew nothing of what Tommy had suffered before meeting Charles nor of his experience in 'no man's land'—that information would never pass the lips of either man!

Charles was feeling vexed, for the life of him he couldn't think of a way of gently breaking the news to Eira. He wouldn't see her now until she finished her rounds and returned the pony and trap to the colliery stables, he would *have* to work out something by then.

There had been rumours at the Six Bells that General Haig was about to open a confrontation with the Germans somewhere along the Somme valley to try to relieve the pressure on the Allies at Verdun by diverting the attention and resources of the Germans further west.

German army advances from the North through Belgium had been swift and had carried them almost to the outskirts of Paris before their supply lines had become overstretched allowing the Allies to thrust them back to a line joining Soissons, Compiegne, Albert and Arras in and around the Somme area. The British first Army was garrisoned here under General Haig so the rumours were not entirely without credibility and it was very possible that Charles and Tommy were being called back at this time to strengthen the numbers that would be needed to undertake such a push.

The need for more foot soldiers in support of any such assault was plain to see but there would be a commensurate need for more medical orderlies to retrieve and tend the victims that would inevitably follow such hostilities. Conscription was now in full force making it necessary for all eligible men to register for duty fit or not and in parallel with this recruiting teams were about daily at home trying to persuade older men to volunteer. Ammunition factories were running at full stretch yet recruiters were even trying to poach *their* men!

Charles broke the news to his Brother as he collected his things from the cottage and bundled them into his kitbag for the long walk to Eira's parents house. Throwing the bag over his shoulder he took leave of Tommy after having agreed to meet him at the station to catch the early train for the return trip to Gloucester. Charles felt irritated that they had only been given two day's notice to return but there it was, this was war!

He had been walking for some twenty or so minutes when he heard the sound of the pony lightly clip-clopping along the track behind him. There were few ponies in the valley and even fewer that ever came this way so he knew almost instinctively that it must be Eira. Stepping to one side he allowed the burdensome kitbag to fall at his side as he turned to watch her approach, her long black tresses flowing on the breeze and undulating in rhythm with the bouncing motion of the trap.

She drew the pony to a halt and at once it turned its head and nudged Charles by way of recognition and greeting. Charles caressed its nose and scratched behind its ear as he had done so many times in the past without even being conscious of the act. His eyes and all his attention were on his treasured Wife. The pony lost interest and diverted its attention to a handful of ants that were scurrying about its feet in search of anything of use to their community.

She looked unblinking at him, her countenance displaying the anxiety that was troubling her; she had called in at the cottage and had been told by Tommy that the pair had received their marching orders. She had set off without delay to catch up with her husband to help him to the house with his kitbag.

"I've got some bad news." Started Charles.

Eira put her fingers to her pursed lips, she could see the consternation in his eyes and could sense that tears might follow.

"I know Charles, you must leave for the war again the day after tomorrow. I've been expecting the news so don't fret, I'm not foolish enough to think that because we're now married the Army will give you up to me!"

She forced a smile which was galaxies away from how she was really feeling but she new that if *she* could be strong they would *both* weather this parting and go forward in faith and in hope.

Charles could sense her inner strength and felt relieved that she was not devastated, he realised that he should have known it would be this way for he had partnered a paragon of British womanhood who lacked nothing of courage, faith and vision for the future. Little wonder then that the Nation he served was so rich in its culture and beliefs!

They held each other tightly and whispered messages of such sweet tenderness and love that they both felt it together. Tethering the pony they made their way to a honeysuckle sweetened glade and there, on Charles Army greatcoat, made perfect and passionate love binding themselves to each other in ecstasy engrossed only in themselves and the child they were would conceive that day.

He climbed the trap to take his seat beside her and as she set the pony to work he suddenly understood that the steadfast, unyielding, uncompromising fairer sex were far, far more likely to influence the direction the future would take than the outcome of any conflict, any battle, or any war!

His chest swelled with pride and admiration for his love of her and for her simple acceptance of him and his inadequacies as a husband that he knew to be far too many.

∇

The parting at the station was more difficult than Charles had ever imagined a parting could be. The recollection of their moments of unbridled passion of a few hours ago had returned to him over and over again and he realised how, in that moment, he had come to see his hearts companion in a different light, had come to love her more deeply that he thought possible, had come to realise that he *never* wanted to be parted from her.

He made up his mind in that moment that somehow he *would* survive the horrors of the war he found himself in, that he would devote himself to his comrades entirely until this thing was done, that he would return to his bride and *never* part from her *ever* again!

The countryside slipped by un–noticed this time. Both men were wrapped up in their own thoughts, their own little kingdoms. There was no first class travel this time, no greetings from the railway hierarchy, just the humdrum passage of mile after mile that increased the separation of the pair from their newfound Arcadian pleasures and drew them inevitably closer to attrition and abject discomfort.

Gloucester station was a hive of activity. Soldiers were everywhere, many of them little more than boys Charles thought as he passed among them and joined the queue that trailed along the platform from the Provost Marshal's Office with Tommy at his side.

"Fredericks? Ah yes." remarked the red hat MP. "Your unit is now attached to the First Army and is billeted West of the town of Albert, here are your orders and your papers!" He thrust out a sheaf of paper all hand written—*"NEXT!"* he barked impatient to clear the queue.

Charles received his orders from an adjacent clerk, he was to report to RFC Headquarters Command at St. Omer well to the northwest of Albert, there he would transported to wherever 46 Squadron happened to be. (Squadrons tended to move according to the day's gains or losses in territory). The two parted company at Boulogne the MP's directing Charles to climb aboard a RFC tender whilst Tommy was despatched with hundreds of other soldiers to join a waiting train. The pair hugged warmly and promised each other they'd keep in touch through letters to Charles' Mother. They parted with a simple handshake and a vow to meet up again when all this was over!

Amidst the confusion of the hustle and bustle at the clearing yard, the parting was short but heartfelt. Neither lad wanted to prolong the farewell and so were gone before each felt the sting of separation bite into their hearts, they had become closer than any Brother, but it was not all over yet!

▽

The tender bounced its way along the main road from Boulogne to St Omer without a break. The two other occupants were both subalterns and clearly well to do excluding Charles from their animated chatting almost as soon as they had all mounted up. They talked passionately about hunting to hounds and flying and it was obvious to Charles that they had been at school together and had volunteered in response to a visit by a recovering pilot on leave after being shot down. From the conversation it was clear that the pilot had also attended the same school but had lost his enthusiasm for the horrors of aerial combat after having watched several young men perish at his hands, one of them screaming to earth in a pyre of fiercely blazing matchwood. He was called an 'ace'.

The two young and inexperienced subalterns claimed they 'couldn't wait' to emulate the successes of their 'ace'.

St Omer was a charming town built on the gently sloping side of a hill. The airfield and Command Headquarters, was a few miles to its Southwest and was served by an adequately paved road which the tender now trundled up halting at the gates to be identified before proceeding to the Adjutant's Office.

The air was filled with the sound of aero engines either being run up for test or being run up in aircraft before departure to the squadrons as allocated replacements. One of the functions of this large headquarters base was to assemble aircraft shipped in from blighty and despatch them to duty at the numerous airfields along the Western front.

"Ah yes—Jenkins!" The Adjutant exclaimed, "You're just in time. 46 Squadron are to the Southwest of Arras at a field called 'Izel-les-Hameaux'—charming little place—served there myself before Gerry over-ran it and I copped it in the leg." He tapped his pipe against his wooden limb. "Still, we've got it back again now though it's a bit churned up! Arras is a bloody ruin—nothing there but rubble but you'll find the village at Izel very friendly—good wine and nice people too!" He looked at Charles with steady, sad eyes and noticed his medal ribbon.

"Good God man, you've got the latest bloody bravery gong—stout fellow! You're just the sort of chap we need—done much flying?"

"None at all Sir." Ventured Charles wondering what on earth all this was leading up to.

"Oh well, no matter, you're just about to old chap!" Quipped the Officer,

"Get your kitbag over to the quartermaster and he'll arrange for it to go by transport to Izel then meet me here and I'll take you to the crate you'll be flying in, don't be long, it'll be dark soon and you need to be down whilst the pilot can still see the ground or the return to earth might be a bit exciting!"

Charles felt disheartened by this news, he had never been *near* an aeroplane in his life, had never even been close to one let alone *fly* in one and here is this mad Officer suggesting in casual 'matter-of-fact' terms that they might crash!

The quartermaster looked at the order that Charles had relayed from the adjutant, sniffed, took the kitbag and handed Charles a long leather overcoat, regulation scarf and gauntlets and a leather flying helmet with goggles, Charles almost passed out!

His knees had started to knock by the time he returned to the adjutant and he had taken to pressing them tightly together to stop them sounding like two coconuts banging together when he was standing still. This in turn only served to put pressure on his bladder which was now screaming for relief.

He began to wish he were in the trenches—at least that was something he understood and although it was unpleasant he could deal with it, now he was to be propelled into the unknown and he would be flying *toward* the bloody Gerries!

The 'plane he was to fly in looked as if it had been left behind by the Romans and very likely designed by the Wright Brothers, it took on all the similarities of a large bicycle as he approached it but didn't look as strong. There was a large open basket shaped blister at the front with a machine gun set on a large curved rail and a wicker seat with a leather belt on a rope. The pilot sat behind and slightly higher up under the upper wing, there were wires everywhere and the centre of the fuselage looked at if it had been shot away ages ago and no-one had bothered to patch it up!

Charles felt even more disheartened but consoled himself with the thought that there wasn't much for a German fighter to shoot at and anyway, they would probably think it wasn't worth shooting down—leave it alone and it would probably fall out of the sky on its own!

The pilot looked to be no more than fifteen years old, Charles determined he would not ask what experience the boy had on the grounds that the answer might be less than fortifying!

The pilot shook hands with Charles and briefed him on the emergency procedure in the event of a forced landing which, in essence, amounted to 'Don't jump out until the aircraft is close to the ground and don't forget to undo your safety belt or you'll get towed along which might spoil your boots!'

The pilot went on; "The safety belt goes around your waist and the rope attached to it will allow you to stand up so that you can shoot *down* on a Gerry a/c if we get close enough."

The 'plane didn't appeal to Charles as something that would have the ability to get above anything but what did *he* know?

It seemed that the pilot had been given some important despatches to deliver to 46 squadron command regarding an impending imminent movement to be executed at that section of the front. The Adjutant at St Omer had decided to add Charles to the flight knowing that the regular squadron medical orderly was incapacitated with dysentery and that, if a push was about to be initiated, the squadron would need him urgently.

Charles climbed in the front as he had been instructed being extra careful not to put his feet through the flimsy floor. A strong odour of gun oil seemed to have pervaded the whole space and was somewhat overpowering, perhaps it would become less noticeable once they started moving he thought.

The boy pilot climbed into his seat and tapped Charles on the shoulder,

"If I tap your right shoulder it means there's Gerry on the right, if I tap your left it means he'll be on the left!" There was a brief silence before he added with a wicked grin,

"If I don't tap your shoulder at all it means I've probably jumped out!"

Charles' heart was in his mouth. Several times in his life he had wished he was *anywhere* but here; his wish had now assumed a whole new meaning.

'I think he expects me to shoot this bloody gun!' Charles mumbled but dismissed the thought as fanciful and re-focussed his attention on worrying.

The radial engine behind the pilot was hand cranked into life by one of the ground crew spewing dense clouds of foul smelling smoke and the odd flame from the exhaust, it did nothing to bolster Charles confidence in the machine.

Wheel chocks were pulled by yet another ground crew member and the contraption started forward but was arrested by men hanging onto the wings, the pilot gave a thumbs up signal to the ground chief and the wing walkers steered the 'plane away from the hangars and other parked flying contraptions to a space clear of obstructions. Here they chocked it again and with several men draped over the tail the pilot tested the engine to full power. There was an immediate deafening increase in engine roar but it must be said that Charles didn't notice much by way of any more wind being generated.

The pilot seemed to be satisfied anyway and signalled to be released by his helpers whereupon the craft gathered speed slowly and had soon reached a slow walking pace! The throttle was opened wide accompanied by some backfiring and more smoke before the full ear-splitting roar was once again evident. Charles was being bumped around fearfully in the front as the flying machine gained speed, soon they would be at a fast walking pace! Charles sank as far back in his seat as the basket would let him as the hedge at the far end of the field became alarmingly apparent, it occurred to him that if they hit it he would go through it whilst the pilot would pass over the top. He shut his eyes.

The bumping suddenly stopped. Charles opened one eye to find the hedge twenty feet below, 'my God' he thought ecstatically, 'we're actually bloody airborne!' The sense of relief he experienced was immeasurable.

The sensation of flying freely through the air was exhilarating, he couldn't compare it with anything he had ever done before, it was so smooth and the wind whistling through the wires and various holes in the fabric covering gave the aeroplane a personality all of its own. They gained height steadily travelling with the sun at their backs, the landscape below had taken on unfamiliar shapes and hues and was laid out in a manner never before experienced by Charles. He could see roads bordered by hedges, crops in fields, animals grazing, houses, churches, schools, pools, ponds, rivers and here and there concentrations of pock marked ground laid bare by gunfire. These concentrations grew in number as they progressed toward their destination until there was nothing but craters and decimated derelict settlements, they were nearing the battle front!

Charles started sweeping the sky all around them as he had been told, they were now within reach of enemy fighters! Almost dead ahead and slightly on his right he could see several seagulls wheeling around as if chasing each other. He watched them and wondered why they didn't seem to get any closer, that's when the pilot tapped him on the right shoulder and motioned vigorously in their direction, at the same time the seagulls turned towards them.

Charles gulped and cocked the machine gun in readiness just as he had been shown. He had never shot a gun in his life and he certainly didn't want to shoot one at another human! He could see now that there were four aeroplanes all bi-planes and all the same, he watched spell bound as they zoomed by at high speed the black Imperial German crosses clearly visible on their wings and sides. Swivelling his head to follow them he saw the leader peel off and turn sharply back in their direction, he turned to point to the lone aircraft just as the pilot stuffed the nose down almost catapulting him upwards out of the gun bay. Clinging to the sides of the 'plane so hard his knuckles turned white Charles slumped into the bottom of the basket and felt he was being pushed through the floor of the gun bay, as the pilot hauled back on the joystick with both hands forcing the aeroplane in a tight turn towards the invader, he felt a thump on the back of his head. Turning he could see that the pilot was making frantic squeezing gestures and pointing to the gun.

Snapping into action he aligned the sights with the rapidly closing attacker, the penny in his pocket was warming! Closing his eyes he squeezed the trigger.

Rat-tat-tat-tat-tat the gun cracked off jumping all over the place. Charles opened his eyes and the German had gone.

He swivelled left then right, looked up and down but there was no sign of him. The penny got warmer warning Charles that the adversary was still in the chase, Rat-tat-tat-tat came the staccato stutter of machine gun fire again but this time not from Charles' gun. The attacker was coming up from behind them where he knew he couldn't be shot at. The boy pilot shut the throttle and simultaneously hauled the aircraft into a vertical turn as the surprised German slipped by beneath unable to kill his speed or manoeuvre as quickly, converting the turn to a dive the flimsy plane fell headlong at the hapless Gerry as the penny tried to burn its way to freedom.

Without being conscious of it Charles felt irresistibly compelled to squeeze the trigger again and held it tightly, fingers locked, as the machine gun bullets ripped along the length of the Albatross beneath him, he hadn't even taken aim!

Smoke and a streaky black film appeared from the engine as the craft peeled away in the direction of the ground below rolling slowly on to one wing as the nose fell.

Charles watched in horror as it broke into a spin, winding away turn after turn leaving a plume of curling black smoke to mark its path to inevitable destruction! He felt devastated, he had taken a human life!

His pilot wheeled the aircraft in search of the remaining attackers but Charles was unable to divert his attention from the sight of the stricken German 'plane now falling like a liberated sycamore seed, he was disgusted with himself and reviled the action that had led him to not only pull but *hold* the trigger whilst bullets tore into what was, in that moment, a defenceless adversary!

His revulsion with himself gave way instantly to joy as he observed the human bundle separate from the doomed aircraft and take form below the most beautiful silk parasol he had ever seen!

With a sense of overwhelming relief Charles snapped back to the present and joined the search for the other Germans but it seemed they had disappeared. His pilot was to explain later that this frequently occurred in aerial combat, aeroplanes just seem to appear and just as suddenly disappear, the trick was to be alert for the first evidence of them.

Charles thought how ironic it was that the lack of speed that had initially caused him alarm permitted the extreme manoeuvrability of this flying contraption and had been instrumental in saving the lives of both men. The 'bag' had perhaps been the result of sheer luck but who knows, could the devil's trinket have influenced the outcome? Charles shuddered involuntarily as he recalled the coin's almost animated behaviour during the short skirmish with the foe.

As if from nowhere, three flying machines appeared on the right of them giving Charles a violent start, he jumped for the machine gun handles and was about to cock the firing mechanism when he felt another thump on the back of his helmet. Snapping his head around in curiosity at this interference he was surprised to see the pilot shaking his head and pointing animatedly at their company, swivelling his head to the craft now close in formation he could clearly see that they wore the roundel markers of British aircraft, *that* was why their earlier adversaries had dispersed.

He watched them in spellbound fascination as they held their distance skilfully in echelon at their side with enviable precision. It would have been difficult not to notice the black streaks of oil that had emanated from the engines and were creeping along the side of the fuselages and had somehow managed to deposit themselves on the pilots faces. The closest pilot to him grinned nodding his approval at Charles' success and immediately took on the semblance of someone from the black and white minstrel show as his beautifully white teeth and pink gums stood out in stark contrast to his oil blackened face!

Their escort remained with them, they had been returning from a routine sortie and had encountered no enemy aircraft themselves until setting out to return to Izel-les-Hamaeux when they had seen the German Albatross formation set upon the 'Gun-bus' as it was affectionately known. The gun bus was a 1914 design aeroplane that came into service as a fighter in 1915. It had proved unpopular in combat but was still used as an observation platform from time to time to report enemy activity such as troop concentrations and movements. Its slow speed was ideal for this but made it prone to attack from small arms fire from the ground so it wasn't very popular with its crews except when used to carry orders between squadrons such as this one was doing.

The engine suddenly went quiet, quiet that is when compared to the roar it had been making for the last hour and a half. Charles turned to see what this new development meant, the pilot was jerking a gloved finger in the direction of the ground below. Looking over the side

Charles couldn't make out what he was supposed to be seeing so turned to the pilot again shrugging his shoulders in a gesture of puzzlement. The pilot held out his gloved hand in a flat attitude and slowly pushed it down, Charles immediately realised they were about to land.

Looking over the side again, all he could see was open fields and trees that had been stripped and scarred by gunfire. The only predominant features were mounds of displaced earth with a trench or two still discernible here and there, where the *hell* were they going to set this beast down?

The aircraft wheeled slowly and continuously to the left effecting a complete reversal of direction and as the wings levelled, the nose went down a little further. From the five hundred feet that they now had above the ground Charles could make out a large clear field with an air sock and hangars to one side. Behind the hangars were wooden mess huts, several of them. Their appearance suggested they had once been chicken houses or something of that nature!

The ground seemed to be rushing at them at a thousand miles an hour, he gulped again and wondered whether he should shut his eyes, instead he pulled his strap tighter.

With a couple of solid bumps they were down and trundling toward the hangers, Charles relaxed, it hadn't been so bad after all—just a whole lot of new and terrifying experiences condensed into too short a space of time!

Their escort, the three 46 squadron Camels, landed neatly together and made their way to their waiting ground crews at the hangar apron shutting down their engines before they rolled to stop just feet from the expectant airmen.

Charles considered that they were either very used to this drill or very stupid, it would not be long before he learned that the whole process was an amalgam!

The black faced pilots sprang from their machines as a jockey would from a horse and strode over to the gun bus grinning like fools. The taller of the three pilots, a Captain and without doubt the leader, remarked enthusiastically.

"I say you chaps, jolly good bag that—watched you fool that Gerry into early retirement what?"

The boy pilot returned a warm smile and replied, "We were lucky to get enough bloody speed in the dive to fool the Hun into opening his throttle to catch us, that gave us enough energy to pull off a zoom over him so he couldn't help passing through underneath. The sharp shooting was from this chap." He jerked a thumb at the silent Charles.

"Don't know about passing underneath old bean," the Camel pilot giggled, "I'll bet that kraut was passing bloody water!"

The group laughed as the pilot addressed Charles,

"See you have a Military Medal old fruit, not seen you around before, are you on temp. loan or something?"

"No sir." replied Charles drawing himself to attention. "I'm here to take up duty as one of your medical orderlies!"

"Medical orderly?" Quizzed the flyer in astonishment, "D'You mean you're not *aircrew?"*

"Medical." Repeated Charles.

"What the bloody hell were you doing acting as gunner then? Not that you weren't impressive at it so to speak, Christ we could use more like you, fast as we get replacements Gerry goes and bloody wings 'em!"

"Not my cup of tea at all I'm afraid Sir, I'm better trained to take bullets *out* of people than put them *in*!"

"I'll be damned!" Exhorted the flyer, "Small wonder you have such a fine decoration old thing!"

He placed a friendly hand on Charles' shoulder and continued,

"Sorry we've got to leave you—must go and wash up—we're on the late patrol tomorrow so perhaps we could meet up after dinner and crack a bottle of bubbly in the hangar to celebrate your bag—what?"

"Yes Sir!" Charles concurred though not wholly in accord with the notion.

The gun-bus pilot shook Charles' and with a smile of genuine admiration added,

"Well done Corporal, not everyone could pull off what you did today, between us we got a Gerry 'plane that won't be able to shoot up our lads anymore. Look forward to meeting up with you later!"

Charles thought about this remark and felt a little better about the outcome of the encounter, after all, the German pilot had survived. He got to thinking about how the German had been able to escape thanks to the insistence of his superiors within German High Command that had decreed that all aircrew must be issued with the means of escape from stricken aircraft.

It was not so in the Royal Flying Corps, here the High Command considered that the wearing of parachutes might encourage aircrew to abandon an aircraft that might otherwise have been saved. The horrific result of this policy had been all too clear as crews were forced to witness their colleagues perish in 'flamers'—burning aeroplanes from which there was no escape to safety. Rather than suffer the slow and abject agony of burning to death, many such wretched aircrew had resorted to jumping over the side to meet their demise. Falling, falling, falling silently, until they had passed from the sight of men and their names had become whispers in the past!

CHAPTER 12

Arrival at the Squadron

C HARLES REPORTED TO THE Adjutant and filled in the myriad of 'Men Joining' forms before taking himself to the Airmen's mess. Here he located his camp bed and foot locker before repairing to the ablutions block for a good sluice down in the makeshift shower, so far he hadn't seen hide nor hair of any other airmen and wondered where in hell everyone was!

Arriving at the mess hall the answer became immediately obvious for the place was a hive of ravenous jackals all feeding their faces. He joined the dwindling Queue at the servery and picked up a warm plate from the stack that had been placed at the start of the extended single, scrubbed wooden table that contained this evening's fare of culinary delights.

Shuffling along the line he received a huge dollop of coarse, semi smashed potato from the first 'cook', a small mountain of mixed cabbage and carrot, a slice of bully beef from the next and from the last 'cook' in the line a scoop of thick, lumpy gravy that very closely resembled trench mud!

"want puddin'?" asked the last cook.

"What is it?" enquired the reticent Charles, uncertain whether his constitution would be able to cope with the digestion of what he had already received let alone a military pudding!

"Spotted dick!" came the surly response.

"No!" exclaimed Charles firmly.

"No *what* mate?"

The 'cook' was clearly seeking a platitude.

"No bloody fear!" said Charles smiling and managed to wrench a chuckle from the server.

The repast lay so heavily on Charles as he made his way back to the mess hut that he decided to have forty winks whilst his body dealt with the ingestion of the gastronomic uncertainty he had just absorbed.

The hut was now a hive of activity as its occupants made ready to invade the village a mile or two away to take wine at the several Cafes and make sheep's eyes at whatever females happened along!

Charles made his way quiet as he could to his camp bed preferring to rest before introducing himself, he felt very, very tired.

"Whato mate!" exclaimed an airman donning his tunic at the adjoining billet, "Where'd *you* come from?"

"Joined an hour or so ago, name's Charles Jenkins."

"Welcome to the pit mate, can't stop now, see you later—name's John."

The airmen piled out of the hut as one leaving it to Charles and total silence.

Charles flopped onto his camp bed and was asleep almost as his head reached the pillow.

He awoke in complete darkness to the sound of a fearful commotion at the wooden steps that led up into the hut. He had never heard such a string of vociferously expressed expletives in all his life yet he had worked shoulder to shoulder with simple, uneducated men who were prone to using a coarse expression or two!

"Good God!" He exclaimed out loud and immediately wished he hadn't. The commotion ceased.

"You in there Corp-oarawall?" Shrieked a familiar voice to the accompaniment of a chorus of chortles.

Charles kept silent, it was the boy pilot and his compatriots and from the sound of the confusion beyond the door they were flying high but not in aeroplanes!

'Oh bugger' thought Charles realising belatedly that it would have been better if he'd kept quiet when awoken.

"Coar—per—*rawl!*" Bawled a half-dozen voices in unison, "Come out, come out *wherever* you are!" a small pause and then,

"Few don't come out, we're coming *in!*"

"Oh *bugger!*" muttered Charles as he swung his legs over the side of his cot, again he wished he'd kept his mouth shut.

He threw on his tunic buttoning it up to the neck as he made his way tentatively to the hut door.

"Who is it?" he enquired stepping through the doorway pretending he didn't know, he had no idea why he'd done that.

"Come on corpril." muttered the boy pilot throwing an arm around his neck,

"We're taking you into town to cebrilate our combined good fortune, no, *five*tune!" he announced. Turning his companions he gesticulated drunkenly, "Shot down a bloody Gerry you know!"

"Piss off you clot!" someone remarked ungenerously.

Charles couldn't help thinking that they'd be better off going to bed to rest in readiness for their flying operations tomorrow but these were officers so they *should* know what they were doing!

The boy pilot held out the long leather Sidcot that Charles had worn when manning the gun-bus saying,

"Put this on old chum, that way no-one will know you aren't aircrew and you can pretend to be an Occifer like us!"

The group set off with Charles in tow over the field towards the village at Izel-les-Hameau Charles sober and steady, his companions stumbling and more than a little erratic in gait as they puffed and wheezed their way over the rough ground.

Most of the establishments in the village were dimly lit, electric light being used very sparingly in these harsh economic times. In customary French manner the furniture for the benefit of patrons spilled into the unlit street to better accommodate the frequent invasions of large numbers of service personnel.

There seemed to be no lack of food and drink despite the war and the French waiters appeared jovial, amenable and surprisingly hospitable.

As the group rolled its way through the street and passed restaurant after restaurant seeking the bar that the Officers had adopted as their own, Charles found himself amazed at the variety of sumptuous looking meat and vegetables that the soldiers were tucking into. Music spilled from accordion players wandering between bars hopeful of picking up a few coins for their renderings and perhaps, occasionally, the odd tot of calvados. Had it not been for the distant rumble of gunfire, it would have been difficult to comprehend that there was a war raging in the trenches not so far away!

It was the first time Charles had tasted Champagne; until now his social drinking had been limited to the heavy malt taste of cask brewed ale—the difference was something of a shock to him. His hosts had insisted upon it however and refused to accept any kind of contribution toward its cost.

The dissimilarity that Charles had failed to grasp however was in the *strength* of the beverage which took him completely by surprise. The effect of the much stronger fluidin had completely conquered his shy nature to the point where he found himself telling raucous jokes and recounting funny stories to the appreciation and entire merriment of his companions.

The evening wore away in pleasantries as the young men exchanged vivid and heartfelt memories of their home towns and upbringing and it didn't seem to matter to the Officers, who had all been sired and raised in relative comfort, that their guest was a straightforward lad of meagre beginnings and poor academic tutelage.

One of the Officers, overcome by the lateness of the hour and copious drafts of champagne, had placed his long brown uniform boots on a chair before him and had submitted to the enticements of the sand man. His companions smiled their understanding of his demise and were about to order yet another bottle of bubbly when the peace of the evening was shattered by the sound of trench whistles blowing, a sound that Charles was well accustomed to hearing but which was completely alien to the fliers. The officers looked one to the other in astonishment.

"Must be a bloody push on!" exclaimed Charles in reluctant recognition, he knew at once that the evening's frivolities were at an end.

"What d'you mean old chap?"

"They always blow bloody whistles when they want you to do something bloody dangerous—there's a bloody push on!" Charles ejaculated, "Heard it hundreds of times!"

"Who's bloody push, ours or theirs?" enquired the voice again.

"Don't matter—they always blow bloody whistles and we find out which way we're supposed to go by watching which way the others are running!"

A Scammel tender groaned its way up in the street, its radiator boiling as they always seemed to do. Military Police stood on the open platform at the rear and were bellowing orders to all who were close enough to hear.

"Back to camp you lot—AT THE DOUBLE—all leave is cancelled. Anyone not reported back at camp one hour from now will be treated as a DESERTER!"

The announcement was punctuated with yet more blasts on the trench whistle then repeated ad hoc as the tender trundled its way through the village repeating the process all over again. Officers were not included in such orders but on hearing them were expected to repair to base for instructions with all haste.

The slumbering aviator needed something resembling an earthquake to rouse him but finally rejoined his companions in an insensible stupor as they set off in the direction of the airfield. It became clear to Charles at once that, although these men were good navigators in the air, they hadn't the slightest notion of where the airfield was now.

"This way—follow me!" He suggested and was surprised at how, with relief and good grace, they did so!

The airfield was alive with activity as the group rolled through the gate and past the Guard House.

"What's afoot?" One of the company enquired of the guard Corporal as they shuffled their way along. The Corporal snapped smartly to attention and saluted the enquirer.

"There's to be a new assault Sir, beginning in the early hours and every man will be needed—it's the biggest push the allies have made yet and they say it could end the war!"

"Bloody good job too!" muttered the almost lucid enquirer. "Not sure if my allowance can stand much more of these frightful Champagne binges!"

The Corporal watched the dishevelled group shuffle off wondering how on earth they would be fit to fly in the looming conflict. He shook his head in disdain and turned his attention to the streams of returning soldiers, barking orders at them to sharpen up 'and look quick about it!'

Charles knew that he would be better off not even trying to sleep, he knew that there would be work for him aplenty in the hours to come and that the quickest route to a clear head was to keep moving and drink lots of coffee. Slowed by the muddling effects of too much alcohol he put fatigue behind him and busied himself with preparing stretchers and the medical kit that he and his contemporaries would be sure to need whatever the outcome of the approaching encounter. He felt glad that he wasn't in the shoes of the fliers knowing that they would somehow have to clear their heads of the remains of the champagne, fly a machine that was intrinsic in its lack of stability and obedience and wanton in its aerial behaviour to face an enemy as determined on the ground as in the air to see them perish.

He downed enough coffee to float a canoe that night and was feeling more or less over the effects of the champagne as he witnessed the first fingers of dawn creeping over the dew moistened grass airfield. The air was fresh and reviving on his nostrils sweetened by the fragrance of dew on grass reminding him of the early morning walks to the mint.

My God, had he *ever* done that?

The airfield sprang to life as mechanics began pushing flimsy aeroplanes from hangars and lining them up in good order for wily sergeants to inspect and approve as fit for flight. As soon as they had been ranged and chocked in position, armourers set about crawling all over them hanging bombs, fitting gun belts and drums of ammunition. The order was out that every aircraft must engage the enemy that day, they were to carry more munitions than they were ever designed to tote. The Generals were determined to deliver maximum destruction to their unseen adversaries in the shortest possible time, thus denying them the opportunity to prepare for, or respond to, the onslaught.

The lack of power from those small early engines and the added weight of extra munitions would combine to produce yet more instability for the unfortunate young pilots to contend with. The Hierarchy knew nothing of nor gave a toss for the problems of the aircraft or the safety of the unfortunate boys that would fly them! *'C'Est la Vie et C'Est le Guerre!' 'Pour le Royaumme mon brave!*

At a single stroke, every gun in the combined allied artillery battalions let forth together, smashing the night sky and the peace of the opening day. It was evident that all hell was being released in a cacophony of conflagration and ear splitting resonance underscored by lightning-like flashes that dominated the early morning piercing the blackness of the night and bathing the faces of onlookers in a ghostly silver hue as they paused to take in the awesome power of this new offensive.

"This is gonna be a big one, my oath it is!" exclaimed one of the mechanics, "Just look at them gun flashes—they're stretching for mile after mile along the front as far as the eye can see!"

"Yeah!, I pity the poor krauts on the other end of it, there won't be too many places to hide with all *that* lot coming at 'em!"

"It's not just the big guns—Kitchener's chuckin' *everything* in!"

"Yeah! He means business that's for sure—just hope the brass know what their doing this time!"

The onlookers fell silent, robbed of conversation by the noise and the spectacle before them, they watched the night sky respond to the overwhelming power of the muzzle flashes. Although just a few moments into the offensive the men had already accepted the horrendous din and had begun to close their minds to it.

The penny that had lain dormant in Charles' pocket began to wake once more as the prospect of human suffering edged towards reality. Charles became mindful of its evil presence and wished he could rid himself of its all consuming power but he knew that he had not the mental fortitude to dispense with it, he had already tried and failed—the hold that it had over him had long since become absolute! He thrust its presence from his thoughts and set about his work with renewed vigour, but the Devil's coin was not going to be so easily ignored!

The young pilots made their way to their mounts without enthusiasm or visible emotion, they were fully aware that many of them would not return from the foray they were about to set out upon. Each young man knew only too well that many of his kind would not return that day and prayed to whatever God he placed his faith in that it would not be him!

Those 'fellows well met' that had been with Charles the night before had taken just a few hours of rest and precious little sleep but to all outward appearances seemed to have surmounted the effects of the champagne binge—or perhaps had learned the secret of concealing them, for they looked quite fresh and alert.

One by one propellers were hand swung and engines spluttered to life, more clouds of dense, acrid smelling smoke fouled the air as they did so. One by one aircraft taxied to the runway, formed themselves into squadron groups and took off in close formation.

Six groups of aeroplanes formed the assault force that morning; each group comprised six hulls made up of four single seat fighters and a pair of two seat fighter-bombers. The groups departed in steady order, each so heavily laden with armaments that the entire length of runway was needed to get them into the air.

All the while Allied guns maintained their offensive, they continued even as their own aircraft turned to close upon the enemy from the flanks. It would be something of a miracle if they got through without some of them being hit by shells from their own side! Somehow those raw pilots pressed their attack through and delivered bombs that were calculated to silence the enemy and give the already advancing infantry a chance to take territory the allied hierarchy had set their sights on.

Even as they ran the gauntlet of enemy anti aircraft gunfire, (known by all as 'Archie') and the deadly splinter fragments they threw out, machine guns and small arms bullets from the defending trenches ripped into the wood and fabric structures severing wires and peppering control surfaces. Intrepid flyers struggled to penetrate the fiercest anti aircraft barrage that had ever been encountered. Aircraft fell stricken from the blood coloured dawning sky one after another in smoking, flaming, spiralling palls of helpless, hapless futility. Flying machines transformed into coffins of a another kind whilst the power in the Devil's penny ascended feasting upon the horror of the endless carnage.

Charles felt sickened.

He could sense the presence of the devil's talisman and feel the aura of evil that emanated from it as it became enlivened by wretched souls tumbling to their ultimate destiny, he would need no report from mortals to tell him how the conflict was upon that day! Charles descended into consuming depression as he thought of the sacrifices he knew were being made at the front and contemplated with deep sadness and regret the fate of those he could not see.

He detested the realisation that he was safe and unthreatened in the remoteness of the airfield whilst men were bleeding to death from wounds that would not be attended for lack of trained medics. Pleas for help and cries of anguish would pass unheard. Memories of better days, of sunny afternoons, lazy days of cricket and long walks and dearly loved families and friends would pass into the mists of time as weary fingers let slip the tenuous grip that had held so long, so dear, so resolutely to a once strong but now fading life.

Charles, disgusted by his situation and his association with the devil's coin, thrust his hand into his inner pocket and grasped the evil trinket between two fingers with the full intention of ridding himself of its influence once and for all. He removed it from the pocket, drew back his arm and made to throw the coin from him in an act of helpless desperation but even as he released his grip upon it the coin remained fixed in his fingers like sticky toffee paper. His arm fell to his side in abject resignation as he resigned himself to the certain knowledge that he was no longer the custodian of the coin. The coin had become the custodian of him!

He resolved to accept his lot and do whatever he could to confound the coin, to cheat it of its evil need of malevolence, suffering and the forfeiture of human life wherever he could.

He could see that the coin had become much more than the devil's token, that its influence, its embodiment, its *power* emanated from the devil *himself!* Colour drained from his cheeks as this new revelation sank in. In desperation he let his mind flash back to the recent carefree moments he had spent with his bride. To the long pleasant walks they had taken in the forest surrounding his Mother's house and to the frequent embraces he yearned for but could no longer be sure he would ever enjoy again.

The distant hum of what he knew were aircraft returning diverted his mood from self pity to alertness lending strength to his sagging spirit. Drawn back to the present he realised that he had been standing outside for the entire duration of the sortie and was more than a little cold from the early morning damp.

'Too late for that hot cuppa now!' He mumbled to himself beating his arms across his chest and stamping his feet to restore circulation and vigour to his stiffened muscles. 'Better get the medics together!'

As he started in the direction of the mess huts there came an ear splitting, colossal '***thump***' close by and behind. Flying tufts of earth and grass smacked into Charles bowling him over, he knew without thinking that it was the blast from an exploding bomb and was at once taken aback by this truly unexpected occurrence. He stood up and shook himself but even as he battled to figure out what was happening there came a second and a third explosion in close order. The 'stand to' siren began its warning wail; senior NCO's dashed here and there blowing whistles and directing everyone to take cover—the airfield that had despatched aircraft to harass the enemy was itself under attack!

It was clear that the marauders were bent on exacting revenge on the allies and intended to do so by denying the returning aircraft a place to land and replenish.

The noise of the attack became deafening as the enemy aircraft swept at low level over the unprepared airfield. Fighters with clearly visible black imperial crosses on white backgrounds machine gunned everything and everyone they could bring their weapons to bear upon whilst the bombers turned their attention to the hangars and the large circular field that was the landing area. There seemed to be enemy aircraft everywhere. The foe had even commissioned long outdated machines pressed into service from retirement and loaded with hand held bombs that were even now being thrown over the side by the pilots! There seemed to be *hundreds* of them! Zooming and weaving to miss each other as well as the small arms fire that was being unleashed from soldiers on the ground in a attempt at defence against this unexpected reprisal!

The onslaught came to an end almost as abruptly as it had began, one by one, each of the raiders ran out of ammunition. Retreating engines grew quieter akin to the sound of bees departing to form a new colony.

Scruffy soldiers emerged from cover to stand in horrified silence gawping at the destruction before them. Hardly a building had been left undamaged and two of the most important hangars were blazing from end to end. At the far end of one of them and very close to it was the ammunition dump, a concrete covered structure in the shape of an arch with its two sides enclosed by corrugated steel sheets that were sound enough to the eye but not designed to withstand the heat from the blazing hangar that they were now being subjected to.

"Get a bloody move on you lot!" Barked the Sergeant Major at the idle men,

"Get over to the ammo dump and start shifting the ammo!"

The men leapt into action and made toward the dump—if the ammo went up there'd be nothing to fight *or* defend themselves with and Gerry could come back and pick them all off at will.

The men formed themselves into three human chains side by side and literally threw the ammunition from one man to the next, each aware that if they didn't get the job done quickly, they would *all* perish from what would be an eruption of giant proportions. Few, if any, would survive.

Those at the head of the chain removing the ordnance that was closest to the burning hangar, became exhausted quickly and had to be relieved every few minutes by men from outside. The searing heat being radiated from the corrugated steel wall baked their bodies making it almost impossible to breathe, quickly sucking strength and the will from them.

Searing hot ammunition scorched unprotected hands and raised fear among all that the unstable explosives might self detonate and wipe out the entire crew. Several tons of ordnance was moved to the relative safety of open storage in what seemed like an eternity of time yet in reality had taken no more than a handful of minutes. The station fire crew, absent when most needed, arrived with their ancient Thorneycroft fire engine and set about dousing the ordnance and the men transporting it with copious drafts of freezing cold water!

"Bloody marvellous isn't it!" Quipped one of the more vocal of the chain,

"We just get to the end of movin' the ammo' and the bloody fire jacks show up and drench us!"

Men sagged exhausted to the ground but took heart and jumped to their feet as the little NAAFI refreshments van arrived with scalding hot tea and toast—not so much for the refreshment, which was welcome enough, but for the arrival of the starched white apron clad lasses that would serve them. A smile from a cheery female was a tonic that few of them would want to miss.

Charles had not been idle.

Throughout the fracas brought about by the aftermath of the inferno of burning buildings and movement of the munitions, he had led his small band of medics in the rescue and treatment of the wounded and injured. The station had been allocated a single Doctor, a very young second lieutenant fresh from College and of extremely limited experience. He had been appointed to the air station principally because it was not expected that he would be called upon to do much more than tend the sick bay with its daily parade of coughs, colds and minor ailments.

The shock of seeing so many men with torn bodies and missing limbs had been too much for him to deal with and had it not been for Charles more than one man would have perished in the aftermath of the attack.

For Charles, the situation had seemed like an image of the colliery incident except that this time he knew how to cope with amputations and the dressing of injuries with skill and determination without faltering nor pausing to take in the enormity of the task he was undertaking. Some of the men in his team were very young and inexperienced but under his guidance and solid example they rallied, coped and held on to their stomachs. The surgeon stood aside and watched Charles dismayed by his own lack of tenacity and overshadowed by the competence and dexterity of the corporal before him as he moved swiftly from one casualty to another advising subordinates of the procedures needed, sewing torn flesh, releasing and re-applying tourniquets, administering morphine and shrouding the fallen.

Through those moments of personal despair and feelings of inadequacy, the surgeon was learning about war, about courage and about himself!

He shook himself from his apathy and closed to Charles' side.

"L-Look here old chap" he stammered. "Sorry to have been so useless to you just now—bit outside my experience you know but I'm ready to try now—what would you like me to do?"

Charles looked at this boy of an Officer and saw something in his eyes that he had seen in no man—genuine remorse and self loathing, his heart went out to him.

"I've left several amputations because of the need to attend the men with the best chance to live Sir will you help me with those?"

The surgeon turned pale and replied thinly,

"Y-Yes of course—you will help won't you?"

Charles nodded, "Come on Sir, let's get to it!"

One by one the pair moved from man to man for there were many of them, most were sedated with morphine that Charles and his helpers had administered but some were writhing in agony and had lost far too much blood. One by one limbs that could not be saved were removed and the soldiers made as comfortable as possible and as each man was attended to the surgeon grew in confidence and competency.

The last casualty was the most serious of all. His left leg had suffered compound fractures caused by an explosion at close quarters, fractures that had penetrated the skin and which extended so far up as to have smashed the hip. The medics had tried to apply a tourniquet without real effect and pressure pads that had been applied to the area around the hip were barely doing the job of stemming blood loss.

With great care Charles eased the pressure pads from the hip and what he saw caused him to recoil. That the leg would have to come off was not an issue—it was plainly obvious—but what **on earth** could be done with this ghastly hip?

He turned to the surgeon and started to shake his head, there was little that could be done to save this man. Feelings, overwhelming feelings of regret remorse, and sadness flooded through his breast and his eyes began to cloud—he had never faced certain failure before.

What happened next was a lesson to Charles that he would *never* forget. A lesson that taught him that no matter *how* desperate a situation might seem there is *always* hope so long as there is *faith!*"

The young surgeon, the same fellow who had been dumbstruck when first faced with adversity, now concentrated his mind and his skills, fused them with years of training and threw in the resolve that he had inherited from his parents, resolution that is often referred to as the 'stiff upper lip' and took control of the situation as he was always meant to do.

For an hour and a half they worked, two pairs of hands as one and somehow, with the encumbrance of the leg removed and the skin taken from it to close the terrible socket that remained, the two men completed their Herculean task.

Now they would have to wait.

Now they must stand back whilst nature and the tenacity of the man's will to live decided what his future would be for his life would hang in the balance for some while and there was nothing more that mortals could do!

For more than a couple of hours the penny had been smouldering with ferocious hatred in Charles' pocket but Charles now knew that, although the coin demanded mortality as payment for its gifts, it could not stop Charles from using the skills that had come about from his ownership of it to *save* life.

Charles fingered the coin and smiled for now he *knew* that its hold over him was less than absolute!

"Sounds strange for me to be saying this to you Sir," ventured Charles as the two men made their way to the wash room to clean up, "But very well done in there—I know we couldn't have achieved such an outcome as that without the skill you brought to the table. That man, if he lives, will owe *you* his life!"

"It's an embarrassment to me Corporal that you must call *me* sir for, if not for you I may have remained frozen with fear and many of these young fellows may have died!" He went on,

"Only through watching *you* did I find courage enough to put my training to use. I both admire and respect your skill and can't help feeling your talents have been somewhat overlooked!"

Charles turned crimson, he had never received recognition such as this from an Officer since his days in the trenches with Tommy.

My God, he thought as recollections of Tommy returned to him, that feels as though it was a long time ago.

"Is everything alright Corporal?" The surgeon enquired.

"Oh yes, yes, Sir. I was just thinking back to similar experiences a while ago and remembering an old friend. Sometimes you can't help worrying about folk!" His voice trailed into silence.

The surgeon looked at him and said nothing, young as he was he had seen that look before and even without the wisdom of years he knew that his unwitting mentor needed space to settle his contemplations.

Charles collected himself.

"Time we did the rounds and made sure that the patients are being looked after! This way Sir"

He led the way to the makeshift ward with its lines of beds. His team of medics, so few of them, were busy tending injured soldiers but each man paused as the two walked in. Who started the process is uncertain but from the far end of the ward someone began to applaud which appreciation was quickly taken up by all that were conscious and still had two hands to clap with.

The surgeon half raised a hand to acknowledge the salutation but swiftly modified the gesture to a signal of 'hush' and the ward returned to the business of attending the sick.

CHAPTER 13

A Strange Episode

F AINTLY FROM THE DISTANCE came the drone of approaching aero engines but this time the station was ready—they would not be caught napping again. Mercifully, the munitions had been declared safe and were almost all back in the relative safety of their shelter. Machine guns now bristled the airfield perimeter in large numbers in readiness to repel further waves of attackers. As the first aircraft drew closer, one of these opened up severing shards of wood and canvass from the lower wing and ripping its fabric covering.

"Cease fire!" bellowed the Sergeant Major at the top of his voice simultaneously belting the trigger happy gunner across the top of his head with his swagger stick, a curly, twisty stick not unlike a school master's cane.

"Can't you see their *our* lads returning?"

"Silly little bugger!" he muttered as he stood back to watch the returning allies land.

It was clear to all that they had taken a lot of punishment. Many of the aircraft had barely enough of their fabric covered wings left to keep them in the air, the ripped material flapping like a myriad of banners and creating an angry din that could be heard above the engines by men standing in worried silence on the airfield.

'There *must* be more!' Charles remarked to himself as one by one the 'planes landed. 'Surely there must be more?'

Of the thirty six plus planes that had departed from the airfield just twenty two had returned and those in appalling condition. The bedraggled aircraft were marshalled one by one to the dispersal apron. Exhausted pilots and crew dismounted, faces and clothing blackened by overworked leaky engines into which particles of dirt and powder from exploding munitions had leeched.

Through blackened somnolent countenances, deep wrinkles cradled fear widened eyes. These individuals would never again feel the irrepressible exuberance of youth nor know the vitality and zest for life they had possessed before this day. They would never again experience the unbridled affection they had once held for their fellows, adversaries or other. These youths had set out in innocence and returned as hardened men; had this day been robbed of feelings dear to mankind and had been condemned to an underworld of fear and mistrust.

The station medics were kept busy patching the wounded but few of them were aware that there was damage here that no man would ever address nor yet had the knowledge to mollify!

"Come on you lot!" barked a Senior NCO from beyond the infirmary gesticulating in the direction of the aircraft, "Get this bloody lot into the hangars for repair—they'll be needed again later!"

The mechanics groaned and gave each other knowing glances illustrating in no uncertain fashion their feeling of disdain for the order and the irritating notion of getting wrecks flying again that day.

"Must be bloody joking!" remarked an unguarded tongue.

"What was that? Step forward and show yourself!" Bellowed the outraged NCO but no man would be brave enough or foolish enough to identify himself. As long as the Sergeant was uncertain upon whom to place the mutinous remark it was best to leave him guessing!

It was some hours before the first aid tasks had been wound up but finally Charles found himself free. He stepped from the ward into the sunlight of a clear late afternoon breathing in the sweet smell of airfield grass and clearing his lungs and nasal passages of a mixture of perspiration and unpleasant pungent medical odours.

He breathed a sigh of relief and was about to turn toward the mess tent for a cup of tea when he was confronted with a strange phenomenon.

Before him stood a young French girl of probably no more than twenty summers. She eyed him in the coy and appealing way that only French maids can, her young eyes wide as she sought to find the English she needed. Before she could complete her search Charles enquired.

"What on earth are you doing *here* mam'selle?"

"This is a British Army post and no civillians are permitted here!"

She averted her eyes from his and stuttered.

"Pardon M'sieu, I 'ave milk for you but I cannot put it from the cart. Ze personne at ze—'ow you say? *eh oui,*—gate say to take it 'ere—you will 'elp non?"

Charles looked over her shoulder to the small cart behind her, it was drawn by a very tired looking horse that, by appearances, may have once been owned by

Methuselah. On the cart that it pulled sat two large milk churns that were clearly destined for the quartermaster at the commissariat.

"'Course I'll help mam'selle, follow me."

The girl took the horse by its bridle and tugged gently clicking her tongue as she did so. It trundled obediently forward but entirely without enthusiasm.

"I am Yvette m'sieu, from ze farm locale!"

Charles looked at her and felt a tickle in his breast

"Charles!" he replied sheep like. He felt guilty.

"I shall call you Sharll m'sieu—*D'accord?*"

Charles didn't know what to say, he hadn't been in the company of a woman for some while and found it difficult to keep his eyes from her. Thoughts of his wife came flooding into his mind—he had tried to keep his thoughts of her suppressed so that he could get on with the war and not brood over their absence one from the other. He felt sure that by doing this he would be able to devote his entire attention to his work and not be distracted by things he couldn't have nor by futile wishes for impossible dreams to come true!

He could not deny the feelings of longing that seared through his body nor the arousal he felt at the mere scent of this girl. He shook himself.

"M'sieu?" quizzed the maid, "You are *bon*?"

"Oui mam'selle—very bon." Charles surprised himself, he had no idea where he had learned this French and was slightly exuberated by the experience of it.

"*Parlez vous Francai m'sieu?*" The maid too was surprised and a little delighted.

"Non mam'selle!" He blurted not wanting to be found a fraud.

"I shall teach you Sharll. When I come every day you will meet me *non?* I will learn you very good!"

Charles smiled, what harm could that do, it would be something to look forward to and learning French would be an achievement even if he never got the opportunity to use it again. That last bit opened his eyes, he realised that once he left France (supposing he survived the war), he would never set foot back here again—ordinary folk would never have the privilege of foreign travel.

"*You* lad—*Corporal*—stop making sheep's eyes at that maid and get that milk off the bloody cart!"

It was the quartermaster Sergeant, six foot sixteen tall with a chest like a beer barrel, the Sergeant had watched the ensemble come to rest outside the store and was indignant that this ruddy corporal was more engaged with conversation than with the job in hand.

Charles' mind sprang into the present.

"Yes S'arnt!" he snapped and jumped to the task.

He was amazed at how heavy these churns were and realised he would be unable to get them to the ground without help.

"Can you give us a hand?" he asked stupidly.

"Give you an'and?" Spat the sergeant in scorn, "**Give you a ruddy hand***?—where the bloody 'ell d'you think you are?*" The Sergeant had turned purple with rage.

Charles complexion turned crimson as he realised what he had done.

"Sorry Sergeant!" he said snapping to attention, "I'll get one of the lads from the mess tent!"

The Sergeant glared but refrained from any kind of reply; his dignity and stature had been sorely damaged and to grace this fool with a response would not serve to restore good order and Army discipline!

The maid covered her young lips and giggled discreetly at this peacock like display though her heart went out to Charles, she felt the rebuke had been a little over played. She held the horse steady and stared at her feet in bashful silence as Charles scuttled off.

Charles walked her back to the main gate chattering the whole time completely unaware that engines had been started and that something was afoot once more. A sudden backfire hauled him to his senses, he had best make ready for whatever was to come. He bade the maid *au revoir* with a promise to be at the gate to meet her the following day and made his way to the first aid orderly's quarters chastened by the thought that some other Sergeant might yet chastise him for enjoying the company of a pretty girl in preference to the needs of the service.

As he passed by the maintenance hangars he couldn't help but marvel at what he saw. The wrecks of aeroplanes that had gone in were being hauled out with repaired wood, replaced fabric and new paint!

Those airplane fitters must be bloody magicians, he thought to himself as he watched the machines being ranged in the open for the armourers to load with bombs and other ordnance. His thoughts diverted to the pilots and gunners that must man them again and his heart sank. How on earth were they to cope? Where would they find the courage and stamina to go through all that they experienced this morning all over again?

Without any warning the sirens started to wail and NCO's began running around like headless chickens in an effort to complete the task of getting the aircraft ready. Charles could see black dots on the horizon and at once knew that the airfield was about to come under attack once more. He stood as if rooted to the spot as pilots once more raced for their steeds, ready or not they must get airborne and engage the enemy to protect the airfield and the wounded still recovering in the makeshift field hospital.

As Charles set about resuming his journey, a two seat RF4B moved across his path, the observer position behind the pilot unoccupied.

The pilot already had his goggles down and was shouting something to Charles but the din of the engine and the thrust from the propeller was carrying his message away.

Charles shook his head in bewilderment at which the pilot became truculent. He signalled furiously to Charles and jerked his thumb at the empty gunner's seat.

Charles was dumfounded, the pilot *surely* couldn't expect him to get into it—could he? The pilot cut the throttle and the 'plane drew to a halt. Now there was no mistaking it, that's *exactly* what the pilot was ordering!

"Oh Christ!" gulped Charles as he thrust his foot into the toe hold in the fuselage, "OH ***Christ!***" He clambered in.

There was no coat to keep him warm but at least there was a leather helmet and goggles, even as he put them on the aircraft accelerated to full power and was wallooning down the runway like a mad whippet!

Charles was petrified, there was supposed to be something to attach him to the aeroplane but where the hell *was* it? He was already shivering from the cold air rushing through the open hole that was the gunner's position but thrust that to the back of his mind as he turned his thoughts to how the gun worked. It was not unlike the gun he had used before, round magazines and a large heavy cocking lever but everything seemed much bigger. He slapped on the first magazine, pulled the cocking lever and released the safety catch and there it was—the penny was burning in his pocket.

There was no time for such diversions for Charles knew that his life and the life of the young man driving would depend upon him putting his personal feelings to one side and defending the aircraft in which he was a reluctant crewman!

The ground below seemed years away and had taken on an unreal appearance, his musings were interrupted by the sound of a whistle. He looked around his silly little fortress and his eyes lighted on a tube with a whistle in the end—yes, there it was again. He picked up the tube and removing the whistle stuck the open end of the tube to his ear.

"The fighters are going in before us to break up the formation, we must concentrate on hitting the two seat bombers and come in from above and to the side!" the pilot paused for air, "You OK with that?—over!"

Charles nodded his head before realising that the pilot couldn't see him. He put the tube to his mouth and shouted,

"OK!"

The pilot jumped sideways and rubbed his ear. "Silly Sod!" he mumbled.

Charles could hear the unmistakeable rattle of machine gun fire. He swung himself and his gun around the circular fixing rail to bring the approaching enemy into his line of fire. Almost immediately a German two seater flashed past giving Charles a small window of opportunity which he took without thinking. His machine gun blasted out its deadly staccato. Charles saw holes appear in the airplane's side and just had enough time to take in the expression of terror on the face of his opposite number who had seemingly frozen his finger on his trigger, the gun was discharging shots randomly and without effect. The pilot swung Charles' airplane violently around to give chase, its wings forming an angle vertical to the ground. Charles was finding the gun ridiculously heavy as the gravity forces fought the airplane's movement but found himself staring down onto a bomber that was clearly unaware of their presence. He lined up the gun and emptied the rest of his magazine into the unsuspecting foe. The gunfire cut through the centre of the upper wing and snapped its main spar but Charles saw no more of it as his own 'plane jerked upright and aligned itself with its previous adversary. Bullets came at them as Charles fought to change the magazine, one of them splintering the frame between the pilot and the gunner. Snapping the magazine finally into place Charles cocked the gun again and let the entire magazine empty into their adversary catching a lucky shot into one of its suspended bombs. The force of the explosion and shards of what had once been a flying machine hit him before there was sound of any kind. Charles could now see the ground beneath his feet, there was very little of the aeroplane's covering left surrounding him but a quick look around showed the tail and the wings to be intact. The spare magazines had gone, fallen through the ripped fuselage, there was nothing left to fight with yet the penny blazed in his pocket in expectancy—something else was about to transpire.

Charles wished he had a parachute but they had been forbidden by a hierarchy that did not fly themselves! He blew down the Gosport tube but there was no reply. Stretching as hard as he could he just managed to tap the pilot on the shoulder but again there was no response.

Charles realised that the pilot must have been wounded but was powerless to help him. His heart sank.

The aeroplane droned onward slowly losing height, there was no smoke, no fire and no loss of stability. They appeared to be drifting away from the combat area but in which direction? Charles lapsed into a feeling of helpless resignation bordering on tranquillity, there was nothing he could do to influence his situation The devil's trinket was still blazing in anticipation of *something* but *what?*

Charles thrust his hand into his pocket and touched the coin, perhaps he could rid himself of it now, what he felt turned his blood cold for there in his pocket was a spent enemy machine gun round! Had the penny stopped it and if so why was the coin not damaged?

In any event Charles was aware that, yet again, the coin had intervened to save him.

Crack! Crack! Crack! puffs of black smoke were appearing all around them. Charles looked ahead and below and to his horror realised they were flying through enemy anti aircraft fire *towards* enemy lines!

He started to laugh insanely, what *more* could happen to him? That's when the engine stopped!

The aircraft pitched steeply nose down making for the ground with the noise of an express train. Wires between the wings shrieked and twanged and Charles felt he should have been aware it was all over for him but, as had happened to him before, he felt serenely calm and collected. Another bang, this time the noise and the explosion were simultaneous and the 'plane pitched nose up losing speed rapidly. It began to porpoise, nose up until it stalled then nose down until it had flying speed again when the process repeated itself, the ground drawing ever closer. Charles braced himself, the impact could not be far away. Visions of the downed German pilot he had seen burned to death all that time ago flashed through his mind—was this to be his fate?

He wished he had written to his Wife, he wished he could have told her one last time of how deep his love for her was, he touched her fair skin in his mind's eye and suddenly there she was! 'Don't worry' she seemed to be saying, 'don't worry, I am carrying your child, you will always be in my heart.'

"Not now, not this time!" he shrieked and clambered out of his gun port toward the motionless pilot. Stretching himself along the top of the fuselage he pulled himself forward inch by tortuous inch. The 'plane didn't seem to be porpoising now but had steadied itself in a shallow glide at what seemed to be a very slow speed until Charles noticed the ground whistling by just a few feet below. Edging forward he reached down and took the stick from the pilot's grasp. He eased it slowly back halting the aircraft's decent and slowing its speed still further. Ahead of him loomed a large bank of earth thrown up around a shell crater.

"God in heaven help me!" he pleaded unaware that he was uttering anything audibly and pulled back further on the stick. The wheels clipped the top of the bank just as the 'plane stalled shooting him forward like a bullet from a gun. He hit the water in the crater absolutely horizontal and skimmed across it like a flicked stone to slide up the far bank grateful that the soil had not yet hardened!

He was not even scratched!

There was heavy gunfire ahead and behind him, he must be in the barren strip between the lines, in 'no man's land'. From the noise of the gunfire relative to his position he figured he was somewhat closer to the enemy than to his own lines. He knew that the enemy would come for him after dark and that, if he was to save his skin, he would have to stay one step ahead of them.

Soaking wet and covered from head to toe in mud he crawled around the water toward the stricken aeroplane keeping his head and body well below the parapet thrown up by the shell that had made this wonderful, life saving crater. The impact had broken the fuselage where it had been weakened in the aerial engagement and the forward section had separated and sagged into the crater just far enough for Charles to get to the pilot. He was dead.

Charles slumped back into the quagmire, he had hoped that he would have been able to help his unfortunate companion but the wind had been taken from his sails. Pulling himself together he kicked himself into action—his chum might be dead but he could *still* play a part in this interminable conflict!

Charles unbuckled the restraint that was binding the pilot to his hearse and dragged him clear of the 'plane and across to the far side of the crater where he lay him chest down with arms outstretched. In an act of compassion, he turned the pilot's head to the side to keep his face from the sickly mud and eased his goggles on to his forehead. Even through the blackened face he recognised the young man who had flown him from St Omer to 46 Squadron headquarters at Izel-les-Hamaeux on his return to the war in France.

Charles took from his pocket the Military Medal that he had been awarded and pinned it to the pilot's chest—it meant nothing to him now; he felt guilty to be alive when this young man had perished so gallantly in the service of his country. 'Our Father' he began .... the prayer was painful and punctuated by frequent pauses as Charles fought to hold himself together.

Darkness had already started to fall, he must move and move *now!*

He obliterated all traces of his movements within the crater leaving only the marks left by the pilot's body—with any luck the Germans would think there had been only one occupant in the stricken aircraft and might be fooled into leaving things at that.

The gunfire had now lapsed into silence and although the darkness was not complete Charles knew it was time for him to make his move. His khaki battledress stained with mud would offer him a good chance of blending in with the terrain so it was now or never!

He pulled himself to the top of the parapet as close to the crashed aeroplane as he could to make use of the cover it afforded and glanced over his shoulder toward the enemy trenches—no movement yet—no movement that he could *see* anyway. He slid over the top making as few movements as he could and reached back to brush over the giveaway scuff marks in the soil, he could hear shouting now, *German* shouting—had they spotted him?

He wriggled along beneath the upturned tail with the intention of keeping the hulk between himself and the enemy as long as he could as an aid to concealment when, to his horror, the entire dusk covered sky was illuminated in a deathly silver light.

'Bugger!' he thought and lay motionless face down in the soft soil. The shouting was now getting closer and he was not yet far enough away from the 'plane to be missed, what the hell to do?

Throwing caution to the wind he made his way forward like a sidewinder snake wriggling its way over desert sand

and leaving such a trail as none but the blind might miss. The flare, floating earthward on its parachute, gave way to darkness once more. Charles seized the opportunity of renewed cover, thrust himself to his feet and ran for his life covering more than a hundred yards in record time! Fear lends wings to weary legs!

Pouf! the spent flare was replaced and the night had become day again. Charles threw himself to the ground but the German yell that he heard told him that the game was up—he was now the hare and the hunters were hot in pursuit. On to his feet again and *run*, run like the wind and don't stop! He weaved from side to side so as not to be an easy target and was surprised that he could not hear machine gun fire. A bullet whizzed past his ear so close that he could hear the peculiar whirring, buzzing sound it made unlike anything he had ever heard before. He could even feel the air move as it sped by. More flares and now the thump of mortar fire but it didn't seem to be exploding anywhere near him, his heart was racing and there were spots before his eyes. He threw himself headlong into another crater grateful for its cover and the chance to catch his breath—his lungs were blazing!

His chest heaved as he drew in the reviving air and he was aware that he was gasping. His hip felt strange, sort of sticky damp but he paid no heed to it, fear of capture was uppermost in his mind, he must escape at all cost.

He had been under mortar fire before and was perplexed as to why there was no flying earth or shrapnel until it finally sank in that the mortar fire was being directed not at *him* but at the enemy and *that* was why they had not caught up with him. The Germans stopped discharging flares aware that it was these very flares that were giving the Allies light to accurately hit their quarry by. With the returning darkness Charles threw himself over the top of the crater and ran headlong for his own lines but he was now being impeded by the excruciating pain in his hip. Throwing a glance over his shoulder he could see the Germans had resumed the chase—it wasn't over at all and they were gaining on him!

Thump, thump went the allied mortars again this time shooting blind and not missing Charles by much! Now whistles were sounding, lots of them and not too far ahead, bullets began whining past much too close for comfort; Charles fell to the ground again but this time feigning injury in the hope that the Germans might believe they had got their man and break off the chase. Charles knew they were now close enough to see him even in the poor light and close enough to see is close enough to shoot. His hip was hurting a lot more now and any kind of movement brought sheer agony, he knew he could run no more. He thrust a hand into his ripped trousers and knew at once that he had sustained a fairly serious flesh wound that had been drenched in stinking crater mud. Visions of gangrene pervaded his mind causing him to wretch such as he had never experienced before, he knew full well what such mortification could do for he had encountered and tended this affliction in others.

Time was up for him—no more running, no more escape, no more freedom. In a last desperate act he removed a bootlace and applied a tourniquet as high as he could on his leg but he knew as consciousness slipped away that such things cannot work on hips. As he slipped away, the blackness of the night lifted for him to give way to a silent white light, a smooth calming light that seemed to be calling softly for him to come. He could see his Father and his Father's Father standing at the head of a column of smiling faces he did not know. His Father reached to help him from the mud, he looked so clean!

His Grand Father was showing him a child, a boy, so fresh and new, already with a smile. The infant proffered a tiny hand as if to say 'I need you.'

CHAPTER 14

New Horizons

F AINT VOICES WERE COMING to him form a distant place, he could hear them but was unable to comprehend a single word. The voices grew louder yet still he was unable to put meaning to the words, they were coming so fast and his head was hurting from the strain of trying to pull his mind together.

He forced his eyes to open and the bright white light above the operating table made him wince but he was unable to move an arm to shield himself from its penetrating glare. The surgeon stared dispassionately down at him, his faced unmasked and his once white robes stained red with blood.

"Ah M'sieu, you are awake at last, we were not sure you would return to us!"

"Where am I?" faltered Charles confused that he could now put meaning to the words that were being spoken.

"You are in the French held sector of the front—you are in the battlefield of the Somme—but how is m'sieu feeling?"

"Not sure, a little woolly I think!"

"Not surprising *Mon Amis,* you have lost a lot of blood and you were lucky to have been rescued and saved by our brave French Soldarmes, if you had not arrived at the hospital when you did we could not have saved you—you owe your life not only to the brave troops who kept back the Germans but also to the field medics who cleaned and closed your wound and brought you to safety!"

The surgeon paused and looked deep into Charles' eyes as if wanting to tell him something but thought the better of it and continued.

"Our French *braves* watched your *avion* crash and reported you as certain dead—imagine their surprise to see you running through the mine field with the Germans close behind like the hare and the hounds—it is a wonder indeed that none of you were blown to pieces!" He smiled again.

"There is nothing but shreds of your uniform left, a picture of a beautiful girl and this." The surgeon held up a bright new copper penny trapped between finger and thumb, "It is very strange how it is warm when it has not been in a pocket for some while—very curious!"

He placed the penny with the photograph in one of Charles' boots—all that remained of his kit.

"Now you must sleep and get better." The surgeon instructed.

Charles had not noticed that he was being administered morphine as they talked. As consciousness slipped away once more Charles drifted willingly into oblivion.

It was some while before he came to again. He was laying on a low camp bed his body bound tight by blankets and was part of a long row of such cots each bearing a wounded man. The ambience of the room was pervaded by continuous groans of agony and incessant chattering in French as delirious soldiers re-lived the moments in which they had been injured. Now and then a man would shout at the top of his voice which was as un-nerving to his neighbours as it was exhausting to him.

Charles attempted to raise himself and roll onto his right side to get a better look at his surroundings but the effort evoked unexpected searing pain, a pain so consuming that the shock of it forced him to pass out once more.

He came to several minutes later, a nurse was cradling his head and pressing a small glass of water to his lips. He drank the water grateful for its coolness and its sweet reviving taste, the pain was less now and his mind was beginning to clear.

"W-w-what has happened to my side?" he stuttered, his voice heavy and faltering from the mixture of shock and lingering pain.

"Pardon M'sieu, I say no English, *Le Medicine* tell you!" the nurse apologised. Rising, she shrugged her shoulders and with a look of genuine regret lay his head back on the coarse pillow and left.

Charles' wound, although severe, was not deep enough to have shattered any bone which was merciful indeed but the nature and extent of it had caused him to lose a great deal of blood before being tended by the field medics and dragged by what was left of his tunic across the remaining mud of no man's land to the safety of the French lines. He had no recollection of his rescue at all and had no idea of whether or not his superiors at 46 squadron had any notion of what had happened to him. For all he knew he may already have been posted as 'missing, believed lost in action' or worse posted as a deserter.

His blood ran cold at the thought of the latter, he could be shot for that and how on earth was he going to prove where he had been and what he had done? He groaned and realised at once that he had joined his French comrades in re-living their indelible horror!

Despite his mind's unease and his pain, Charles was coping well with the situation he was now in and apart from the distractions of a headache and hunger, he was otherwise in relative good spirit. He didn't *really* believe he could have been posted as a deserter.

The surgeon was a long time in returning. He seemed to take ages peeling back the dressings, prodding here and prising there and going over his own handy-work with meticulous attention but in due course he declared himself to be pleased with the outcome. Charles had watched many surgeons go about their tasks and felt reassured by this man's thorough, confident manner and the positive instruction he was offering his subordinates, although it was all in French Charles' just *knew* that he was in capable hands.

"I think M'sieu, that if you continue to make good progress, you may return to your unit in two days and finish your recovery there. Now you must tell me your details so that arrangements can be made for your transfer—you were not alone in your *avion* I think?"

"No." Replied Charles, "I was just a press-ganged gunner, the aeroplane was being flown by 2nd Lieutenant Tern-Scott. I left his papers in his pocket so that the Gerries can give him a proper Officer's burial—that's all I could do."

"He was dead this man?" enquired the surgeon.

"Yes Sir—there was nothing I could do for him."

"Lieutenant Scott died from injury when the *avion* crashed?"

"No Sir, he was dead before we crashed—from machine gun fire."

"You were lucky to have escaped the crash *mon Amis!*"

A picture of the young pilot's lifeless face flashed through Charles' mind and he felt sickened that the outcome of their second flight together hadn't been more favourable.

The surgeon saw the cloud pass across Charles' eyes.

"That will be enough for now *mon Amis*, I will have your unit informed that you are here and I will give them the details you have given me. *Merci mon Amis et Bon Chance!*"

Charles nodded, why on earth had he not mentioned how hungry he was, it could be *hours* before he was fed. He became irritated with himself with the realisation that he had no idea of the time or even the day for that matter.

∇

Charles was growing apprehensive now that he was tucked up in the squadron ambulance and on his way back to the unit. What was he going to tell the Adjutant—it was very unlikely that anyone would regard his story of events as anything but a tissue of lies designed to illuminate his bravery and his standing in the unit. Who in his right mind would believe a Corporal medic when he claimed to have been coerced into being a bloody combat gunner in an aeroplane?

The deep frown on his face must have conveyed something of his unease to the Lance Corporal tending him who remarked.

"Penny for your thoughts mate?—Cheer up, it might never 'appen!"

Charles smiled, if there was one thing about the British Tommy that he had learned and understood a long time ago it was their irrepressible cheer whatever the circumstances.

It had come as a surprise to Charles when he was told that he had been in a coma for three full weeks after being taken to the French field hospital, he had lost a lot of time from his life but at least he *had* a life. He had only been out of the coma for four days but notwithstanding that his recovery had been astonishing. Loss of blood had been the main culprit in those early hours after rescue and there had been far too little blood available to transfuse in the needed quantity. Once his young and virile body had adjusted itself and overcome the initial effects of shock however, it set about replacing the lost cells and the anti-bodies that he had lost and nature took over.

The Albion ambulance trundled through the main gate without stopping and made its way to the sick bay bouncing like a small boat on a high sea.

"Bloody ruts!" scathed the Lance Corporal, "Been like this ever since the push. So much bloody ordnance has come in by road that the airfield is chewed to bloody bits!"

Charles wasn't interested, the rocking around had jarred his wound and good medical progress or not it was too painful to ignore.

He had never seen the sick bay look so sparkling clean. There were quite a few occupied beds giving the ward staff work enough yet every one of them was draped in crisp, clean white sheets. The nurses and ward orderlies were turned out in equally clean, smart uniforms almost like they were on parade but there was no time and certainly no inclination toward such ceremony in the middle of a war.

Charles was feeling a little nauseus as he was transported into this unusual environment, he was still vexed about what the immediate future held for him. The stretcher party were instructed to halt just inside the entrance to the ward whilst the Adjutant, accompanied by the Station Commanding Officer approached.

Arriving before the stretcher, the Adjutant halted and brought himself stiffly to attention; clearing his throat he began an impassioned liturgy.

"Corporal Jenkins", he addressed Charles, "You have been absent from your appointed place of duty for eight days—what have you to say?"

Charles was stunned, he was to be charged after all.

The Commanding Officer took a pace forward and together he and the Captain removed their headgear and tucked it under their left arms. Neither man was smiling.

Charles was torn apart, his mind racing. 'Oh my God!' he thought, *'I've been tried and convicted my absence*—they only *ever* take off their hats to announce the *supreme* penalty.

His heart sank to his boots in desolation and hopelessness. Was he never to see his beloved Eira again? Would he never hold her soft body to his nor listen to her sweet singing nor delight in her soft spoken Welsh lilt ever again? Visions of her radiant smile brushed across his mind, closing his eyes in desperation he wished above all he could escape this dreadful evil. His senses reeled as the full realisation of his predicament came to him, how much kinder it would have been to everyone at home if he had died in that aeroplane. Why had his creator chosen to save him as he had? He must have been aware that Charles would have given his life for that of the pilot without a second thought, he *still* would. His head started to swim—why was everything fading? Voices around him were softening, becoming less distinct, why won't they let me sleep?

The fragrance of her fresh scrubbed skin came to him as real as if she were at his side. He reached out to brush her hair from her eyes—why did she let her hair do that?

Charles somehow didn't make it all the way to unconsciousness. Through the turmoil of his thoughts he could hear orders being given and though he was unable to comprehend what they were, he could sense that the situation was urgent. He felt the prick of a needle and an oxygen mask slip over his face. He knew as soon as the mask touched him that he was going to wretch—he couldn't stop himself.

Regaining his senses little by little, Charles could see that there was no measure of scorn in any of the faces staring anxiously down at him, indeed, there were only expressions of consternation and concern.

"He's coming to!" announced the surgeon.

Turning to the Commanding Officer he advised, "I suggest you keep your ceremony as brief as you can so that we can clean this lad and let him rest."

"Very good Doctor!" the C.O. replied and turned to the Adjutant.

"Carry on Major."

"Sir!" he snapped and turned once more to Charles.

"We had hoped to greet you with the ceremony you deserve lad but it's clear that you've suffered a great deal and we've taxed you beyond your strength. Perhaps you would allow us to simply say welcome back to the station and wish you a speedy recovery?—well done!"

"Well done indeed Jenkins, we are all proud of you." rejoined the C.O. He executed a casual salute even though his cap was still under his left arm.

The sense of relief that surged through Charles'as this information was received was overpowering. The presentation of the ward, the smartness of the orderlies and nurses, the attendance of the two senior Officers had all been in *honour* of his return—not to rebuke, chastise or convict! Tears rolled in silence down his cheeks as emotion got the better of him.

It took several operations over the next few days to close up the damage that his wound had suffered and it was some time before Charles was able to try walking again. With the aid of crutches and what seemed like endless excercises under the eye of a physical training instructor, he began the process of rehabilitation.

After what had seemed like an eternity, Charles was released to continue his daily walks alone under the proviso that he remained on the board walks that surrounded the field hospital. He however, had other intentions in mind. He had never forgotten the promise he had made to Yvette that he would meet her at the guard house and however late the event he was going to keep that promise.

Had she hated him for not being there? Did she still deliver the milk? Had she moved on or been replaced?

A thousand questions surged through his brain though he couldn't reason why, she meant nothing to him and he wasn't *that* desperate to learn French. Despite the uncertainty he felt, he hobbled to the end of the boardwalk knowing that he was going to try to make good that promise—late or not and in the face of the pain he knew he would have to encounter. The ground was still rutted badly from munitions movements and was somewhat soft but at least the crutches didn't sink so far as to halt him as he left the boardwalk. Going was not so easy now and the effort of it was taking its toll of Charles' strength but he pressed on aware that he was now not so far from the gatehouse.

"You all right Corporal?" called the gatehouse duty Sergeant as he watched Charles' difficult progress toward him.

"Not too bad Sergeant, a little pain but I have to keep the exercise going!"

The Sergeant lowered his voice as Charles hobbled the last few feet to the wooden building. "Sooner you than me lad." he muttered.

"I'm surprised they didn't tell you to stay on the boards and just exercise around the hospital." observed the Sergeant.

"Actually they did." replied Charles, "I wanted to find out whether the milk girl still delivers here—I was supposed to meet her a few weeks ago but got wounded and ended up at a French hospital so couldn't make it!"

"So *you're* the chap?"

"Sorry?" ventured Charles.

"You're the chap that shot down those 'planes and got shot down yourself!"

"Oh! Yes." Charles admitted feeling a little foolish.

"Well done mate." congratulated the Sergeant, "The maid asked after you a couple of times but none of us knew it was *you* she was talking about."

"She asked after me?" repeated Charles, his heart gave a little flutter.

"Every time she came through she asked but we haven't seen her for a day or two; the tender has been going to the farm to pick up the milk."

"Oh!" exclaimed Charles and fell silent. He stared at the gate and the track beyond, there was no way he was going to be able to hobble to the farm even if he could get permission to leave the camp.

"The tender driver goes alone." the Sergeant spoke as if Charles wasn't there—almost to himself.

"Could probably do with some company—a sort of guide if you take my meaning." He winked now that he had charles' attention.

"If you're interested I could ask him to take you and if you won't be missed at the hospital for an hour or so you could go along for the ride."

Charles' pulse raced.

"I'd love to go Sergeant, I've been bored to death hobbling round and round the hospital and the change of scenery would be bloody welcome."

"Yeah *right,"* chided the Sergeant."Off you go then—be back here at 0830 tomorrow morning. If you can't make it, get the hospital orderly to give the guardhouse a ring and let us know."

Charles smiled as the Sergeant disappeared into the guardroom,

He was, as ever, amazed at how resourceful Non Commissioned Officers were.

Getting consent to go outside seemed to be an impossible task. None of his superiors in the medical fraternity appeared empowered to even consider such a request and appeared frightened by the very thought of having to make a decision upon it. Each Officer he approached adopted an expression of bewilderment crowned by 'Court Martial' eyes. Charles decided for them, he would go *anyway.*

It was not characteristic of him to flout regulations in this way but he felt *compelled* to make the effort to keep his word and thus it was that he appeared at the gate next morning at 0830. The tender was already there loaded with the empty milk churns in readiness for the trip to the farm and with its engine still running. The driver, a corporal himself, was talking to the Sergeant and taking from him a sheaf of papers clearing the removal of crown property, including the tender, from the station on local sortie.

"Morning Corporal!" smiled the Sergeant, "Glad you made it. The driver's happy to take you along for the ride, d'you have a pass?"

"Got one here somewhere." muttered Charles sifting through his pockets.

"Sarge!" The driver intervened his voice strained, "I don't have all day and milk won't keep!"

"Oh! all right—bugger off the pair of you!" The sergeant sighed and signalled them to be on their way.

The driver helped Charles into the truck then climbed into the driving seat. With a horrid crunch and a screech of grating gears the truck lurched forward jerking both men into the back of their wood and canvas seats. Charles looked at the driver and was about to comment when the man cut in.

"Not my normal job this and I'm a bit rusty I'm afraid, normally drive the C.O.'s car but the regular driver's got dysentery—just my bloody luck!" He moaned. Charles smiled.

"Name's Stan." The driver added.

"Charles." returned his passenger still smiling. It didn't matter in the slightest to him how the vehicle was driven so long as it was on its way to the farm. The going was similar to that of his return from the hospital in the ambulance in the way that the occupants were being thrown around as the tender bumped over the ruts of previous journeys. Steam began issuing in a continuous plume from the radiator cap.

"Bloody boiling now!" cursed Stan, "One of these days we'll get issued with some decent vehicles that can do the job proper!"

Charles gathered that complaing was a way of life to his host who seemed to find satsfaction in it, he was making the most of the opportunity.

"Bloody good job the aeroplanes don't bloody boil like this or they'd never bloody come back!" he exclaimed.

Charles grinned but said nothing.

"You're the chap who got shot down aren't you?"

Charles looked sidelong at his host searching for some sort of emotion that would explain the need for the sudden change of tack. He decided that it was nothing more than conversation.

"Yes, a lot of guys got shot down that day—I was lucky—I came back."

"What's it like being an air gunner, I'd be bloody terrified if it was me."

"I'm not really a gunner Stan nor even a flyer, I'm a medic. I just got caught up in the battle somehow and got *mistaken* for a gunner."

Stan looked long at him in disbelief, so long that the tender left the track and started to mount the bank that now flanked its sides.

"Shit!" shrieked Stan and wrestled the heavy vehicle with its impossible heavy steering back to the rutted track.

He turned to Charles again face as radiant as a beet, wearing a really sheepish grin, he apologised.

"Sorry mate—what you told me surprised me so much I thought you had to be pulling my leg!" he paused to think about this then went on,

"D'you *really* mean to say that you got into one of those bloody stringbags *voluntarily* with no training and no idea what you were letting yourself in for?"

"I suppose so." replied Charles before adding, "The pilot knew me by sight from a while back when he was giving me a lift to join the squadron and somehow I accidentally become his gunner when we were attacked by a German fighter. He must have thought I was a proper gunner or something."

"Good grief man, you must have been bloody terrified!"

"Not really," replied Charles, "There just wasn't *time* to be scared, it all happened so quick and I didn't have chance to think about what I was doing *or* where I was."

"Phew!" The driver wiped his brow. "You must be stark raving bloody bonkers!"

"Here we are!"

The farm buildings looked as if they had once been magnificent but were now tumble down and ramshackle in appearance; they had clearly been subjected to more than their share of explosives.

"Not sure where we're supposed to collect the milk from. Must be someone here *somewhere.*" Muttered the driver looking around the deserted yard in the hope of finding answers. He honked the hand squeezed bulb of the bugle shaped horn and switched off the boiling engine which shuddered to rest then ran ran backwards for some seconds amidst clouds of steam and dense blue smoke.

Palls of blue smoke continued to rise in a lazy arc from beneath the engine cover; it seemd the engine was informing its master of its reluctance to be dispensed with.

"Bloody truck!" spat Stan as he alighted and kicked the solid front tyre, "Bloody useless truck!"

Charles sat and waited. The mud in the farm yard looked as though it would swallow his crutches without trace and in any case if the maid wasn't there he had no reason to get out.

"Can I 'elp m'sieu?"

The question, aimed at the driver, was strange considering that the tender had visited the farm every day and from the empty churns on the back was clearly there to collect milk.

"Oh, yes, I've been sent to collect milk for the air station."

"But you are not the usual m'sieu—'ow do I know I can trust with you?"

Charles' heart leapt for joy, it was *her* it was Yvette.

He undid the light chain that closed the side opening to the truck, swivelled around and lowered himself backwards to the mud. Dragging his crutches from the floor of the cab he propped himself up on them before starting his way to the others.

"There is another m'sieu?" The maid enquired. She was uncertain about this, there had never been two men collecting the milk before.

"Yvette, it is me!" exclaimed Charles.

She looked at him in disbelief.

"Sharl?" she stammered, "But-but, they say to me that you are dead!"

"Been in hospital for a while Yvette and I still have a little trouble getting around but here I am." He threw out his arms in a gesture of resignation losing both his crutches to the mud.

She laughed and it was music to Charles' ears. His grin threatened to split his countenance in two.

"I'm so sorry that I didn't meet you as I promised, I got shot down and was in a French hospital for a while." The expression that clouded his face illustrated how truly cut up he felt at not keeping his promise.

She placed her hands on her hips and drawing back her shoulders she looked him over with narrowed eyes, her display of mock irritation melting to coy innocence as she attempted rebuke.

"Sharl, you 'ave 'urt my feelings, you 'ave make me feel sad."

"I am so, *so* sorry Yvette—please don't hate me." He found himself begging.

She laughed displaying a set of perfect white, beautifully formed teeth.

"I forgive you Sharl, now I will learn you French when I see you, Non?"

"That would be really good Yvette, I will look forward to it."

Stan coughed.

"Don't want to trouble you folk but we are supposed to be collecting milk you know, shall we get on with it?"

"This way m'sieu." Yvette signalled Stan to follow her. Charles stood for a moment and watched them depart before stooping to retrieve his crutches.

He felt alive and in high sprits for the first time in weeks as he climbed back into the truck.

Stan and the maid returned hauling a low wooden truck laden with half filled milk churns which Stan hoisted onto the rear of the tender.

"D'you reckon you could back the truck over to that door?" enquired Stan nodding toward the place where the milk was stored. "It'll save me having to trudge through the mud with this bloody broken down trolley!"

"Give it a go," replied Charles, "But you'll have to crank it—I don't want to have to get down again if I can help it!"

The two exchanged very little by way of conversation during the trip back to the station. Stan because he was near exhausted and Charles because he was deep in thought about the course his life was taking and what he had felt on meeting Yvette again. His initial emotion had been one of elation but the journey had given him time to reflect and the joy was all too fast being tainted, degraded by overpowering feelings of guilt and apprehension. This was not right, this attachment was just not *right*. It wasn't that he didn't love his bride anymore, he knew he *did*, So what *was* it? Why did he feel so comfortable and happy in the company of this young French farm maid and why did he feel with such passion that he wanted to take her in his arms and smother her with kisses?

Unable to resolve the issue he turned on himself releasing suppressed anger that would have better been left in the past. His thoughts turned to the action he had taken in revenge against the Colliery owner, an action that he now bitterly regretted. An action that had led indirectly to the hotchpotch of events that had transpired to creat his present dillema. He felt a barrier, an unwelcome wedge forming between him and the memory of the girl that should be his *only* love. His mind churned in ceaseless turmoil; finding no solutions to his dilema and unable to bear the torment of his guilt he sank into misery and a desperate sense of loneliness.

Sleep was fugitive to Charles that night as his brain, robbed of the diversions of a working day, continued to seek answers to the strange consuming passion he felt in his breast. He tossed and turned but the more he tried to shut out his problem the more his mind returned to it. He got up and paced the small annex into which he had been moved to complete the final period of convalescence.

Pacing the floor, the snores of his compannions in the annex served only to remind him of what a boon a clear conscience is and how blessed is an uncomplicated existence—it did nothing to sooth his jangling nerves!

He made his way back to his cot, although he knew he would be unable to sleep he felt it must surely be better to rest his body rather than exhaust it before the day ahead.

Despite his reservations, as the night dragged on Charles managed to drift into a restless slumber that was invaded by recurring dreams of his Father and Grandfather. Just as in the dream he had experienced during his near death encounter, his Grandfather was proffering a boy child for Charles to see but when Charles reached out to take the child his Grandfather shook his head and faded from sight.

There are nights when it would be better to forgo sleep, to bend before whatever troubles the mind and appraise the course life is taking; consider alternatives and disregard the need for respite, but few are able to shelve perversities and pursue such action. For most it is a matter of waiting either for the morning to come or lay still in the hope that sleep may yet come! Charles enjoyed no comfort in his cot; half sleeping, half waking he continued to battle conscience against desires, moral against temptation. His beleaguered mind weighed fidelity and devotion for the people he loved against the powerful inbuilt natural urges that pester, even *dominate* every moment of a young man's life.

He felt powerless in the face of this challenge and knew now that being shot at and shooting at others was as nothing in comparison to slaying the giant that was passion for the opposite sex!

The reveille sent its piercing call through the half light of morning surmounting the sporadic distant gunfire from the front but for once it was not unwelcome to Charles. He was glad the night was over for now he would be able to lose himself in daily routine and not think unless he had to.

Charles had become concerned that he had received no mail from home for some time so as a diversion, he decided to while away a little time in finding out why. Making his way to the censor's Office he was confronted by the desk orderly.

"Mornin' Corporal, what kin I do you for?" the private asked with a cheery grin.

"Has there been any mail for me—Corporal Jenkins?" he enquired.

The orderly eyed him suspiciously.

"If there's been any letters or parcels mate they'd have been dished out by now—you expectin' something?"

"I was shot down a couple of weeks ago and billeted in a French hospital so there must be some back mail for me *somewhere*!"

"Hang on a minute, I remember you—your mail came back from the mess marked 'missing in action' so it was returned to the senders. Oh *Gawd*! mate—your folks will have had the dreaded dead telegram as well!"

Charles' heart sank, visions of the distress this declaration would bring to his Wife and family sent his senses reeling, had he not enough problems without this? He demanded to see the censor Officer at once as was his right in the circumstances.

"I'll go and see what I can do Corp, the old man's a decent enough chap and I'm sure he'll do something." declared the orderly and disappeared into the rear of the office. Charles's wound was now paining from standing too long but he knew that to take the orderly's seat would be an unwelcome intrusion. He bit his lower lip and shifted his weight a little.

It seemed like a long time had passed before the orderly returned.

"I've told the old man about your problem and he's going to send a counter telegram right away—it's the best he can do!"

"Thanks mate." replied Charles relieved that action would be put in hand to inform his kin of the true situation. "Thanks for your help."

He turned and hobbled out into the part dried mud.

Charles spent most of that day fashioning a letter to Eira explaining the reason for his silence and that he was safe and in reasonable health. He left out the details of how and where he was injured and the true extent of his wound saying only that he would soon be well and that he wished he could be with her. Throughout the letter writing his conscience kept needling him until he felt he would go mad. Throwing down the pencil he thrust the letter into an envelope without sealing it and hobbled back to the censor's office.

"One last favour lad." asked Charles of the orderly. "Can you get this off as soon as possible it's to my Wife."

"Certainly old mate," winked the orderly, "I'll get the old man to censor and approve it right now—it'll go tomorrow!"

"Thanks again." said Charles departing into the cooling evening air. He felt a little more at ease with himself satisfied that he had actually *achieved* something.

He slept well that night. There were no strange dreams and his conscience left him well enough alone which was a blessing indeed for there was more bad news to contend with on the following day.

He was woken at the usual early hour and had spent some time in the wash tent before presenting himself at the mess for breakfast. Making his way through the canvas flap that formed the entrance to the mess the Sergeant on duty there put a hand on Charles' shoulder and announced.

"C.O. wants to see you lad. He'll see offenders for punishment at 0900 and wants to see you straight after so be there at 0930 latest."

"Any idea what he wants?" enquired Charles fearful that it might have something to do with his visit off camp without permission.

"Haven't got a clue Corporal, he'll tell you soon enough but at least it can't be to do with discipline or you'd be on defaulters!" He smiled and turned his attention to two privates who were arguing in the queue.

"Belt up you two, if you can't be quiet then bugger off and finish your beef outside!"

Charles hated it when he was told to present himself to a superior. He liked to keep himself to himself and such a summons meant that he had been noticed and that usually led to something unpleasant.

"Good morning Jenkins, very pleased to see you." Greeted the Commanding Officer. Charles had known him as Major Hemming on his arrival at the squadron but it was clear he was now a Colonel.

"Sit yourself down and make yourself comfortable." Looking beyond Charles he instructed the private guarding the entrance to leave them and was silent until the man had retreated.

"I have some very good news for you Jenkins. Your recent conduct has been brought to the attention of the Senior Field Officer who has, in due recognition, awarded you a clasp to your Military Medal. Your courage and exemplary conduct have also been recognised by our Allies the French who have awarded you the coveted 'Croix de Guerre'—a singular honour indeed but one of which you are fully deserving!" He cleared his throat.

"Since arrival at this station you have proved yourself to be of outstanding courage and devotion to duty and are an example to us all. In recognition of your contribution to the war effort and in view of the nature of your injury, which medical opinion believes to be of a permanent nature, I am happy to inform you that you are to be repatriated to Great Britain as soon as transport is available for you with a most honourable discharge from further service."

The Colonel continued but Charles had ceased to listen, his heart was in his boots once more as he thought of losing Yvette. The feeling of loss was overwhelming and not at all what he had expected. His morals, his conscience, his resolve to do the right thing had all evaporated as if they had never existed; he reached for the arm of the chair for support as his head began to swim.

"Orderly!" Barked the Colonel rising from his chair and racing to Charles' side, "Some assistance if you please."

The orderly burst through the door accompanied by the armed sentree who had reasoned that his Colonel had been attacked.

"Help this man to his mess and call the surgeon, I fear he may not be as recovered as was suggested."

Had Charles not been so diverted by the news that he was to be sent home, he would have learned that he was to be sent into Devon to complete his recovery to a large country house that had been converted into a special convalescence hospital. It was of no consequence to him for uppermost in his mind burned the need to see Yvette and nothing else seemed to matter.

The next day the news got worse, as a result of the Colonel's concern about Charles' near faint, he was to be confined to camp for further medical observation until the reason for his relapse could be determined and a satisfactory course of treatment defined. Charles cursed his rotten luck—confined to quarters for pity's sake—what next?

The nurses that tended him were sweet enough and very sympathetic to his misery without being aware of the reason for it. Watching them bustle back and forth made Charles realise they had their hands full with the sheer volume of wounded they were tending and a plan began to take shape in his head. He would wait until the ward was quiet during breakfast, pack his bed sheets with his pillows and sneak out. By the time they realised he had gone he would be safely away.

It worked like a dream, movement was slow but that helped to leave him un-noticed as he made his way to the motor transport section. The tender allocated to collect the milk was standing in the roadway, its engine ticking over as the driver returned to the office to sign for its custody. Charles mounted it from the passenger's side and slid across to the driving position; he was away in a trice not even noticed it seemed. He Slowed at the guardhouse as the Guard Sergeant stepped to the edge of the boardwalk and held out a sheaf of loose papers for the him to see. The Sergeant waved him through without checking, as was the usual routine, then returned to his tea.

Charles put his foot down hard on the accelerator and pressed the tender for every last ounce of speed it could give in a bid to put distance between himself and the camp. He knew he had burned bridges, had set wheels in motion that could not be reversed. He didn't care.

The old tender whined its way into the deserted farmyard, what would he do if Yvette wasn't there, had he taken this frightfull risk for nothing? He needn't have fretted, the noise of the approaching vehicle brought her from the milking parlour, waving she turned and made her way back inside, she clearly hadn't recognised it was him. Charles reversed the tender to the parlour door, stopped the engine and climbed down. The effort was not easy to him and in spite of his impaired mobility he decided to manage without his stick, it made him feel old.

"Yvette." he called not wanting to walk in without invitation. The place seemed quite still apart from the occasional cow-call and very gloomy in the half light.

"Yvette." he called again, a little louder. She appeared as if from nowhere.

"*Please* M'sieu—you will frighten the animals!"

"Sorry Yvette, couldn't make out where you were—it's me!" Charles waited for what seemed an age.

"*Sharlie*" it is you?"

"Yes Yvette."

"But where 'ave you been, I teach you the French but you are not 'ere, you are not 'ere *at all!*"

"I know Yvette, sorry *again*, It's not that I mean to keep letting you down, things just seem to get in the way." He lied.

She had a very strange look about her. Her eyes, always bright and lively darting here and there taking in every movement around her, were dulled and lacked lustre. She seemed to have them fixed on a point away to Charles' left to the space that formed the doorway.

"Is something wrong Yvette?" He asked trying to be as gentle as he could.

She smiled bringing life to her eyes for a brief moment before replying.

"You did not know Sharlie—they did not tell you?"

"Tell me *what* Yvette, is there something I should know?"

"Mon dieu Mon Amis." The statement was flat, there was no feeling in it.

"I cannot the milk take anymore, that is why your comrades collect. I do not see the things you see but shapes—nothing but shapes and shadows!"

Her gaze was still fixed on the opening but now tears were gathering at the corners of her eyes imparting polish to them once again.

Charles was stunned.

He had set out driven by a helpless desire for this girl but now felt both passion *and* pity for her. He couldn't, *wouldn't* use her, desire remained sure enough but now there was something *more* than desire, there was a heartfelt need to help her in whatever way he could. He took a couple of steps forward and held her to him, with the contact she placed her arms about him and raised her face to his unseeing eyes searching for whatever she may find, the war had taken her family *and* her sight but not her perception of the man that stood before her. Somehow she *knew* that she could trust him and was ready to give herself to him whatever the future might hold.

"Yvette, *my* Yvette. I have loved you from the very first moment I saw you and somehow I'll take care of you."

All feelings of sexual desire had now gone, dispelled as if they had never been. Charles had a *new* and more pressing duty, a duty to help this desolated maid to a future. He cursed himself for thinking only of himself when he absconded and for seeing in his mind only the conquest of a desireable young woman.

Visions of a different future tortured his thoughts, what on earth would transpire when this helpless girl realised that he was a deserter, that he was likely to be tried, lined up and shot!

How the hell would he help her then? How would he be *able* to help?

The noise of machine gun fire suddenly shattered the moment, Yvette leaped away from Charles.

"What is it Sharlie—it is so *close!*" She cried.

I think the airfield is being attacked again Yvette."

He cocked his head the better to listen. Now he could hear the drone of an aero engine much closer than the others.

The machine gun fire intensified. The lone aero engine grew closer, much closer, Charles saw in his mind a lone novice pilot, a terrified lad separated from his group and confused about where he was. Charles drew Yvette to him out of instinct.

The vision was correct. A young German pilot on his first foray, a mission to destroy 46 Squadron and its airfield, had somehow become separated from his '*staffel*'. The youth caried a single bomb slung on a hook beneath his aeroplane and it had failed to release over the airfield when the drop mechanism was pulled. It remained dangling at an odd angle beneath the aeroplane waving and weaving in the slipstream like a fish on a hook just hauled from the water.

The pilot was petrified, the bomb was stll there, he *knew* it was, he could feel it bumping against the underside of his hull, what in hell was holding it? Machine guns barked and stuttered out their poison reducing his wings to shreds of shattered cloth and splintered wood. The knowledge of the hung bomb and the probability of it being detonated by the thumping it was getting added to the terror of the machine gun attack. The boy had wet himself.

In a desperate effort to save himself and to avoid the hundreds of bullets being thrown at him, he weaved his creeking steed from side to side to the accompanyment of the bomb beating out a death march under his feet. It could hang no longer.

Charles heard the whistle of the liberated bomb and it didn't matter.

He drew Yvette tighter to him and placed his hands behind her head pulling it to his chest, if this was the moment they were to die then it would be together. Was the penny in his tunic burning for *them* or for the *German?*

The building disintegrated amidst shards of splintered timber propelled like spears in all directions. Charles felt the sliver pierce him at the same moment that Yvette sagged in his arms.

He had wanted to protect her with his own body, had wanted to hold her tight to keep her safe from the thing that was screeching toward them but he had failed to do the one thing that might have saved them—he had failed to take cover! The spear of sharp wood that now bound him in blood to the maid he had vowed to protect sucked the strength from his legs, the couple sank locked together to the cold floor, to blackness.

If life spares you, it is because it wants you to suffer some more!

That was the thought that Charles held in his head as he returned to consciousness. He had been bound to this maid in life by a trick of fate, had been bound in affection to a girl he had adored but had never really known; bound now by a simple splinter of wood.

She gazed at him as in life but the wide eyes that had held his heart were cold, distant, unseeing, they held only an expression of surprise and unanswered questions. Her mouth was part open as if she had been about to speak when death had found her. Charles yearned for release from this dreadfulness that he had brought about by his failure to take the right action at a critical time, he wished above all that he had perished with the girl. Now life would hold nothing but imaginings of what might have been, of self persecution for not having protected her when he *knew* the power of the devil's talisman and could have kept her free of its influence. He was bleeding, he knew that, but it didn't matter. He eased the girl away to find that the barb had penetrated the soft flesh beneath his breast bone, the wound was superficial. He cursed the luck that seemed to leave him alive when more worthy folk around him perished. The penny, that *bloody* penny was gloating in its success.

The emotion that engulfed him was as painful as it was prolific. He raised himself to his knees and buried his head in his hands. Why couldn't he just die and be released from the torment that successive afflictions had furnished him since this thing he could not be rid of came to him?

What now? Where was his future? Why hadn't that silly little bugger of a German pilot done an apposite job and finished them *both* off?

Raising his head he gazed at the girl for the love of whom he had deserted, stared through tears that could not dampen the wrath that consumed him. He vowed upon his life that he would come back to this God forsaken, shell ridden, pock marked miserable land one day and speak her native tongue! He would learn to speak French as she had wanted him to.

He tore a small section from his thick shirt to form a simple bandage to keep his wound clean, there appeared to be a lot of blood around the wound but at least it now seemed to have stopped. Looking around at the shattered remains of the building, Charles was surprised to find that there had been no fire following the explosion. The realisation was of little importance, what he was really looking for was a fitting place to lay to rest this special person that had come to mean so much to him. She had been born, brought up and loved by her folk in this place before conflict had taken the lives of her parents and it was here that Charles decided to place her to rest with her memories. He would lay her to final and everlasting peace and a reunion with those that *she* had loved.

He made his way to a small orchard on the south side of the farm buildings. Here there were bluebells fresh sprung from the soil in illustration and solemn promise of the inevitable cycle of death and life re-kindled to which all living things must subjugate. He knew at once that this was the place, there was no more fitting a bower than the carpet this innoccuous little flower of blue would place about the resting place of this maid whenever spring returned.

The spot beneath the apple tree seemed perfect. His chest blazed with pain at every turn of the spade and his leg was hurting but he would not rest until this task was done. He didn't hear the creak of the pedals as the bicycle approached, he was deep in his own sorrow.

The Gendarme dismounted allowing the *velo* to fall to the ground as he reached for the notebook and pencil in his tunic. He paused to regard the activity before him; as a precaution he un popped the flap on his holster and loosened the revolver, he was unsure of the situation and the half-naked man digging, but well aware that a grave was being prepared.

"M'sieu!"

He called keeping himself at a safe distance, his hand now on the pistol butt.

Charles swung around startling the policemen who snapped the revolver from the holster promptly dropping it to swing on its white lanyard. He snatched it back and was visibly shaken. He had been recalled to service from retirement when the younger men had been taken for the war and was short of youth and its inherent dexterity.

Charles held up a hand in reassurance. The Gendarme looked as if he might pull the trigger by accident.

"Je suis Soldarme Anglais!" he blurted not knowing that he had learned this much French.

The Gendarme looked relieved and lowered his revolver.

"Ah *bien* M'sieu." he replied, "Vous parle Francais?"

"Non!" said Charles, his French now seriously stretched.

The policeman looked at his feet for a moment, collected himself and went on.

"I 'ave un message a bomb is dropped 'ere, I arrive to . . . ." He paused and stared at his feet again as he searched for the right word.

"Investigate?" ventured Charles.

"*Oui* M'sieu, exactement—to investigate. You know of this?"

"Yes," said Charles, "I was with the Mademoiselle of the farm when the bomb exploded. I was trying to shield her but she is dead."

The two men looked at each other for a long moment whilst the officer decided the bonifides of the statement. He returned the pistol to its holster and made his way toward Charles noticing for the first time the injury to his chest.

"You are injured also M'sieu!" he observed.

"It's nothing Officer, the shaft of wood that killed m'amselle also pierced me."

"Where is Mademoiselle now M'sieu?" enquired the Gendarme.

"She's laying in the milking shed. I laid her comfortable while I found a place for her."

"Mademoiselle and you were *friends* M'sieu?"

"Yes, I came with a lorry to collect milk!"

Ah *bien,* J'ai Comprehend! Per'aps you could take me to 'er?"

The two men walked the short distance to the ruined building. Charles became visibly shaken as he rejoined the maid. He hadn't realised that he'd left the stake in her body. The Officer baulked at the encounter, shook his head in sorrow and removed his kepi.

"C'est la Guerre!" He announced.

Both men closed to within a few feet of the lifeless girl. Charles stared longingly down at her, "Where is my sweet now?" he asked himself the words hard with bitterness.

The Gendarme removed the stake from her back, Charles felt wretched, felt physically sick and had to resist a powerful urge to hit the officer.

"Together we will lay this poor creature to her rest." The officer instructed.

CHAPTER 15

Going Home

THE TENDER TRUNDLED ITS way back to the airfield a little more willing for the better treatment it received during the madcap outward journey.

There was no Sergeant to be seen at the guard house half of which was a smoking ruin. Fires were burning in buildings around the airfield lending an eerie glow to the fading half-light of dusk. Charles made his way to the motor pool, or at least to the place where the motor pool and workshop had once been. The buildings and every vehicle in the compound had been reduced to smoking, unrecognisable ruins. He gaped in disbelief at the chaos that he remembered as a well organised and orderly airfield.

There was barely anything recognisable left, aircraft had been destroyed, the hospital flattened, hangers demolished and the ammo' dump reduced to a huge crater, a twenty feet deep hole in the ground.

"Get that bloody truck over to the medics and get the wounded to the French!" someone bawled at Charles, it was a voice he knew.

He couldn't place it but he *knew* he knew it!

He could see the bodies placed side by side, lined up on the ground in rows, some covered head to toe, some writhing in agony. All else left his mind as he helped the orderlies pack a dozen or so men into the tender, they had little choice but to be rough, time was now of the essence, there would need to be a score or more of such journeys if these men were to be saved and time was running out.

The task took Charles well into the early hours of the morning and would have been much longer had the French Field Hospital Unit not pitched in by providing more vehicles and a host of medical attendants. It was a strange thing for Charles that he was passing in and out of this place so soon after being a patient here. There were few faces that Charles remembered from his time there, the one he remembered best was the surgeon that had tended him who seemed well pleased that Charles was mobile so soon. At his insistence, a French nurse was allocated to help Charles with the transportation of the wounded.

"I present to you mademoiselle nurse Collette?" The Surgeon smiled as he introduced Charles' helper. Charles was speechless for the resemblance to Yvette was stunning, overwhelming.

"*Enchanted M'Sieu!*" She extended her hand.

My God, she even *sounded* like Yvette.

Charles nodded, took her hand and and gave it a weak shake, he knew he should have kissed her on both cheeks but was frozen by the likeness of the nurse. The resemblance was uncanny, he was pursued by the strangest feeling that this girl was a reincarnation of his former friend. He stared at her unable to say anything in response to her greeting, the girl placed her head on one side conveying with clarity her bewilderment.

"M'Sieu?" she enquired trying to evoke some sort of response from Charles.

The Surgeon explained to the nurse in French that Charles had been shot down and that he may be suffering from the effects of trauma so to be patient with him. He also explained that Charles spoke no French outside simple greetings so communication between them would be limited and sometimes might be difficult. Collette nodded her head and shrugged her shoulders in acquiescence, this wouldn't be the worst thing that had ever befallen her, just awkward and uncomfortable.

The Surgeon departed grinning as he shot a glance at Charles whose mouth still hung open. He had placed an entirely different assessment on the event.

Charles gave his head a shake to try to clear the hanting images of Yvette.

"Pardon moi M'selle." he blurted in his best French, "Parle Vous Anglais?"

"Non M'sieu, J'regrette." She smiled in apology, she remembered he could speak no French.

He searched his brain for the word for lorry, it came to him in a flash as he recalled a distant conversation with Yvette, she spoke it in his mind as clear as if she had been there.

"Allez la Camion." He said gesturing for the nurse to accompany him.

"Par certainment M'sieu." She responded with a bunny dip pleased that she had understood him and stepped forward.

The noise in the tender made conversation with the girl impossible so the trip back to the airfield passed in silence giving Charles the opportunity to think about things and to adjust to this uncanny meeting with the French nurse. They made a further five trips to that day so the pair were kept busy well into the small hours of the morning the strain exhausting them both. Sleeping in the back of the tender was as short as it was uncomfortable for Charles but welcome nontheless

Charles jumped down and cranked the handle until the motor gave in and started, driving the tender from the compound he made his way to the field hospital every bone in his body aching. Wounded were still being brought in from the front, Allied forces had been forced to retreat and the battle was said to be getting too close for comfort. There was no possibility that the hospital would be able to cope with the flood of arrivals so he and his ancient tender would definitely be needed again.

"Better report to the temporary Staff Sergeant—he's and infantry bloke but bloody good at getting things done." Suggested the admissions orderly.

"He's over there!"

Charles approached from behind the man, he was sure that he had met him somewhere before, there was something familiar about his build and the way he held himself.

"Morning Sergeant." He ventured as he drew close. The Sergeant wheeled around. The action produced a minor shock for Charles for the Sergeant was none other than his old comrade Tommy.

"Good God Charlie—what the hell are *you* doing here, I thought you'd be a bloody General by now!"

"Still a Corporal Tommy but *really* pleased to see how well *you've* done. I was posted here at the airfield as one of the medical staff."

"Who'd have bloody thought it?" remarked Tommy watching the movements around him like a hawk as the conversation progressed. Charles went on,

"There's no shortage of medics now that the French are here Tommy but a lot of the drivers were put out of action during the last raid so I'm acting as a driver, I'm getting the overflow of casualties to the French Hospital."

"Bloody good for you mate, it's great that you are happy to pitch in and help."

"What the hell d'you think you're doing lad?" He shrieked at a boy soldier who had been carrying more medical supplies than he was able to manage and had tripped in the mud.

"Get your arse up and take that lot to the pharmacy!"

"Sorry Chas. Better get over to despatch and pick up your next lot of wounded."

"Sure Tommy—by the way, I brought a French nurse in last night she's my first aid attendant, any idea where I might find her?"

"Yep. She spent the night with the Brit nurses but she's at the hospital right now waiting for you—didn't know *you* were the driver she was looking for."

He winked.

Charles turned, smiling over his shoulder he told his chum.

"You haven't changed a bit Tommy, Sergeant or not you're as cheeky as ever!"

Collette looked flustered and a little distraught as Charles caught up with her outside the nurses quarters but brightened as soon as she recognised her driver.

"I zought you 'ad gone wizzout me M'sieu." She stumbled in broken but recognisable English, grabbing his arm tightly. "We go to ze 'ospital now?"

"This way," he gestured and she took off at once propelling him with her, it was clear she was glad to be out of this place.

By the end of the day both attendants were once again exhausted but even then Charles had the good sense to suggest that Collette remain with her colleagues at the French female hostel rather than spend another night in a strange environment among folk who were unable to comprehend her native tongue.

Charles thought long and deep about this new aquaintance as he trundled the tender back to the airfield. He liked her certainly but sweet as she was, she was not Yvette; that phase of his life, that inexplicable attraction for a woman that was not his Wife, was gone. He would never allow it to be repeated for now he was able to see the relationship for what it could only have been, a diverting infatuation fuelled by lonliness and the need of female company. He shrugged and turned his thoughts to the flashes of the guns and the thunder that accompanied them. They seemed to be a lot closer than he remembered from the journey back the day before, what was happening out there?

The question was answered more quickly than he was expecting for on arrival at the remains of the guardhouse he was intercepted by a breathless Tommy and ordered to leave the tender and make his way to the hospital with all haste. There had been a huge influx of wounded from the front as the Germans had intensified the push, so many that the depleted medical staff were unable to cope and needed the help of whatever medical personnel they could find.

The scene around the hospital was chaotic, there were vehicles *everywhere* off loading man after man. *Lines* of vehicles the attendants of each competing for urgent attention for the unfortunates incarcerated within, there was no shortage of drivers now.

Charles made for the hospital orderly only to find him swamped by soldiers pleading for attention to the wounded they had brought in. He made his way to where he could see one of the surgeons taking a breath of fresh air beyond makeshift hospital. A short but critical respite between what had been for the man a succession of continuous operations.

The surgeon wore an expression of intense exhaustion, his hands were shaking as he clutched at the cigarette he had plucked from cracked lips. The once spotless white gown that hung about him was drenched with blood and he looked more than twice his twenty four years.

"Excuse me Sir." Charles broke through the man's isolation and secured his attention. The Surgeon raised his head to peer through jaundiced eyes at the stranger that had severed his solemn reflections. Eyes that seemed to be focused on something beyond the enquirer, he said nothing.

"I can see you're tired," proffered Charles, "Don't mean to break your rest but I wanted you to know I'm a fully trained medical orderly with operating theatre experience and I want to help, can I help you?"

"What sort of theatre experience?"

"Open wounds, broken bones, amputations . . . . !"

The surgeon cut him off.

"I need to get back, if you think you're up to it we can use every bit of help we can get, come on, let's see what you can do!"

"Thanks, I'll do my best."

The surgeon looked a little brighter now. "You look pretty tired yourself Corporal," he drawled, "you sure you're up to this?"

"Don't worry about me Sir, I'll hold up just fine." Charles responded as the pair made their way through the flap to the dozen or so operating tables beyond.

The scene was one of carnage beyond anything Charles had ever experienced, carnage beyond comprehension; he beat back the urge to shriek in protest at the condition of these unfortunate souls who had volunteered their services at the call of their Country, given limbs, eyes and minds for their altruism in exchange for slaughterhouse treatment. There was no time to reflect further for the surgeon had taken post and was busy trying to put right what his fellow man had callously perpetrated.

Charles found a robe and mask in the pre-operation room adjoining the theatre, throwing it on he joined the surgeon and true to his word and his nature used the skills that he had accumulated to the very limit of his spirit.

The medics worked for three days and four nights taking rest wherever they could but for periods never longer than a couple of hours, the need of the wounded remained ever acute.

The 'big push' finally failed to sustain; as tables turned the Allies began to thrust back the oppressor, the horrendous pressure on the hospital eased allowing the exhausted teams to step out into the sunshine and breath untarnished air again. The guns were quieter now, further away and less intense as the enemy licked their wounds and buried their dead. It was time to think of the morrow.

"The old man wants to see you Charlie."

Charles took his head from his knees and looked up, Tommy wasn't smiling.

"What for?"

"Don't know mate, better get over there."

"Bugger!" Cursed Charles, he was thinking of taking a few hours in his cot and this intrusion was irritating in the extreme. He forced himself to his feet.

"Gonna get a bloody wash first." The statement was final and didn't invite comment or counter.

"Sit down Jenkins, I know you are tired so I will be brief." The Colonel scrutinised Charles with surpising alacrity.

"There are some letters here for you, it seems your family is overjoyed at the knowledge of your survival and there is some news that I hope will delight you." He paused and awaited a reaction but finding little continued.

"Right, to press on then. I have been informed that you are to be repatriated to England a few days from now and as of this moment you are to stand down from duties and take rest. You may wish to write home with your news."

The Colonel handed Charles a bundle of letters and one loose one.

"I'd like you to read this in my presence Jenkins if you would be so kind?"

Charles took the bundle and with his thumb nail slit the tape that had been used to re-seal the loose letter following scrutiny by the censoring Officer. The date had been obliterated. It began.

'My Dearest, Dearest Husband.

You will never know the joy I felt at finding out you had not been killed after all. To receive such a telegram was something I always dreaded, I thought my life was over and had it not been for the child I have been carrying for you I think I would have ended my days. Yes Charlie my sweet, sweet Charlie, you are going to be a Daddy, very soon now I think. Your Mother thinks so too. She has been such a friend to me, more like a Mum to me than my own and we have become very close. She was heartbroken when her letters came back unopened marked Missing in Action and like me didn't stop crying for days when we heard you were still alive, silly isn't it? Your Brother and Sister are well and send their love. Tom never said much when your Mother told him but I know he was hurt bad.

I will close now as there is so much to do. Remember always that I love you and miss you and can't wait until I'm finally at your side.'

Charles at last knew why he had felt so uneasy at seeking a relationship with Yvette, felt indescribably relieved that he had not betrayed the true and undiminished love of his Wife. He wanted nothing more than to go home now, to leave this sickening holocaust of a war perpetuated by glory seekers with little care for the horror it meted out to those that had to fight it face to face.

A plethora of mental images of his family waiting faithfully at home and the heartwarming words of the letter stirred deep emotion within him, emotion that welled up and overflowed like the spill from an overfilled dam.

"Congratulations Jenkins, I hope it's a boy as proud and true as you."

The Colonel broke the silence and in doing so snatched Charles in the nick of time from what would have become a miserable breakdown.

"Yes, Thank you Sir, I hope it's a boy too. We both want a boy."

"Report to Sergeant Fredericks and get your transport movements and release paperwork from him."

"Yes sir." Charles rose to his feet and took the hand that the Colonel had extended and shook it. As he set off toward the door the Colonel added without rancour.

"By the by Jenkins, I know what you had been about to do on the day the airfield was attacked. The Adjutant had seen you depart with the tender and came to see me. In deference to your bravery and general conduct we agreed that no action would be taken until your return to give you a chance to explain yourself. You know of course that the attack on the airfield had far reaching consequences and every able bodied man was needed. Your contribution to the effort and dedication to the care of the wounded after the attack far outweighed your indiscretion and when the adjutant lost his life I felt too weary of it all to want to take any action."

He added as an afterthought, "Just wanted you to know."

Charles was astonished, he had believed it to be the action of the penny alone that had brought about his good fortune that day and that no-one beyond himself had any knowledge of the misdemeanor.

$$\nabla$$

To be on the way home, making his way in a troop train in a slow crawl over the ravaged French countryside, was an indescribable joy. To know that each clack of the wheels over loose joints in the track brought him that little bit closer to home changed his outlook on life altogether.

In the solitude of what once had been a fine orchard adjoining the East side of the airfield Charles had opened each of the remaining letters from his bundle. Heaven knows when Eira had written that first letter with the promise of a child to come, for the last but one letter told him that he was the Father of a strapping healthy young Son delivered by his Mother. Eira had said she wanted to wait for Charles' return before naming him since when name after name had passed through Charles' mind, there were so many men he would like to have honoured by gifting their name to his son and thus make sure they would be remembered long after they had passed.

The exercise kept him distracted for many an hour and had served to sharpen his appreciation of release to happier circumstances whilst others would have to press themselves once more into the valleys of death.

Charles had long since erased from his mind the privation, the odours of rotting bandages and mortification, that had pervaded the iniquitous hospital. He was homeward bound in a railway carriage that was clean and comfortable, he could sleep whenever the desire took him and there were few passengers with the energy to bark orders. He felt he could put up with *anything* knowing that within a week or so he would be home. *Home,* how sweet that sounded.

He stepped down through clouds of escaping steam from the single railway carriage that had brought him to Guilloshen, his heart racing with anticipation and his mind so distracted that he forgot to retrieve his kitbag from the guard compartment.

"Hang on Lad!" the guard called after him, "You've forgot something!"

He didn't want to turn back, not now. The steam, moved along by the breeze, was clearing and through its lifting wisps he could see Eira waiting beside pony and trap beyond the station entrance. He dropped his greatcoat and ran leaving the coat on the platform where it fell and the guard holding the kitbag.

There was no silver band, no greeting party, no celebration as there had been before, the war had gone on too long and taken too many young men. People were tired and dispirited by the lies and false promises of an early victory and glory for all. Almost every family had given a life to this futile conflict, some more than one, they were not inclined to celebrate homecomings whilst their own kin remained at the battlefront.

She cradled their infant to her in the traditional Welsh shawl rocking it gently to and fro, her countenance illuminated with a broad, radiant smile and dazzling white teeth as she watched Charles take the last few paces toward her. Charles was captivated, in the ever present distraction of battle he had forgotten how beautiful she was. It was as if they had met for the very first time and his heart was skipping just as if it *had* been the first time. Eira was dressed in her Sunday best of midnight blue velvet and pure white lace and looked as though she had stepped fresh from the bath. Her raven black hair spilled over her shoulders in a wavy cascade adorned by a small matching hat and gossamer fine net. The infant in the shawl across her chest prevented Charles from taking her up and squeezing her to him, instead her free hand entwined with his, their fingers interlocked as they had always done before he had been forced to leave her. She was crying tears of joy through her smile. His Son was fast asleep, he knew only peace, love and hope but what would the future hold for him?

"Charlie I have *so* much to tell you, I've got some *fantastic* news for you!" she enthused, "Your step Dad has taken over from Doctor Moody—of course you won't know—Doctor Moody passed away three weeks ago and has left us his cottage and the stables and *everything!* Mrs Moody has gone to live with her Sister in Bournemouth so we can move in *now*, today! We can go there now if you want to?" She paused almost breathless and waited for his reaction.

Charles was stunned, the Doctor had been a wonderful friend and had taught him so much not only about medicine but about courage, honesty, loyalty and honour and now this. He felt overwhelmed by the generosity of this wonderful man and hoped that he would be as well received in death as he was respected in life.

"Think I'd like to go home first and see my folk, we can go on to the cottage straight after, that OK?" He couldn't believe his good fortune.

"So the pony and trap is *ours?*" he enquired.

"Certainly is Charlie, it's not the same pony of course, the pony you used to drive was requisitioned for the war effort straight after she gave birth to this one!"

Charles rubbed the pony's neck. "Looks sturdy enough, how's its temperament?" he asked.

Eira looked askance at him.

"Charlie, if you don't leave that dratted pony alone and kiss me at once I'm leaving you!" She exclaimed, eyebrows meeting in irritation.

They trotted the pony to his Mother's house, a veritable mansion it seemed when viewed in comparison with the cottage they had been brought up in. Charles let out a whistle.

"Wow, Mum's really come up in the world."

"Aye, but better yet she's happier than I have *ever* seen her and she and Doctor Williams make a smashing team, you should see them, you'd be really proud."

The two chatted non stop as the journey progessed. Tom was farm manager and his Sister was at school and doing very well. Eira's Dad had been forced to withdraw from working underground at the Colliery because of a back injury but unlike the old days when he would have been thrown aside as Charles' Father had been, the new colliery owner had found work for him on the surface. He was happy, contented and close to retirement.

Charles had been reunited with his Mother for only a few minutes before she insisted he took a bath, he understood the reason well enough, he could smell himself! Her house was well appointed and possessed a proper, separate bathroom *and* toilet WC, something Charles had never experienced in the days in simple their cottage.

He made the most of it. Hot water that came from a tap? Only royalty and the very wealthy could afford such luxury. His Sister thought him a stranger and kept her distance, had she known the part this stranger had played in her early moments she might well have thought him less so, but life unfolds in its own fashion and values are often confused by misunderstanding.

$$\nabla$$

Charles had been impressed enough by his Mother's good fortune in having found not only a good man but also a splendid house. He knew that Doctor Moody had always preferred a cottage and with no offspring, size was of no consideration so he was expecting a somewhat less well appointed dwelling. His recollection of it was limited to its frontal elevation, he had never had cause to visit the inside so had no preconception of what it might be like. Now as Eira urged the pony into the driveway and past the stable, Charles was shocked to find that it was much larger than he remembered.

Eira took the large wrought iron key from the ledge in the thatch covered porch and unlocked the front door. Pushing it open she stepped back grinning from ear to ear and motioned for Charles to enter.

It was *huge.* The rooms cascaded gently downward from right to left, at the extreme right was a generously proportioned living room with a large inglenook fireplace with stone bench seats set at each side of an iron fire grate that contained a blazing log fire. From here a small downward step led into the dining room through a split stable type door, next was the entrance and reception room where Charles now stood and last, from another small step was the kitchen. It was breathtaking,

"We could get our living room *and* the kitchen from our old cottage into just the kitchen alone here!" Charles remarked turning to Eira eyes wide with delight and anticipation.

"Wait 'till you see the *upstairs* Charlie, there's three huge bedrooms *and* a bathroom up there! Ours is right above the living room and guess how you get to it?" She looked at him expectanly. He noticed how radiant and beautiful she was and how the flames from the fire reflected in her peach smooth skin.

"Haven't got a clue love, but I bet *you* want to tell me!"

"Come on!" She urged grasping his hand and tugging him toward the living room. They stepped up from the dining room to where the fire was blazing.

"There!" She exclaimed, pointing to the right hand side of the inglenook.

Charles was delighted for there before him curling around behind the stone inglenook, was a stone built spiral staircase disappearing upward. Fascinated he made his way up the uneven stone steps to the room above, it was a giant bedroom with a ridiculous large bed that looked so comfortable he felt like jumping straight into it. The timbers that supported the old lath and plaster ceiling had distorted from the weight they suspended so that they were now bent from the walls downward toward the centre of the room and sagged a good six inches. He loved it and thanked God for the day that good fortune had brought this wonderful gift into his life. He made his way back to the living room.

"This is fantastic Eira, Doctor Moody left all this to *us?*" he quizzed, hardly able to believe their extraordinary luck.

"There's *more* Charlie, he left a sum of money to see you through proper medical training, I don't think he knew you were a medic in the Army. Anyway, the money is there for you if you want it. Well, what do you think?"

Charles wheeled and snatched her into his arms.

"I want us to spend the rest of our days here with our boy!" He exclaimed in sheer joy.

That night, Eira emptied Charles' pockets in readiness to wash his uniform and erradicate the odour accumulated from the long journey home and the lack of any kind of amenities other than miniscule toilet cubicles that contained nothing other than the most rudiment facility.

Coming across the coin she recognised it at once as the talisman that Charles had always been so reluctant to be parted from. Examining it carefully, she was surprised at how clean and shiny it still looked yet it bore no sign of the polishing that takes away the crispness of the features.

It felt cold, very cold and she somehow felt that it was repelling her, urging her to put it back, to leave it be. She placed it on the table but still her eyes would not leave it, there was something wrong. Shivers ran down her spine; in her mind's eye she could see men reaching out, crying for help, pleading for relief, moaning, many men, dying men, *thousands* of men all reaching, reaching, reaching.

Her head began to swim; she stepped back in horror, what *was* this dreadful thing that her husband was so reluctant to part with? She threw a cloth over it to conceal its revolting lustre. Was it *really* mocking her?

Charles stepped out of the bath at the very moment that Eira had sensed the evil of the trinket. Moments before, he had been ecstatic at the thought of being not only home but in his *own* home, of being with Eira and his Son, of being out of the Army and that dreaded war. Almost delirious in ecstasy the last thing he was expecting was the ice cold cloud that twisted through his mind and robbed him of his moment of contentment. A black veil had without warning encompassed him, wrenched him from euphoria and hurled him headlong into depression and despair. The moment he had stepped from the abundant hot water of the tub he had been singing, but that moment had passed, had vanished and been replaced by emptiness, he knew at once that the Devil's coin was at work but could not know why.

He felt drained, emptied, devoid of any kind of lasting or meaningful compassion for those he had left on the battlefields of France. Hatred now reigned where love had dominated just a few short moments ago, he knew the coin was sucking at his very soul and he knew equally well that he was powerless to resist it. Depression deepened.

Draping a towel about himself he sat on the edge of the cast iron bath his had supporting him on the back of the chair that held his fresh civilian clothing not caring that moisture was seeping into it.

Despondency at the front had always been a heavy burden as he had endured the everyday horrors of conflict yet he had been able to bear it because of the firm knowledge and solid belief that there were better days to come. What if the penny had turned on *him* now that it was removed from the holocaust that it had from the outset steered him toward?

What if the penny was now bent on exacting revenge on him for removing it from the carnage of battle and the easy conquests it could secure for the force of evil that had created and now controlled it?

Oh my God! What if it had chosen to take revenge not on *him* but on his *family?*

Eira picked up the shrouded penny and dropped it into the small tin that Charles had been carrying his medals in. At least it was out of sight, out of mind and didn't bother her now. She would tell Charlie of it later.

Charles came out of his stupor as if he had been released and towelled himself down, he would talk to Eira about the penny. Why did he now feel better? He put the episode behind him, completed towelling himself and dressed himself in the civilian clothing that Eira had put out for him. How on earth had it got damp in places.

The infant reposed in the same shawl now re-arranged at his Mother's back and was sleeping. With the child secured in this position Eira was able to work at most of the daily chores without worrying about her child. She had long ago learned that there was an added benefit to this method of carrying in that there was something soothing to the infant about the motion imparted to it as the mother moved around. Perhaps it was reminiscent to being carried in the womb.

Eira sensed the presence, *felt* it. A cold shiver gripped her. The infant was awake now; facing into the room behind its mother he could *see* it but was not yet developed enough to react to it. Eira wheeled around, there was nothing for *her* to see but still she *knew* it was there in that very room, it was there with *them*.

Men were screaming again, pleading for mercy and relief, eyes displaying pain, torture, misery. She shut her eyes tightly and placed her hands over her ears. The infant was awake and craning its neck to see it again, fascinated by this hideous apparition.

Eira knew she must move the tin further from sight, she didn't know *why* but taking her hands from her ears she picked up the object and locked it securely in a compartment within the writing bureau that the Doctor's wife had left for her. Locking the lid she removed the ornate key and thrust it into her pocket. She would find a hiding place for that too.

The apparition looked on, seething with resentment that the malevolence it had planned to administer in this place had passed beyond its influence. It transferred its attention to the infant that was facing it again, fiery eyes boring deep into the enwidened eyes of the innocent child. It would return for the coin; it would wait for a moment of opportunity no matter how long it took. It would have revenge.

Malevolence propelled it toward mother and child but its power here was spent, its token nullified by a woman's intuition. The apparition had observed the penny intently from the moment of its inception, had steered it and taken delight in the evil that its token had wreaked and would not rest until it was at work for him again! The power had been subjugated for the present but the devil would return to exact revenge far beyond comprehension.

The End—or is it?